TALES FROM

DRAGON PRECINCT

Also by Keith R.A. DeCandido,
from eSpec Books

The Precinct Series
DRAGON PRECINCT
UNICORN PRECINCT
GOBLIN PRECINCT
GRYPHON PRECINCT

Coming Soon
MERMAID PRECINCT

Forthcoming Titles
PHOENIX PRECINCT
MANTICORE PRECINCT
MORE TALES FROM DRAGON PRECINCT

Other Titles
WITHOUT A LICENSE

TALES FROM
DRAGON PRECINCT

Keith R.A. DeCandido

eSpec Books
Pennsville, NJ

PUBLISHED BY
eSpec Books LLC
Danielle McPhail, Publisher
PO Box 242,
Pennsville, New Jersey 08070
www.especbooks.com

ISBN: 978-1-942990-90-1
ISBN (ebook): 978-1-942990-89-5

Interior Design: Danielle McPhail
Sidhe na Daire Multimedia
www.sidhenadaire.com

Cover Design: Mike McPhail

Art Credits - www.Shutterstock.com
Dragon Medallion © Marina Yakutsenya
Quill © sequarell - Fotolia.com

Dedicated to John J. Ordover, who bought
Dragon Precinct *back in 2004 and suggested the title,*
which tied it all together so perfectly.

ACKNOWLEDGMENTS

For the new edition:
Hugely massively amazingly big thanks to Danielle Ackley-McPhail, Mike McPhail, and Greg Schauer of eSpec Books for giving the series a new home.

From the original edition:
First of all, I must thank the editors who published five of the stories in this collection: Rosemary Edghill ("Getting the Chair" in *Murder by Magic*), C.J. Henderson & Patrick Thomas ("Crime of Passion" in *Hear Them Roar*), Danielle Ackley-McPhail, Jennifer Ross, & Jeffrey Lyman ("Fire in the Hole" in *Dragon's Lure*), Lee Hillman, L. Jagi Lamplighter, and Danielle & Jeffrey Lyman again ("House Arrest" in *Bad-Ass Faeries*), and Jean Rabe & the late, great Martin H. Greenberg ("A Clean Getaway" in *Pandora's Closet*).

Secondly, thanks to everyone who supported the Kickstarter for the initial release of "When the Magick Goes Away" (many of whom are listed in that story's acknowledgments).

Thirdly, massively huge thanks to Neal Levin of Dark Quest Books, who rescued this series from oblivion with the release of *Unicorn Precinct* in 2011 followed quickly by the re-release of *Dragon Precinct* that same year. It was Neal's idea to do a short story collection, and I jumped at the chance to do some stories I really wanted to do, but which would only work in shorter form—like Torin and Danthres's first case, or stories showcasing the other detectives, or following up on the surviving members of the heroic quest from *Dragon Precinct*.

Fourthly, thanks to my awesome agent Lucienne Diver, my amazing editor Elektra Hammond, stupendous cover artist Jenn Reese, delightful designer Danielle Ackley-McPhail, and also for general grooviness: GraceAnne Andreassi DeCandido, Wrenn Simms, Tina Randleman, Dale Mazur, Ænder Steven Harris, Sally-Rouge, Andrea Bergan, Heidi Molano, T'Anna Harrington, Kat Toomajian, and my fellow members of the Liars Club.

TABLE OF CONTENTS

INTRODUCTION

Back in high school, my best friend John S. Drew (still one of my closest friends) introduced me to the wild and wacky world of Dungeons & Dragons. The primary game available back then was Advanced Dungeons & Dragons, before the infamous Second Edition was published in 1989. (Yes, I'm old.) One of the characters I played in a campaign was a red-bearded ranger named Torin ban Wyvald. No idea where the name came from, it just sort of fell into my head, as did his father, Wyvald ban Garin, and his horse, Sylvan Wye (I know where *that* came from: a William Wordsworth poem I fell in love with in college). The character lasted quite a while, as part of a high-level party that included an elven wizard and a dwarven warrior and a cleric who jokingly referred to himself as "the generic cleric," which stuck.

Fast forward to my twenties, when I'm playing another fantasy RPG, DM'd by Leigh Grossman, the developmental stages of what was eventually published as the Wildside Gaming System. At one point, I played a cranky half-elven female warrior named Danthres Tresyllione, a name that I thought sounded very elven. She lasted through several games—which was unusual, as Wildside is a brutal game in which characters tend to die off quickly—and was indeed the second-longest-tenured character I had. (Amusingly, the longest-tenured was a one-handed archer whom Leigh insisted wouldn't last a full game—he kept going for *months*, despite everything Leigh threw at me.)

As I proceeded through adulthood, time for role-playing became increasingly harder to come by. But I really had a soft spot for the characters of Torin and Danthres. I can no longer recall exactly how many stories and/or novels I started that featured Torin and Danthres as the protagonists—though I do know one was a vague adaptation of that college game with Danthres added to the party we played.

More years passed. My writing career developed. And one day in 2003, John Ordover at Pocket Books started to develop a line of original science fiction and fantasy novels, and he was using his regular stable of *Star Trek* authors (like, well, me) for a lot of the books: Peter David's *Sir Apropos of Nothing*, Dayton Ward's *The Last World War*, Kristine Kathryn Rusch's *Fantasy Life*, Susan Wright's *Slave Trade*, and my own *Dragon Precinct*.

The novel was the second one I pitched to John—the first one wasn't working out, as John wanted changes I wasn't comfortable with—and it was when pitching to John that I *finally* hit on what to do with Torin and Danthres. A longtime fan of cop novels and cop TV shows and nonfiction books about cops, and also a fan of high fantasy since I read *The Hobbit* and the Earthsea trilogy as a wee lad, I thought, what better story to tell than a melding of two of my favorite genres?

SF/F is particularly well suited to this sort of thing, as it's a genre of setting, whereas mystery is a genre of plot. And it finally gave me something to do with these two characters I'd come to love.

For the first novel, I did a variation on that college campaign—the elven mage became Olthar lothSirhans, the dwarf warrior became Ubàrlig, the "generic cleric" became Brother Genero of Velessa, and I added Gan Brightblade, Mari and Nari, and Bogg the Barbarian. They were the same type of heroic party they'd been in the game, and in more than one of my attempted works of fiction, but this time they weren't the main characters—they were the victims.

The hard part was coming up with a title for the damn thing. It was John Ordover, my editor, who suggested *Dragon Precinct*, which was *perfect*, as it incorporated both genres in one simple, descriptive title.

I've made a bit of a career out of doing SF/F-laced police procedurals. Besides this series, I've mixed cop novels with superhero fiction (my Spider-Man novels *Venom's Wrath* and *Down These Mean Streets*, my *Super City Cops* series including *The Case of the Claw*) and with TV tie-ins (my *Buffy the Vampire Slayer* novel *Blackout*, my *Supernatural* novel *Nevermore*). I really enjoy the juxtaposition of the down-to-earth nitty gritty of what cops encounter every day with odd fantastical elements.

Sadly, while I had plenty more stories to tell, Pocket discontinued that line of novels. No publisher wanted to take up the series without having access to the first book, and Pocket still had that. I had sold a *Dragon Precinct* short story to Rosemary Edghill for the *Murder by Magic* anthology, which came out around the same time as the novel, and that soon became my avenue for keeping the universe alive. Whenever I got an invite to an anthology, I tried to do a *Dragon Precinct* story for it.

In 2011, Neal Levin of Dark Quest Books offered to continue the series, and *Unicorn Precinct* — which I'd plotted out way back in 2004 — at last saw the light of day. I finally got the rights back to *Dragon Precinct*, so that's been reissued, and the series continued with *Goblin Precinct* and the upcoming *Gryphon Precinct* and *Mermaid Precinct*. But in the interim, I'd done five short stories, and Neal thought it would be cool to put out a collection. Of course, I didn't have enough material for a collection without writing five more stories . . .

Some quick notes on the ten stories contained herein:

"Getting the Chair" was another one suggested by John Ordover, who thought it would be cool to have animated furniture be the witnesses in a crime. Of course, one of them would have to tell a different story, but why would furniture lie?

I originally submitted "Crime of Passion" to one of Esther Friesner's *Chicks in Chainmail* anthologies, but she didn't go for it. Then Pat Thomas and C.J. Henderson told me about this anthology of strong female characters they were putting together, and I had something ready to go, since this one is pretty Danthres-heavy.

For this collection, I wanted to give the other detectives some spotlights, and "Catch and Release" is the Iaian and Grovis story. Really, mostly, Iaian, since Grovis got lots of time in *Unicorn Precinct*. This story also allowed me to finally showcase Cliff's End's prison system, and also do a classic cop story, that of the wrongfully imprisoned perp. Iaian seemed like the perfect detective for that one.

When Danielle Ackley-McPhail approached me about doing a story for *Dragon's Lure*, I was reluctant to do a *Dragon Precinct* story for it, because I'd been avoiding creatures like dragons in the storylines as they were a bit *too* out there for stories about street-level cops. But then the plot for "Fire in the Hole" kinda jumped out and wrote itself down, and I had my dragon story that still fit the idiom of the setting.

Dani is also the genius behind the *Bad-Ass Faeries* series of anthologies, and it's for the first volume that I did the all-interrogation-room story "House Arrest," which is just Torin and a house faerie doing a two-person play.

I'd originally envisioned "House Arrest" as an all-dialogue story, also, but other heads prevailed. I still wanted to try an interrogation-room story that *was* all dialogue, and since Torin had "House Arrest" to himself, I wrote "Brotherly Love" for this collection as a Danthres solo story, with just her and the guy she's questioning without any narration.

In *Goblin Precinct*, I made several references to Dru and Hawk having closed "the Corvin case," without any specifics. That was my placeholder for the Dru and Hawk story that I knew I was going to write for this collection, so if you've read *Goblin Precinct*, "Blood in the Water" is what they were talking about.

I've known Jean Rabe for years, and after I did a story for her for *Furry Fantastic*, she asked for a story for her next anthology, *Pandora's Closet*, stories in which closets hold all kinds of bad things. I loved the idea of a closet that spewed filth all over a home, so I ran with that for "A Clean Getaway."

Given the history (outlined above) behind the members of the heroic quest from *Dragon Precinct*, it only made sense to do a story that followed up on what happened to the three survivors after that novel. The result is "Heroes Welcome," which includes some flashbacks to the heyday of this band of seven adventurers as they fought the minions of Mitos the Mage.

And finally, there's the story I'd been dying to tell ever since I established in *Dragon Precinct* that Torin and Danthres had been partners for ten years: how did they first meet? "When the Magick Goes Away" was originally done as a Kickstarter project, and released only to folks who supported the Kickstarter. It's reprinted here along with the other stories, telling the tale of how these two got thrown together in a case involving the murder of several wizards.

I hope you enjoy this collection that explores some of the side roads and back alleys of Cliff's End, in addition to the usual Torin-and-Danthres-close-the-case tales.

Book 'em . . .

—Keith R.A. DeCandido
somewhere in New York City

GETTING THE CHAIR

Lieutenant Danthres Tresyllione of the Cliff's End Castle Guard stopped short in the doorway of the cottage. Behind her, Lieutenant Torin ban Wyvald, her partner, had to do likewise to keep from being impaled on the standard-issue longsword scabbard that hung from her belt. He found himself staring at the brown cloak with the gryphon crest of Lord Albin and Lady Meerka that Danthres (and Torin, and all lieutenants in the Guard) wore.

Torin was about to ask what she was on about when he, too, noticed the smell.

Danthres was half-elf, so her senses were more acute. Torin could only imagine how much worse the stench was for her — it was pretty wretched for him. He detected at least four different odors competing to make his nose wrinkle, and only one matched the expected stench of decaying flesh.

The guard who had summoned the two lieutenants was a young man named Garis. Like most of the guards assigned to Unicorn Precinct — which covered the more well-to-do regions of Cliff's End — Garis was eager to please and not very bright. "Uh, that's the body, ma'am."

"Guard, I've been around dead bodies most of my adult life. They don't usually smell like rotted cheese."

"Uh, no, ma'am," the guard said.

A brief silence ensued. Danthres sighed loudly. "So *what* is the smell?"

"Ah, probably the rotted cheese, ma'am. It's on the table. Or it could be other food items we've found."

"Who found the body?" she asked, still standing in the doorway blocking Torin. Since she was half a head taller than him, and had a wide mane of blond hair, he had no view of the interior. Under other circumstances, he might have complained. Instead, he was happy to enjoy the less unpleasant aroma of the street a while longer. At least this murder wasn't in Dragon Precinct or, worse, Goblin Precinct, where a rotting corpse constituted a step up in the local odors.

"Next-door neighbor, ma'am," Garis said. "The, ah, smell got to her—"

"No surprise there."

"—and, ah, when he didn't answer the door, she summoned the Guard. I came, broke the door in, and found this body. He's the only one here, and there's only one bedroom upstairs, so he probably lived here alone."

"You didn't ask the neighbor that?"

"Uh, no, ma'am, I thought that you—"

"Would do all your work for you. Naturally. Did you at least have the wherewithal to summon the M.E.?"

"Yes, ma'am, the magickal examiner sent a mage-bird saying he'd be here within half an hour—and that was about a quarter of an hour ago."

Danthres finally moved into the house, enabling Torin to do likewise. He surveyed the sitting room, which seemed to take up most of the ground floor. To his left, a staircase led, presumably, to the second level. To his right was a wall taken up almost entirely with shelves stuffed to bursting with books, scrolls, papers, and other items, interrupted only by two windows. The wall opposite where he stood was the same, those shelves broken only by a doorway. Directly in front of Torin was a couch, festooned with papers, dust, writing implements, and wax residue from candles. Perpendicular to it on either side were two easy chairs, one in a similar state of disarray as the couch, the other relatively clean. A table sat in front of the sofa, covered with a lantern, papers, books, scrolls, candles, bowls, and foodstuffs—including the cheese responsible for keeping Torin's nostril hairs flaring.

Lying facedown on the floor was the body of an elderly man, already decomposing, which meant he'd been dead at least a day. The corpse wore a simple—but not cheap—linen shirt and trousers. Most importantly, the man's head was at the wrong angle relative to the rest of his body.

"The question now," Danthres said, "is whether he broke his neck or if someone broke it for him."

"I'd say the latter." Torin pointed at the body. "Look how neatly he's arranged—almost perfectly parallel to the couch, with his arms at his sides. He was set there by someone."

Danthres nodded in agreement, then looked around. "Probably too much to hope for that it was a robbery. Not that we'd be able to tell if something was missing in this disaster." She turned to look at Garis, folding her arms across the gryphon crest—a match for the one on her cloak—on the chest of her standard-issue black leather armor. "Why haven't you opened a window?"

Garis seemed to be trying to shrink into his own armor, which was a match for Danthres and Torin's, save that he wore no cloak and the crest on his chest was that of a unicorn, denoting the precinct to which he was assigned. "Well, er, uh, I didn't want to disturb the scene. I remember that robbery in Old Town last winter and I tried to close a window, and—well, ma'am may not remember, but ma'am tried to cut my head off for interfering with possible evidence before she had a chance to, ah, to examine it."

Danthres snorted. "That's ridiculous. I never would have tried to cut your head off—there'd be an inquiry."

Torin grinned beneath his thick red beard. "I think it will be safe for you to open it, Guard."

"If you say so, sir."

Garis walked to the window, and found that it wouldn't budge.

"Honestly, they have got to raise the standards during those recruitment drives," Danthres said scornfully. Her not-very-attractive face looked positively deathly when she was angry, and Garis tried to shrink even further inside his armor. Danthres's features were rather unfortunate combinations of her dual heritage. The point of her ears, the elegant high forehead, and the thin lips from her elven father were total mismatches with the wide nose, large brown eyes, and shallow cheekbones she'd inherited from her human mother.

"I'm sure," Torin said before Danthres truly lost her temper, "that it's just stuck." He walked over and saw that there was no locking mechanism. That, in itself, was odd. True, this *was* Unicorn Precinct—people didn't need to virtually seal themselves into their homes for safety around here—but an unlocked ground-floor window was still unusual. Especially if this old man did indeed live alone.

Torin braced himself against the window and heaved upward. It still wouldn't budge.

"It won't work, you know."

Whirling, Torin looked for the speaker, his right hand automatically moving to the gryphon-head hilt of his longsword. The only people in the room were Garis, Danthres, and himself. And the corpse, of course, though he was unlikely to speak.

"Who said that?" Danthres asked. Her left hand was also at her sword's hilt.

"I did."

Torin realized that the voice came from the area of the couch.

"Come out from behind there." Torin walked around to behind the sofa.

"Uh, sir, there's nobody there," Garis said. "I checked."

Torin saw that Garis was right.

"It's the couch," Danthres said. "The couch talks."

"Brava to the woman," the couch said.

"Hell and damnation," Torin said, "our corpse is a wizard."

"And bravo to the man," the couch added. "Yes, my dear, departed owner was a mage. His specialty, as you might have already deduced, is animating furniture. He also hated the very concept of fresh air, so he magicked the windows shut."

Another voice said, "You'd think just once he'd take pity on us, but no." This, Torin realized, was the lantern.

Then the cleaner of the two chairs made a noise. "All you *ever* do is complain. Efrak gave you life, and now that he's dead you spit on his grave."

Danthres turned to Garis. "I don't suppose the M.E.'s mage-bird is still here?"

"No, ma'am, it discorporated as soon as it gave the message."

Another noise from the chair. "It *really* is a shame about poor Efrak."

"It's not that much of a shame," the couch said. "I mean, really, what did he do for *us*?"

"Well, he *did* give us life," the lantern said.

"I don't think —"

"That's *enough!*" Danthres bellowed, interrupting the furniture.

Torin added, "I'm afraid we're going to have to question each of you individually."

"What's the point?" Danthres asked him. "He's a wizard. The Brotherhood will claim jurisdiction, perform their own investigation and keep us completely out of it, like they always do whenever one of their own is involved. And honestly, they're welcome to it. I *hate* magick."

"Don't be so sure of that," said another voice, this time from the doorway. Torin recognized this one: Boneen, the magickal examiner. The short, squat old man was on loan from the Brotherhood of Wizards to provide magickal assistance to the law-enforcement efforts of the Cliff's End Castle Guard.

"Good afternoon, Boneen," Torin said with a grin.

"What's so damned good about it? I was having a perfectly fine nap when one of those blasted children woke me with another damned thing for you lot." Several young children — troublemakers, mostly orphans that had been arrested and pressed into service in lieu of incarceration in the work-houses — served as messengers and/or informants for the Castle Guard. Most of the Guard called them "the youth squad," except for Boneen, who usually had less flattering terms. Garis had no doubt sent one such to fetch Boneen. "And what in the name of Lord Albin is that horrendous smell?"

"A combination of various slovenly habits," Torin said.

"Not surprising," Boneen said as he entered. "Efrak makes the gutter rats in the Docklands look positively pristine by comparison."

"You know him?" Danthres asked.

Boneen nodded. "A tiresome little old man who dabbles in useless magick for the most part. He's not actually a member of the Brotherhood."

Torin blinked in surprise. "I didn't think that sort of thing was permitted."

"With new wizards, it isn't." Boneen reached into the bag he always carried over his shoulder. "But Efrak's a couple centuries old — he predates the Brotherhood, and they let him be as long as he registered with them and stayed out of mischief." He pulled the components for his spell out, chuckling bitterly. "That certainly won't be an issue anymore."

Torin led Garis toward the back doorway, which presumably led to the kitchen. "Come on, let's give him some room."

The primary duty of the magickal examiner at a crime scene was to cast a "peel-back" spell — it read the psychic resonances on inanimate objects and showed him what happened in the recent past. This generally meant he was able to see what happened, how it happened, and, most importantly, who did it.

Danthres followed him into the kitchen, which smelled worse than the living room. The place was an even bigger mess, with several part-full mugs of various liquids (or congealed messes that were liquid once), plates of partly eaten food, and still more papers and books freely distributed about the table, chairs, countertop, and cupboard. The cupboard itself was the source of the worst stench. Torin recognized the sigil on the cupboard door as that of a freezing spell, but he also knew that it had to be renewed every few days—something Efrak was no longer in a position to do.

"Why would anyone want to have animate furniture?" Danthres asked.

Torin shrugged. "It gave him someone to talk to? If he lived alone, shunned even by other wizards, he probably didn't have much by way of social interaction."

"We should talk to his neighbors—starting," she said with a look at Garis, "with the one who called you. Take us to her."

THE PEEL-BACK GENERALLY TOOK HALF AN HOUR OR SO, WHICH LEFT THE lieutenants with the task of questioning potential witnesses. That pool was fairly shallow. The neighbor who summoned the Guard referred to Efrak as a "stupid old man who talks to himself." His other neighbor said that he had very few visitors, usually people seeking out potions or other small magicks that they didn't want the Brotherhood to know about. "Y'know how these young folk are—they think if they don't tell no one, no one'll find out," he said with a wink. That neighbor hadn't seen anyone go in recently, though.

The house was across the street from a park Lord Albin and Lady Meerka had had built a year before as a children's playground. No one there was particularly helpful—the parents were too busy watching their children, the children were too busy playing, and, since they'd only all been there a few hours at most, it was unlikely that they saw anything useful to the investigation of a day-old murder.

Garis, meanwhile, tracked down two of the youth squad and told them to fetch a cadre of guards—in addition to removing the body, they'd need to take the furniture in for questioning.

Boneen came out of the house after a half-hour looking even more sour than usual. "Bad news, I'm afraid. The peel-back was inconclusive."

Danthres's eyes flared. An inconclusive peel-back was a rare thing indeed. "Why?" she asked sharply.

"That damned furniture, that's why!"

Torin closed his eyes and exhaled. "Let me guess, they don't count as inanimate objects?"

"No," Boneen said. The peel-back spell only worked on unliving items. The living interfered with the spell's ability to work—a term which didn't apply to Efrak's corpse, of course, nor would it to, say, a zombie, but apparently did to magickally animated furniture.

"We have to remove the furniture anyhow," Danthres said. "Maybe after that—"

Boneen shook his head. "Won't work. Something about the way that old ass performed the spell interferes with the peel-back. I can tell you two things, though. One is that it's just the lantern, the one chair, and the couch. All the other objects in that house are *properly* inanimate."

"And the other?" Torin asked.

"Efrak died about a day ago, and there was *someone* else in the house yesterday. But I can't tell you if it was before, during, or after the murder." Boneen smiled—a most unpleasant expression that didn't remotely suit him. "Actually, it's good news for you two, isn't it? It means you have an actual mystery on your hands."

"Wonderful," Danthres muttered.

"Oh, I thought you detective types loved a good mystery." Boneen was still smiling.

"Actually, we hate them," Torin said, "with great passion and vehemence. They're irritating, they involve a good deal of effort, and they tend to be exceedingly messy."

Danthres nodded in agreement. "I prefer my crimes simple and my criminals stupid and easily found."

Three guards, each wearing armor with the Unicorn Precinct crest, walked up to the house. One of them said, "Afternoon, Lieutenants. Hear tell we're, whaddayacall, movers now."

Nodding, Torin said, "Yes, we've got a body, two large pieces of furniture, and a lantern to bring to main headquarters. They're witnesses."

"The, whaddayacall, body's a witness?"

"No," Torin said with a grin, "just the other three."

"I'M TELLING YOU, I DIDN'T SEE ANYTHING!"

Danthres growled. "How could you not have seen anything? You're a *lantern*."

"I can only see things when I'm lit. Efrak was in one of his—his moods. He was only using candles."

Danthres sat at the table in one of the interrogation rooms of Castle Guard Headquarters. The headquarters were housed in the east wing of Lord Albin and Lady Meerka's castle, which in turn was located right at the end point of the Forest of Nimvale—the architectural centerpiece of Cliff's End. Four of the wing's interior rooms were lit only by a single lantern and used primarily for questioning people. Torin and Danthres had found that suspects and witnesses tended to get nervous—and therefore chatty—in rooms that had little light and many shadows.

She had to admit, however, that having two such lanterns—the one hanging from the wall and the one sitting on the room's only table—diluted the effect considerably.

"Moods?" Danthres prompted after the lantern remained silent for several seconds.

"Oh, he'd just get into one of these things where he'd be experimenting with some magick thing or other. It was always just a phase— he didn't have *any* discipline, really. He'd always start something, throw himself completely into it for a while, then abandon it unfinished. But every time he did, all of a sudden it was just candles, candles, candles. I'd sit for *days* without being lit—weeks, even. It was just *awful*. I mean, can you imagine having to sit blind all the time?"

Danthres didn't answer—her first rule of interrogation was that she asked all the questions. "What happened the night he died?"

"I told you, I didn't—"

"See anything, yes. But I assume you can still hear when you're not lit, right?"

"Well, strictly speaking, yes, but—"

"So what did you hear?"

A pause. "Well, you see, I wasn't really paying close attention."

"You were sulking because he was ignoring you," Danthres said.

"I don't sulk!"

She pressed on. "You didn't like the way he was treating you, so you decided to ignore him. He was treating you like a child, so you were going to act like one."

"I'd hardly go *that* far, but—well, it isn't fair. I mean, if he was going to make my sight dependent on being lit, the absolute *least* he could do was light me regularly. But no, he couldn't be bothered. He just *had* to study by candlelight. 'It keeps me pure,' he used to say. Honestly, such pretentious garbage."

Danthres got up from her chair and paced around the table, her brown cloak billowing a bit behind her as she did so. "So what happened the day he was killed? You must have heard *something*, you were right there."

"Just another one of those idiots that always comes in. Even if I had been lit, I probably would've ignored him. They just want to use Efrak, you know, try to get around the Brotherhood, like that ever works. Honestly, it's just so—"

"Did you recognize the voice?"

"Not really, but you people all sound alike to me."

"People—or humans?"

Another pause. "You're right, it wasn't a dwarf or an elf—and he spoke Common, so it wasn't a goblin or anything like that. Besides, I'd've been able to tell by the smell, even in *that* pigsty. No, definitely a human."

"I SAW THE WHOLE THING, OFFICER."

Torin smiled as he entered the interrogation room. The guards had placed the couch up against the wall and removed the papers and books, though it was still thoroughly stained and dirt-encrusted. At least, Torin assumed that whatever encrusted it was dirt. He decided not to inspect it too closely, instead turning the seat at the table toward the couch and addressing it.

"I'm a lieutenant, actually."

"Look, I saw everything, Sergeant. It was a human, male, young, black hair, blue eyes. Or maybe it was brown hair, but either way it was tied back in a ponytail, and it was definitely dark red hair. And greenish-blue eyes. Anyhow, he came in and started bothering poor Efrak. He wanted a charm for this girl he was attracted to. Efrak said he wasn't licensed for that kind of thing, and the boy went insane. He punched Efrak right in the face, then broke his neck. He seemed a little surprised after that, actually. Got all angry, and started yelling at Efrak. At least, that's what it sounded like."

Torin frowned. "Sounded like?"

"Well, it was hard to get a good look. Efrak tended to leave stuff lying around, and it makes it hard to see exactly —"

"Good sir, if you could tell me what color my beard is, I'd be grateful."

"It's red, of course. But, I can see fine now. It's just — Efrak had that stuff all over me."

"You don't have any idea what the murderer's hair color is, do you? Or what length it is?"

"Well, not as such, no, but I did hear everything that happened. I can tell you this, too, Captain: he didn't leave right away. I don't think he took anything, just threw some papers around."

"Did you try to stop him?"

"No. I think the chair might have, though. I heard them talking, but I couldn't make anything out. My hearing isn't always great when I'm all covered either, to be honest, but I definitely heard that blond-haired boy break Efrak's neck. Probably."

"It was just an accident."

"Really?" Danthres said, gazing upon the chair with annoyance.

"Total accident. Efrak tripped right after that boy who wanted the love potion left. Poor kid, he just wanted to impress a girl, y'know? Why do boys do that, anyhow? Try to impress girls?"

"Describe the boy."

"He was average height, straight brown hair, blue eyes. No beard, but he was obviously trying to grow one."

"And what happened when he was there?"

"Not much. He came in, asked Efrak for a love potion. Efrak explained about how those things have to go through the Brotherhood and he wasn't licensed. The boy whined the way boys do, and then he left, talking about how unfair life is and how he'd never get the girl of his dreams. Kind of tragic, really. Poor boy."

After several seconds, Danthres prompted, "*Then* what?"

"Oh, Efrak just tripped on the table and broke his fool neck. At least, I assume that's what broke. His head hit the table, and then he didn't get up. Silly old man, he was always tripping over things."

"I HATE MAGICK, I REALLY REALLY HATE MAGICK."

Torin smiled at Danthres's words as he entered Captain Osric's office. His partner was already seated in one of the captain's guest chairs and had made that comment to the head of the Castle Guard. Osric sat behind his desk, his perpetually half-shaven face in its permanent scowl, made all the more doleful by a silk eyepatch over his left eye. He, too, had a cloak and leather armor, both emblazoned with a gryphon crest; however, his cloak was red, and presently hanging on a hook on the wall.

Danthres continued ranting as Torin took the other guest chair. "It's ridiculous. How am I supposed to interrogate someone who doesn't blink, doesn't shrug, doesn't slouch, doesn't smile, doesn't —"

"I get the idea, Tresyllione," Osric said. He turned his right eye onto Torin. "What did Boneen say, ban Wyvald?"

"To stop bothering him when he's trying to have a nap." Torin grinned. "However, I got him to admit that there's no way to tell if Efrak died by accident. The neck break and the bruising on the side of Efrak's head are both consistent with Efrak falling into the table, but how he fell is impossible to say."

"From the sound of it," Osric said, "the only reliable witness is the chair."

"He's the only one who saw everything," Danthres said, "but I'm sure he's lying."

Osric's right eye bored into Danthres. "Why would a chair lie?"

"I don't know, but he's lying. Efrak was murdered."

"I agree with Danthres."

Osric snorted. "As if that's going to convince me. You two always agree with each other when you're sitting in this office because you don't want me to think that you ever argue."

"That's absurd," Danthres said archly. "Torin and I never argue."

"Yes, we do, actually," Torin admitted.

"No, we don't."

"In any case, she's still right. Efrak was murdered. Bodies don't, as a rule, fall down with arms at their side parallel to the furniture. Someone set him down."

"Probably our 'lovesick boy.' I want to put his description out to the Guard."

"What description?" Torin asked. "The chair's the only one who described him."

"True," Danthres said, "but it's the only one of the three who got a good look."

Leaning back in his chair, Osric said, "This still doesn't answer the question of why a chair would lie—what's the motive?"

Danthres shrugged, causing her blond hair to bounce. "Either way, the chair's description is the only one we've got. It's what we have to start with."

"It could take days to find him."

Again, Danthres shrugged. "So it takes days."

The captain pulled out his dagger, grabbed the battered sharpening stone on his desk, and started running the blade up and down it.

Torin scowled under his beard. Osric only started sharpening his dagger when he had bad news to impart.

"The Brotherhood's letting us handle this—assuming we handle it 'quickly and properly.' Translated into Common, that means that we need this case closed by sunup, or they'll step in."

"Fine by me," Danthres said. "Let them have it."

"No." Osric leaned forward again and pointed at Danthres with the tip of the dagger. "It's bad enough that they crawl all over our damn cases from the start when their registered mages are involved, I'm damned if I'll let them step on us because we're not solving the case fast enough to suit 'em. I want this case closed by sunup. Is that clear, Tresyllione?"

"Yes, sir."

"What about you, ban Wyvald?"

"Quite clear, sir," Torin said quickly.

"See if you can get a better description out of one of the other two, if you're so sure the chair's not being truthful."

Danthres shook her head. "They couldn't see anything, they were all covered in clutter. The chair's the only one who got any kind of good loo—"

"That's it!" Torin said.

"What's it?"

Grinning, Torin said, "The chair's motive for lying."

"Did you find that poor boy yet?"

"We're still looking," Torin said as he and Danthres re-entered the interrogation room where the chair sat. "We were wondering if you could answer a few more questions."

"Of course. I'm happy to do whatever I can to aid you good people."

"That's very considerate," Danthres said.

"Indeed." Torin nodded. "You've been much more helpful than your compatriots, in fact."

"Well, that's hardly surprising," the chair said. "They're just a couple of tiresome, filthy little worms."

"I'm glad you said that," Danthres said. "That they're filthy, I mean. We noticed that you were less stained than the other furnishings."

"*Any* of them," Torin added, "ability to talk notwithstanding."

"Oh, well, that's hardly surprising," the chair said quickly. "After all, I was Efrak's favorite chair. He always treated me better than the others."

"Funny, the others never mentioned that."

"Well, they're jealous, is all."

Danthres looked at Torin. "I can certainly understand that."

"Of course," Torin said with a nod. "After all, if I were a piece of furniture in that house, and some other piece of furniture was singled out for such treatment, I'd be jealous also. But if the chair *was* his favorite . . ."

"Yet the other two gave no indication of this exalted status. In fact, they were also surprised when we told them how clean you were." On those last two words, Danthres turned to the chair. "In fact, the couch opined that that was why your poor, lovesick boy stuck around *after* Efrak's death. And why you two were talking."

"That's—that's ridiculous," the chair stammered. "I would never lie like that."

"Unless you had good reason," Torin said.

"Or a shallow one," Danthres added. "Like a promise to clean you up in exchange for lying to us about how Efrak died."

"Shallow?" The chair now sounded indignant. "You think it's shallow to ask for once—just once—to be treated with respect? To actually scrape off the food that dates back to the reign of Chalmraik the Foul? To not leave eight pounds of books on top of my cushions? To maybe *sit* on me every once in a while instead of treating me no different than the table? I'm a *chair*—my function is to be sat on, not used as a receptacle for some stupid old man's garbage."

"So the boy did kill him?" Torin asked.

"It was an accident, but yes. They got into a shoving match, Efrak fell down and broke his fool neck. And you know what? I'm glad that old fool's dead! The man had no respect for us! *None!* And it wasn't just me, you know—but those other two were just *so* grateful to be animated, they let him walk all over them. How he treated the poor lantern—a disgrace, an absolute disgrace, keeping a lantern in the dark like that."

"We're going to need a full description of the boy," Torin said after a moment. "Then I'm afraid we'll have to turn you over to the Brotherhood of Wizards."

At that, Danthres turned to Torin. "What for? Why not just put him in a cell here? He *did* cover up a crime."

"Yes," the chair said in a panic, "why not in a cell here? The Brotherhood'll probably de-animate me or something. I don't want to die!"

"Besides, the Brotherhood gave us jurisdiction," Danthres said. "So it's up to our magistrate to decide what to do with him, not them."

"I'll be a model prisoner!" the chair put in. "In fact, it'll be heavenly—people will actually use me to sit on for once."

Torin shook his head and smiled. "Fine, we won't turn him over."

"Oh," the chair said, "and the boy's name is Brant—he lives a few blocks from Efrak's house. He came by a few times, actually, and always talked to me. Very nice boy—short, blond hair in a ponytail, brown eyes, and a thick full beard."

Torin gazed at the chair, then turned to Danthres. "So much for our accurate description."

"I'll have Garis pick him up," Danthres said. Then she sighed deeply. "I really hate magick."

CRIME OF PASSION

Lieutenant Danthres Tresyllione of the Cliff's End Castle Guard saw that the young guard spoke true. Blood spattered the walls, windows, and even the ceiling of the small house. Rivulets of blood flowed across the unevenly laid wooden floor, pooling in odd places. Both she and her parnter, Lieutenant Torin ban Wyvald, had to lift their brown cloaks of rank to prevent them from being stained. As it was, their boots were going to need a good cleaning, and Danthres wondered if she could talk Captain Osric into requisitioning a Laundry Spell — it was the only way to get the stains completely out.

All of those pools led back to the three bodies sprawled in the middle of the room: one female adult and two male children.

Danthres turned to the guard. Like Danthres and Torin, he wore the black leather armor of the Guard; unlike the lieutenants, he did not wear a cloak, since he was only a foot soldier. His armor was adorned with the symbol of Dragon Precinct, the location of this house — the middle-class section of Cliff's End. "What've we got?"

"Woman's named Tybet Nerban, the boys are her two sons, Leestan and Bykir. She's married to Cebru Nerban — he's the boys' father, and the one who called this in. Says he came home from his morning run and found them like this. I've got him back in the pantry. There's no sign of forced entry, and nothing's been stolen."

While the guard spoke, Danthres took a closer look at the bodies. All three of them had been ripped to pieces — the woman's throat was almost entirely gone, and one of the boys' heads was caved in, which right there accounted for most of the blood. *Nothing bleeds so spectacularly as throat and head wounds,* she thought. The woman's arms were positioned in such a way that it looked like she tried to defend herself — there were some kind of claw marks on her forearms that looked like defensive wounds. *Of course, why anyone would think a forearm would be of any use against something that can rip out your throat is another story.*

Then again, Danthres had been investigating crimes in Cliff's End for a decade. She had yet to find a murder that made sense, especially when children were involved.

"Who d'you think was killed first?" the guard, whose name was Kellan, asked.

Danthres shot the young man a look. "Hoping to get some tips on crime-solving?" she said nastily. She had very little patience with grunts who had delusions of intelligence.

"No, ma'am," Kellan said, uncharacteristically unintimidated by Danthres's tone. *He must be new*, she thought. "I was just curious."

"Not that it matters much, but I'd guess the mother was killed first, since the children are on top. The children were mauled and dropped on her."

The guard winced. "I wonder what's worse — watching your kids die or watching your mother die."

Torin finally spoke. "Hope you never find out, Kellan. I believe you said the father is in the pantry?"

"Yes, sir."

"And the M.E.'s on his way?"

"He sent a mage-bird that said he'd be here in a quarter of an hour." Kellan frowned. "That was about a quarter of an hour ago, actually, and —"

"What is all this *blood* doing here?"

Danthres turned to see Boneen, the magickal examiner, standing in the doorway, an even more peevish than normal expression on his wrinkled face.

Torin grinned as the elderly wizard entered. "Apologies, Boneen, but it seems the owners of the blood sprung a leak."

Glowering at Torin, Boneen said, "Stick with police work, ban Wyvald — you're ill suited to the role of wit." Boneen was on loan from the Brotherhood of Wizards to provide magickal services for the Guard. The loan was at Lord Albin's insistence; that it was Boneen was at the Brotherhood's. Danthres was of the considered opinion that he got the job so the other members of the Brotherhood didn't have to listen to him complain.

However, he did his job of magickal examiner well. His primary duty was to perform a "peel-back" spell that read the psychic resonances on inanimate objects. Generally, this meant he could reconstruct the crime, thus simplifying Danthres's job immensely.

"Let him get to work," Torin said to Kellan. "Canvas the area, see if anyone saw anything." Since this was Dragon, there was at least a chance that one of the neighbors might be civic-minded enough to report if they had witnessed something useful. If this were in the lower-class Goblin Precinct or the docklands of Mermaid Precinct, the chances of finding a cooperative witness were all but nonexistent. "We'll be in the pantry, questioning Nerban."

Danthres started toward the pantry door. "I doubt this'll take long. This looks like a straightforward crime of passion—no forced entry, no sign of any mayhem in the house *except* the bodies, nothing stolen. I'm willing to bet the knife he used to slice them to ribbons is still in the kitchen."

"Uh, ma'am?" Kellan said. "I don't think he did it. He doesn't really strike me as the type."

Stopping in her tracks and whirling on the guard, Danthres said, "And on the very off-chance that some day you wear a brown cloak, I will consider your opinion relevant. In the meantime, get out there and canvas, or I'll put you on the detail that has to clean this house *by yourself*, am I understood, Guard?"

"Yes, ma'am," Kellan said with a nod, and calmly walked out the door.

Boneen chuckled. "You must be losing your touch, Tresyllione. They used to tremble at your every utterance."

Danthres bit back a retort. It wouldn't do to kill Boneen—there'd be paperwork.

The two detectives entered the pantry, leaving the magickal examiner to perform the peel-back.

The room was unbearably hot. Danthres saw that the stove in the center of the room was still warm, the door open to reveal cooling wood. From the look of it, the stove had been in use only a few hours before. The remnants of the morning meal were on the table, probably the result of the stove's use. The only foodstuffs still intact were two biscuits, which smelled heavenly even hours after they'd been cooked.

Standing at the cupboard next to the table was a pale middle-aged man with a wispy moustache. His skinny arms and pudgy belly indicated someone who did not perform physical labor. He seemed to be arranging the items in the cupboard so they would be neater. At Danthres and Torin's entrance, he turned to face them.

"Mr. Nerban, I'm Lieutenant Tresyllione, and this is my partner Lieutenant ban Wyvald." Torin waved and smiled. "We're investigating the death of your wife and sons."

"Of course." Nerban straightened his purple tunic carefully, and sat down in one of the chairs next to the table. "The guard said you would be by. I am happy to help in whatever way I can." Cebru Nerban spoke in a monotone and was careful to enunciate every word.

"What do you do for a living, Mr. Nerban?"

"I work at the bank as a clerk. I came home from my morning run—I run every morning now, I have been doing it for seven weeks, since I do not like how fat I am getting—and when I arrived home I saw that Tybet and the boys were lying dead on the floor. I immediately summoned a guard. He told me to sit out here in the pantry and I have remained here ever since then waiting for you to come and question me."

Danthres had to shake her head to keep herself awake, and was starting to understand why Kellan didn't think Nerban was capable of the crime. *Not that I'm going to tell* him *that at any point.*

"When did you go for your run?"

"Right at sunrise. I always go for my run right at sunrise." He started to arrange the plates on the table so that they were all in a line.

"So you had breakfast before that?"

Nerban shook his head. "I did not, no. I stopped eating breakfast when I started running."

She pointed at the table, with its newly organized settings. "So all this was for Tybet and the boys?"

"Yes."

"What about the extra biscuits?" Torin asked.

At that, Nerban shrugged, an action which put his tunic out of place. He straightened it as he spoke. "I would assume that Tybet made more than she and the boys could eat. She did that sometimes. I always thought it was wasteful, but Tybet never listened to me whenever food was involved."

"So you came back from your run," Torin said, "opened the door—"

"No, the door was open. On nice days like today, Tybet usually left the door open to ventilate the house because it got so hot inside."

"That's safe?"

"Oh yes, this is a very safe neighborhood. This is a very good part of town, Lieutenant. Bad things never happen here."

"Until today," Danthres said.

"Well, yes, obviously, until today."

Danthres asked a few more questions, told Nerban that they'd send someone to take the bodies and clean the blood and then went outside via the back door to avoid disturbing Boneen. Kellan met up with them and reported that nobody saw anyone enter or leave the house — including Nerban himself — and that the door was, in fact, open.

"Two different neighbors mentioned that, actually," Kellan said. "One said that it was great that they left the door open because you could smell the food from the kitchen. The other one complained for the same reason — I got the idea that his wife isn't a very good cook," he added with a smile.

Danthres did not return the smile. "Save the commentary, Guard."

At last, Kellan looked intimidated. "Er, yes, ma'am. In any case, one person heard screaming, but she couldn't make it out, and nobody else heard anything unusual. They all said that the family was very quiet, never got into any arguments, except the children when they got to being raucous the way boys are, and that the Nerbans were nice people. Oh, and that Nerban always went out of his way never to hurt anyone or anything — he wouldn't even kill the vermin in his house."

Sighing, Danthres said, "All right, when Boneen's done, get some guards in here, do a sweep, see if you can find a murder weapon. And don't let Nerban out of your sight."

Torin made a noise like a bursting pipe. "Danthres, that's crazy. Nerban didn't kill them."

Looking at her partner like he had grown a second head, Danthres said, "Of course he killed them. There was no forced entry, nothing stolen, no other damage to the house or anything around it. It had to be him."

"A nonviolent bank clerk is your murderer?" Torin asked dubiously. "That man in there isn't capable of killing anyone."

"I agree with the lieutenant, ma'am —" Kellan started.

Danthres turned on the guard. "At what point did you attempt to grow a brain? Just do what you're told, Guard, understood? Now get that detail together!"

Kellan moved off to do that.

"And as for you, I should think that after ten years, you'd trust my judgment a bit."

"Sorry," Torin said, "but I'm too busy trusting mine. That man didn't kill anyone."

Before Danthres could respond, Boneen interrupted, exiting the house into the sunny fall day. Danthres noted with annoyance that there was no evidence of bloodstains on the M.E.'s person, though his hands were stained black with the residue from the peel-back.

"Of course that man didn't," the old wizard said. "It was a hrancit demon."

"It can't be a hrancit demon," Danthres said.

"Of course it can," Boneen said. "Probably some idiot teenager conjured one and let it run around loose. This entire mess fits with a hrancit demon. They have claws that match the wounds on all three bodies, and they tend toward random unfocused violence."

Danthres shook her head. "No."

Torin sighed. "Danthres, stop it."

"Stop what?"

"I know that look on your face. This is going to be another of your crusades."

Danthres's face contorted into a look of fury. "It's not a crusade, Torin! Boneen, you said that hrancit demons tend toward unfocused violence."

The magickal examiner nodded.

"This was *not* unfocused! There was no damage to the doorframe, the furniture, the rest of the house, nothing!"

"Two witnesses said the door was left open, Danthres," Torin said slowly. "The demon could have just run in and killed them. You're letting the fact that children were murdered cloud your judgment."

That got Danthres's blood boiling. "This has nothing to do with the fact that children are involved! It has to do with ten years of instincts telling me that this wasn't a hrancit demon."

Sharply, Boneen said, "I'll see your ten years and raise you several centuries of magicking. My peel-back showed a hrancit demon. Therefore, it was a hrancit demon. I am now going to go back to the castle and cast a spell that should track this particular hrancit demon down. Once I do, you can fetch it and put it down, the case will be closed, and Captain Osric can praise you both for a job well done after I've done all the actual work."

Before Danthres had the chance to weigh whether or not it would be worth the paperwork to kill the M.E., Boneen then disappeared in a burst of light, which he only did when he felt like having the last word, since the Teleport Spell generally took a lot out of him.

Danthres blinked the spots out of her eyes, cursing her sensitive eyesight. The elven half of her heritage had blessed her with better-than-normal eyesight, but it also meant that magickal lightshows had a more profound impact on her ability to see.

"Come on," Danthres said, starting her walk toward the castle. "It'll be hours before Boneen casts that spell."

Torin nodded. "Of course. He'll need a good nap after the Teleport Spell. And you'll need the time to calm down."

"I'm perfectly calm!"

That earned her a dubious look from Torin.

She sighed. "Look, I know what you're thinking."

"I'm sure you do. I'm thinking about that accused child murderer you almost beat to a pulp two years ago—the one who turned out to be innocent." His voice softened when he added, "And I also am thinking about that elf you killed in Bronnwick."

Danthres continued walking, refusing to dignify Torin's diatribe with a response. She had encountered a mass grave of infants who, like Danthres, were born of a human and an elf but who, unlike Danthres, were not permitted to live beyond one month thanks to the snobbery of full-blooded elves in general and one high-born elf in particular who took it upon himself to keep the elven bloodlines pure.

Maybe I do take it a little personally when children are killed, she thought, but refused to say out loud, not wanting to give her partner the satisfaction. *But Nerban killed his wife and kids, and it's not because I'm still trying to take revenge for all those slaughtered children. No matter what the peel-back said, this is not the work of a hrancit demon.*

A day later, a storm front had moved in, blanketing Cliff's End in rain. Boneen had yet to find the hrancit demon. Torin and Danthres were spending their morning in the squadroom of Guard Headquarters, located in the eastern wing of the lord and lady's castle. Torin had acquired a stuffed-up nose thanks to the inclement weather, and was partaking of a mug of tea, while Danthres—whose sterner constitution allowed her to stave off the cold—chewed on one of the pastries that Sergeant Jonas's wife always made, which was soggier than usual thanks to the weather. Torin expressed surprise at the M.E.'s inability to track the demon, which prompted Danthres to fly off on a rant.

"It's not as if we're dealing with a subtle beast, here. A hrancit demon habitually runs amok, ripping to pieces anything that happens to get in its way or looks at it funny. It usually leaves *dozens* of bodies in its wake. I remember hearing about one in Treemark—it killed over fifty people before a local wizard managed to banish the thing. Yet somehow *this* hrancit demon has only targeted one woman and two children and nobody and nothing else in all of Cliff's End. I'm telling you, we should be questioning the husband."

"Boneen said it was a hrancit demon." Torin followed his statement with a sniffle.

Danthres pointed her pastry at Torin as if it were a dagger. "Don't you dare throw that old fool into my face, Torin, or it'll be more than your nose that's stuffed up. Boneen is a cranky old idiot who hates being forced into this job."

"Who still takes pride in his work," Torin added. "He's never given us reason to doubt his peel-backs in the past. But," he said quickly before Danthres could give him a sharp reply, "let's allow for a second that you're right, that it is a crime of passion." He sneezed, then took a sip of his tea. "You really think the husband did it?"

"Let's get him in the interview room. I promise that inside of an hour, he'll tell us precisely how he did it."

"In a dull monotone, no doubt. Honestly, Danthres, you talked to him—he's a *bank clerk*. In order to commit a crime of passion, you have to *have* some. Furthermore, even if he did kill them, he wouldn't have slashed at random parts of their bodies, and he wouldn't have left the corpses just lying haphazardly in the middle of the floor. The entire time we were there, he was neatening things, putting them in order. That is *not* someone who carves up three people like he was hacking his way through the jungle."

Danthres stood fuming for several seconds, covering the action by chewing the rest of her pastry—which, owing to its sogginess, took longer than usual. After swallowing it, she said in a low voice, "I hate it when you're right."

"No wonder you're always in a bad mood. I'm *usually* right." Torin grinned broadly, his teeth showing through his thick red beard. Then the grin fell. "Of course, that doesn't explain why Boneen saw a hrancit demon in the peel-back — or why he can't find it now." He took another bite of pastry. "One thing we haven't considered — that someone conjured the hrancit demon for the express purpose of killing the Nerbans and then banished it."

Shaking her head, Danthres said, "I don't like that — only a particularly powerful wizard could accomplish that, and if that's so, we're going to have the Brotherhood all over this case. That's not the sort of thing that improves my mood."

"Or Osric's," Torin added, then pulled a handkerchief out of a pocket in his belt. Any time magick was involved, the Brotherhood of Wizards tended to interfere in the Castle Guard's investigation, usually to the detriment of the investigation's efficiency. Captain Osric didn't share Danthres's disdain for the practice of magick, but he had a severe hatred for the bureaucracy that administrated it. Torin blew his nose, then said, "Even so it seems to me that our obvious next step is to question Mr. Nerban and see if he might know anything about a wizard with a grudge against him or his family."

For the first time since they got the call to the Nerban house, Danthres smiled. "I knew I kept you around for a reason."

DANTHRES HAD ONE OF THE GUARDS BRING NERBAN IN, WITH PARTICULAR instructions not to take his cloak, assuming he had one to protect him against the rain. He did, and the guard dutifully left it on as he brought the bank clerk into the featureless room with a single lantern hanging from the center of the ceiling.

"Thank you for coming in, Mr. Nerban," Torin said in his most pleasant voice. "Let me take your cloak."

As he removed the sodden cloak from Nerban's person, the pudgy man said, "Thank you. You seem ill today, Lieutenant."

Torin dropped the cloak rather unceremoniously on the table even as Nerban sat in one of the chairs provided. "Yes, I'm afraid this weather has me a bit under it, so to speak."

Nerban immediately moved to fold the cloak neatly. "I am surprised you did not call in sick to work. Today would be a good day to not go into work. I almost wish I hadn't."

"You were at work?" Torin asked as Nerban finished folding the cloak and sat back.

"Yes," he said. "The bank would have let me take another day off to grieve, but I find that the work helps to distract me. Besides, the longer I stay out, the more difficult it will be when I get back."

Torin nodded sagely, taking a sip from his third mug of tea today "Oh yes, I know exactly what you mean. I must admit, that's one of the things that made me reluctant to call in today." Torin then sat directly on the folded cloak. "It would take me ages to catch up on all the work that piles up when I'm out —I mean, you have the existing work, plus the old work. It just piles up."

Nerban did not answer, as he was staring dolefully at the cloak that Torin's rump was now disturbing the neat folds of.

Danthres then spoke up from the corner of the room. "We have a few more questions for you, Mr. Nerban. Did you or your wife know any wizards?"

Her presence startled Nerban, who apparently hadn't known she was there. He looked up from his stricken examination of Torin disturbing his cloak. "Excuse me? Er, no. No, we did not know any wizards. I do not see how that is possible. Wizards do not consort with the likes of us."

"But they use banks," Torin said, sliding off the table, which caused the cloak to fall to the floor in a heap. "Are you sure you didn't help one out with his account?"

Nerban got up from the chair, then bent over to pick the cloak up. "Believe me, Lieutenant, they would not let someone as low in the hierarchy as me work on an account with a wizard. Only the senior officials at the bank deal with those." He neatly folded the cloak and put it back on the table.

Danthres started to move toward the table. "And you've never encountered any wizards anywhere else? There wasn't one tutoring one of your sons, say?" Now Danthres sat down on the cloak. Her armor protected her from the garment's wetness, for which she was grateful.

"I do not believe so. Why are you asking these questions?" Again, Nerban started looking at the cloak with an apprehensive expression. "I never met any wizards until that strange little old man who came with you two. In fact, I thought he said that it was a hrancit demon that killed Tybet and the boys. Can't you just find the demon?"

"Well, that's the problem, Mr. Nerban," Torin said, "we can't seem to locate it. The only way that's possible is if the demon was conjured by a wizard and then banished again. So we thought that perhaps you or your family might have had congress with one."

"Would you like a pastry, Mr. Nerban?" Danthres got up from the table, knocking the cloak askew, though it did not fall to the floor this time. "Sergeant Jonas's wife makes some excellent pastries for us every morning."

Nerban leaned forward and again folded the cloak neatly. "No, thank you. I do not eat in the morning."

"Right, you told us that yesterday. Yet, there were two biscuits left."

Torin added, "The biscuits looked quite good."

"Yes, Tybet was an excellent cook," Nerban said, still in the monotone, though Danthres noticed that his moustache was now twitching. "She saved them for me, but I did not eat them. I told her that I did not eat breakfast anymore. She chose to ignore this, even though I explained why to her."

Torin walked across the room, passing close to Danthres. "I suppose that—" His arm collided lightly with Danthres, but it was the one in which he held his tea. The beverage spilled over onto the cloak.

"Oh, I'm so sorry!" Torin said. "That was clumsy of me.

Danthres reached for the cloak. "That's terrible, we didn't mean to do that."

"That is all right," Nerban said, also reaching for the cloak. "I am sure I can get it cleaned."

Danthres gripped the cloak. "No, we can do that. After all, we're the ones who stained it."

"No, no," Nerban said, also gripping the cloak, "really, I will just fold it, and—"

"I insist, Mr. Nerban."

"Please," Nerban said, tugging harder on the cloak, "if you will just let go of it, I can—"

Danthres, in turn, tugged even harder on it. "We have a cleaning service that did a wonderful job of getting your wife and boys' blood off my boots, I'm sure they can do the same for—"

"Please, just let *go of the damn cloak before I—arrrrrrRRRRR GGGGGHHH!*"

Danthres dropped the cloak and had her sword out of its scabbard in one fluid motion. Next to her, Torin did likewise.

Cebru Nerban reared his head back and screamed to the ceiling, even as his skin rippled and changed color to an unfortunate shade of green, his form expanded, tearing through his clothing, and his hair seemed to disappear.

He had transformed into a hrancit demon.

A second later, the demon seemed to be bound by strings of bright light. *Magick,* Danthres thought with a sigh. Boneen had long ago warded the castle so that any unauthorized magickal creature was immediately bound upon its entry or appearance. So unsheathing the sword had been wholly unnecessary, though that didn't stop Danthres from keeping it out, just in case.

"Well," Torin said after a second. "*That* was interesting."

Blowing out a breath, Danthres said, "I was hoping that disturbing his neatness routine might get a good response, but this was rather beyond expectations."

The door to the interrogation room slammed open to reveal two guards and Boneen. "What happened? My wards are going off like—" He stared at the former Mr. Nerban. "What in the name of Temisa's left toe is *that*?"

Torin grinned. "That, Boneen, is Cebru Nerban. Normally calm enough to lull any sane person to sleep, when he is angered—say by his wife preparing breakfast for him even though he no longer eats breakfast—he changes into a hrancit demon."

"He was cursed." Boneen pointed at the strings of light. "See the orange tinge around the restraints?"

Following Boneen's finger, Danthres did indeed see a slight orange cast to the light.

"That indicates that this is a demon cursed to share its existence with a mortal. My guess is that it was the demon that committed some transgression."

"Makes sense," Torin said with a wide smile. "What worse fate for a demon that indulges in chaos than to be trapped within a human who is the epitome of order?"

Boneen nodded. "And what better punishment than to let it come out every once in a while, to get a taste of reality before being banished back inside Nerban here?" He shook his head. "I shudder to think how this will fall out jurisdictionally. Are they both responsible for the crime?"

Torin shrugged. "That's the magistrate's headache, not ours."

"It seems," Danthres said to the M.E. with great reluctance, "that we were both right, Boneen."

Boneen harrumphed. "Well, of course *I* was right. The remarkable thing is that *you* managed the feat."

Snarling, Danthres briefly held up her sword, then thought better of it. *Paperwork*, she reminded herself.

CATCH AND RELEASE

 the squadroom, that his partner, Lieutenant Amilar Grovis, would not be there. Most days, it was a forlorn hope.

Grovis's desk abutted Iaian's in the easternmost wing of the lord and lady's castle. They shared a view of the Forest of Nimvale through the north wall window. Iaian could only appreciate the loveliness of that vista when Grovis took a personal or sick day. His partner was an imbecilic overprivileged religious zealot whose place in the Cliff's End Castle Guard was secured because his father wanted to make a man of him. His father was Harcort Grovis, owner of the largest bank in the city-state, and he tended to get what he wanted.

Iaian was only two years from retirement. Once he was with the Castle Guard for two-and-a-half decades, his full pension would vest. If he left any sooner, he only got the ten-year pension, which was a quarter of the amount. So Iaian really wasn't in any kind of position to complain when Captain Osric saddled him with this idiot son of a banker.

"You're the most experienced detective in the squad," Osric had said, then. "Who better to teach him the job?"

Iaian knew better than to threaten to quit. Osric had called his bluff ten years earlier during his mercifully brief partnership with Danthres Tresyllione, and again when the captain had paired Iaian up with Forbin after Linder died. Then Forbin was forced to quit after his leg was shattered by that troll, and Grovis had been fobbed on him.

Osric knew damn well that Iaian's comfortable retirement was too important to jeopardize. He'd endure whatever he needed to, including partnering with the biggest idiot he'd ever known. And Iaian had met quite the procession of idiots in his life . . .

Sure enough, this morning Grovis was sitting there at his desk, signing some scrolls—probably the last bits of paperwork from the Abella case—and looking even more like a fish than usual.

Ignoring his partner, Iaian headed to the pantry, where Sergeant Jonas and three of the other four detectives were partaking of Jonas's wife's pastries. Iaian hadn't liked any of the four sergeants who had paraded through the eastern wing since Sergeant Newcastle retired, but Jonas was the least egregious, due to his wife's excellent pastries.

"Mornin', Iaian," Hawk said. His partner, Dru, just nodded, as his mouth was full of fried dough.

Naturally, Danthres said nothing. Iaian had had little use for the half-elf woman when she first got promoted to lieutenant, and nothing in the intervening decade had changed his mind. The feeling had proven to be very mutual.

Danthres's partner, Torin ban Wyvald, was not present, but he was rarely on time. This suited Iaian, as it meant more pastries for the rest of them. Plus it also meant he was never the last one in anymore.

"By the way," Jonas said after swallowing his mouthful, "the barge is coming in tomorrow, and we got the manifest this morning by courier."

Iaian blinked his rheumy eyes. "For Wiate's sake, is it the end of the month already?" Once prisoners were sentenced, the ones who weren't condemned to death served their sentences on a prison barge that sailed around the Garamin Sea. Once a month it came back to Cliff's End to release those whose sentences were up and take on the newly convicted.

Dru had chewed and swallowed, and asked the sergeant, "Anyone interesting on the list?"

Jonas nodded. "Hal Vorlin's latest one-month sentence is up, so figure he'll be picking pockets down Jorbin's Way by week's end. Winn Avar's out."

"Dammit," Danthres muttered. "Another three-year sentence comes to an end. His wife will probably be on the docks welcoming him back with open arms. And then he'll hit her again for walking so slow on the leg that *he* broke."

Iaian frowned. "I thought you and Torin put that shitbrain away—what, six years ago?"

"Seven." Danthres's already ugly face got much uglier when she snarled the way she was now. "And after his three years were up, he went and started beating his wife again a year later. Her brother made another complaint, his wife still refused to admit that Avar caused her injuries, but the magistrate *again* gave him three years."

"Oh, and Iaian?" Jonas said with a wince that made Iaian rather nervous.

"What?"

"Speaking of people arrested seven years ago, Yarbanig's out tomorrow, too."

Iaian almost choked on his pastry. "Already?"

Jonas shrugged. "It was a seven-year sentence, so yes, already."

"Shit. Time really does fly."

"Who's Yarbanig?" Hawk asked.

Danthres frowned. "Isn't he that dwarf actor who was kidnapping children?"

Nodding, Iaian said, "Yeah, took me and Linder a month to track him down. He kept switching theatre troupes."

"He only got seven years for kidnapping kids?" Dru asked incredulously.

Iaian shrugged. "Talk to the magistrate. The kids wouldn't say anything, he insisted he was innocent, Boneen's peel-back wasn't conclusive thanks to the glamours that all those theatrical shitbrains use, so he only got seven years."

"This," Danthres added, "is the same magistrate who thinks a man breaking his wife's bones on a regular basis should only be on the barge for three years. You'd think the second time, he'd lengthen the sentence."

"Same problem in both cases, really." Iaian sighed. "The victims wouldn't testify. Shit." He shook his head.

"What's wrong?" Hawk asked.

"Ever since he went onto the barge, he's been mailing letters to the lord and lady, to Sir Rommett, to Captain Osric, to me, hell, even to the king and queen saying he's innocent. And the letters to me all say that he's gonna kill me when he gets out."

Danthres stood on the dock at noon, hanging back a bit. As always on the first day of the month, there was a huge collection of civilians gathered, waiting for the rowboat from the prison barge. The barge itself never docked, indeed it never got close enough to even be seen from the docks.

Interspersed throughout that crowd were several guards from Mermaid Precinct, making sure that none of the newly released prisoners caused a fuss. On that same boat were members of the prison staff who got a day of liberty.

As a general rule, Danthres avoided this part of the monthly ritual. She would often go on the second day, when the new prisoners embarked for the barge, as she wanted to make sure that all the shitbrains she put away were actually going. Plus, she sometimes enjoyed taunting them and reminding them that she was the one who caught them.

Today, though, she wanted to be there for the arrivals. Especially since, as she had feared, Yona Avar was eagerly awaiting the return of her husband, despite the fact that she'd been separated from him for six of the last seven years due to the violence he committed upon her body.

An irritatingly familiar voice sounded behind her. "Oh, good, I was concerned that the boat hadn't arrived yet."

Turning, Danthres saw the fish-like face that matched the voice. "Lord and Lady, Grovis, what are *you* doing here?"

"I have business with one of the prisoners."

For a moment, Danthres considered asking what prisoner and what business, and then decided that she didn't care enough.

Besides, she could now see the rowboat on approach, so she moved forward on the dock. Grovis, however, moved right alongside her.

Once the sailors tied the boat to the dock, the guards from Mermaid also stepped forward, past Danthres and Grovis, making sure the prisoners moved off the boat in an orderly manner.

Grovis asked, "Why are they all rubbing their wrists?"

Danthres had done this enough times that she no longer even noticed that most of the prisoners rubbed their wrists and walked even more awkwardly than you would expect from someone disembarking from a rowboat. "That's the barge's security. All prisoners wear metal bracelets and anklets that are inscribed with runes. If they go anywhere they're not supposed to—the bridge, or over the side—they start to get heavier. The farther away from the barge, the heavier they become, until the prisoner can't move."

"Hmp." Grovis nodded. "I imagine that cuts down on escape attempts."

Snorting, Danthres said, "Not as much as you might think. There are a *lot* of drowned prisoners at the bottom of the Garamin. Shitbrains who thought they were strong enough."

An unusually tall dwarf clambered off the boat, and Grovis said, "Excuse me, Danthres." He walked right up to the dwarf and put a hand on his chest. "You're Yarbanig, correct?"

"What's it to you if I am, Cloak? I ain't gotta talk to you no more, I served my time on the big boat, and I wanna go home."

"The Castle Guard may speak to anyone within Cliff's End's borders at any time for any reason, and I, as a member of the Guard, wish to speak to you now."

"Fine, I'll listen to whatever stupid shit you gotta say, and *then* I'll go home."

Grovis pulled Yarbanig aside, but said nothing to him at first, waiting for others to get off the boat.

One of them was Winn Avar; the diminutive human looked rather sickly. He didn't do well on the sea, and had begged the magistrate for sentencing anywhere other than the barge. Danthres had taken great pleasure in the magistrate's refusal to grant that request. It almost made up for the short sentence.

Almost.

Stepping between Yona and Winn, she said, "This is going to be your only warning, Avar."

Yona put a hand on Danthres's cloak. "Please Lieutenant, don't."

Ignoring both the hand and the words of the wife, she fixed her glare on the husband. "If you so much as lay a hand on Yona, I will come for you. And there won't be any arrests or interrogations or appearances before the magistrate. I have a sword, and I'm authorized to use it if provoked. So do yourself a favor, Avar, and do *not* provoke me."

With that, she stepped away, allowing husband and wife to go home together. Again.

By this time, the prisoners had cleared out, as had the civilians who were meeting them. Various prison staffers were now disembarking in a more leisurely manner for their liberty. There were a few guards as well. Originally, the Barge Rats were a separate force, hired by the owners of the barge, but Lord Albin bought the barge and the Barge Rats and folded them into the Castle Guard. However, their leather armor was all black and carried no insignia to denote precinct. Their hiring process was also still separate from the rest of the Guard.

"Now listen here," Grovis was saying to Yarbanig. "You've made threats against my partner."

"Oh, *you're* Iaian's partner now, huh? I heard that Linder got his sorry ass killed. No loss, you ask me, just wish I coulda been there to spit on his corpse."

"The point is, you made those threats. And I'm here to urge you, for your own sake, not to act on them."

Yarbanig laughed bitterly. "For *my* sake? My sake don't matter none, Cloak. I lost my sake when your *partner* got it into his stupid head that I kidnapped kids."

"Understand something, Mr. Yarbanig. Iaian is an idiot, a bribe-taker, a very poor example of both a detective and a human being."

Danthres bridled. On the one hand, she agreed with everything Grovis had said. She'd only partnered with Iaian three times, once for half a case shortly before Torin started, once when Torin was sick, and once between Linder's death and Grovis's hire. Grovis was, if anything, underselling it.

On the other hand, that wasn't the sort of thing you said to a criminal just getting off the barge.

Grovis went on. "I rue the day I was partnered with him, and would jump for joy if our captain assigned me to someone — anyone — else." He paused a moment. "But, he is still my partner, and he is a member of the Cliff's End Castle Guard. You said when we began this conversation that you served your time on the big boat, as you so eloquently put it. That means you are a free citizen once more and may do as you wish. But if you choose to make good on your threats to Lieutenant Iaian, you will never be a free citizen again. The moment you decide to make an attempt on Iaian's life, the *entirety* of the Castle Guard will make it their life's work to make sure that you don't live to see the following sunrise. And *I* shall be leading that charge. Do I make myself clear, Mr. Yarbanig?"

The dwarf threw up his hands. "And what do I do about the seven years I just lost? Huh? I didn't *do* nothin', and I just spent seven years on that Xinf-forsaken boat just 'cause your partner's too much of a shitbrain to find the right guy."

"There were no instances of children being kidnapped following your incarceration, Mr. Yarbanig. Lieutenants Iaian and Linder, may Ghandurha grant him safe passage to the afterlife, the magistrate, Captain Osric, and the lord and lady all agreed that you were guilty, and you served your sentence. I strongly urge you to let that go and move on with your life."

"Where to? I can't work nowhere where there's kids. And kids are damn near *everywhere*. Nobody's gonna be hirin' an actor who can't work near kids."

"That is not my concern, Mr. Yarbanig. My concern is that you not throw your life away by trying to take the life of my partner."

The bitter laugh returned. "He took mine. Seems only fair. We done here, Cloak?"

Grovis sighed and stepped aside. "Yes, we are. At least, I hope that we are."

Yarbanig strode past Grovis and headed away from the docks.

Danthres looked upon Grovis with something resembling respect. "I'm impressed, Grovis—that's the closest I've ever seen you manage to approximate being a member of the Castle Guard."

Grovis shrugged. "Whatever I may think of him, Iaian is my partner. And whatever I may think of *that* person," he pointed half-heartedly in the direction Yarbanig had walked, "he has indeed served his sentence. Going after Iaian will only cause him more trouble, not less."

"Let's hope he and Avar both listened." She sighed. "I'll bet a silver that neither of them will, though."

As per usual, Iaian climbed out of the daybed he and his wife kept in their spare room. Theoretically, it was for house guests, but they hadn't entertained in well over a decade, and it had been almost that long that Iaian had been using it as his bed.

As per usual, Iaian listened to the crack of his bones and the whine of his muscles as he struggled to get his aging body moving.

As per usual, he struggled to climb into his leather armor.

As per usual, he wished the next two years would pass considerably more quickly so he could retire, buy that mansion on Shade Way for his wife so she could live out her life in luxury—she'd earned it, putting up with him all these years—while he could do as he wished in this apartment—which he'd earned, putting up with her all these years.

Not remotely per usual, there were two guards from Dragon Precinct, Jared and Simon, standing outside the door to the building in which his apartment was housed. "What the hell're you guys doin' here?" he asked.

"Sergeant Grint sent us," Simon said. "But we woulda come anyhow. We heard about the dwarf, and we ain't lettin' him get near you, Lieutenant."

Jared added, "So you're gettin' yourself an escort to the castle this mornin'."

Iaian sighed. He usually needed the walk to the castle to get his thoughts in order so he could actually face yet another day of tiresome detective work and putting up with Grovis. But all things considered, having the extra protection was probably a good idea. Who knew what Yarbanig was capable of?

Besides, guards helping guards was how it was supposed to be.

"All right. And hey, thanks."

"Nothin' to it," Jared said. "That dwarf gets near you over our dead bodies."

"I feel the same way." Then Simon grinned. "The dwarf'll get near you over *his* dead body."

Iaian chuckled, and they headed toward Meerka Way, and then turned left onto the main thoroughfare of Cliff's End to head to the castle.

"And don't worry," Jared said, "Grint sent Aleta to keep an eye on him. Last we heard from her, he ain't left his brother's place over on Alfar's Way."

While Iaian didn't know that guard, he trusted Grint's judgment. He was a veteran who knew his people. If Grint sent this Aleta person, she was his best guard at surveillance.

They walked up Meerka Way through the rest of Dragon Precinct and then among the higher-class residents of Unicorn Precinct once they passed Oak Way, where modest houses and buildings with multiple apartments gave way to large houses and mansions.

The whole time, Jared and Simon kept an eye out for an unusually tall dwarf, pausing pretty much any time they saw *any* dwarf, just in case.

"Guys, c'mon," Iaian said after they gave a hairy eyeball to the fifth dwarf. "You stop every dwarf you see, I'm gonna be even later'n usual."

Eventually, they made it to the castle, and Bonce, one of the guards assigned to the castle, was running out, but stopped upon spying Iaian. "Oh, good, Lieutenant, now I don't have to try to find you. Sergeant Jonas sent me to fetch you and Lieutenant ban Wyvald."

Iaian snorted. Even with Jared and Simon's slower pace, he still beat Torin in.

Bonce kept going. "We just got a report that a buncha kids were taken from a play area in Unicorn."

Suddenly, Iaian's stomach started churning. "Shit. He only just got out yesterday."

Jogging past them, Bonce said, "I gotta go find Lieutenant ban Wyvald."

Looking at the two guards from Dragon, Iaian said, "You two better come in with me."

As soon as they got into the squadroom, Captain Osric yelled at him. "Iaian! Where the hell have you been?"

"I just heard, Cap'n." He walked in, Jared and Simon trailing behind. The two guards took up position near the doorway, waiting for further instructions. "What happened?"

"Three children were in one of those new play areas they put up on Oak Way. I've sent Tresyllione, Dru, and Hawk down to interview the caretaker and the kids and parents—Grovis, I'm going to want you to go back them up. We need someone who speaks upper class to deal with the parents."

Grovis got up from his desk, which was next to Iaian's. "Of course, Captain." He shook his head. "I can't believe he did this again. Especially after . . ."

"After *what*?" Iaian asked after his partner's words trailed off.

"Never mind," Grovis said quickly.

Osric blew out a breath. "Let's make sure it really was him before we jump to any conclusions."

Iaian pointed to Jared and Simon, who stepped out of Grovis's way when he departed. "These two are from Dragon, Cap'n. Sergeant Grint asked 'em to be my bodyguards, and they also put someone on Yarbanig."

Simon stepped forward. "Last we heard he was staying at his brother's place."

"Find out for sure," Osric said. "Iaian, go with them. If Yarbanig's there, bring him in. If he isn't—well, then we'll have a pretty good idea who did this."

"Yeah." He hesitated. "Cap'n?"

Osric stared at him with his one good eye. "What?"

Iaian took a breath. His plan this morning had been to have Ep, the imp who handled the Castle Guard's files, spit out the scrolls from the original case, but his dreams last night proved that he didn't need to. He recalled the details of that case with shocking clarity. "The last time, the kids always showed up exactly a day later due north of where they were taken."

Nodding, Osric said, "Boneen should get an exact time when he does the peel-back. Then we'll send guards north of the play area tomorrow morning."

"Good." Iaian turned to Jared and Simon. "Let's go."

On the way up, Iaian had let the two play bodyguard, but as they went back on Meerka Way, he didn't want anything slowing them down. He strode ahead of the other two as they struggled to keep up.

When they got to Alfar's Way, Iaian grew livid when he saw that there was nobody standing anywhere near Yarbanig's brother's place — itself one of three small flats located over Finnert's Magick Shop. The shop, Iaian recalled, was owned by a dwarf named Yan who rented the apartments above only to dwarves. Technically, that was illegal, as the lord and lady forbade that type of discriminatory practice. Yan made some noise about low ceilings, but that still made the places available to halflings and gnomes. Iaian wondered if that was still true; six years ago, Yan promised to open up his customer base, but Iaian had never followed up.

"Dammit," Iaian muttered when he looked around and saw nobody in Castle Guard armor save him and his compatriots. "We gotta—"

"Can I help you, Lieutenant?"

Iaian practically jumped out of his own armor at the voice that suddenly appeared behind him. Whirling around, he saw a woman almost as tall as Danthres, but far more attractive. Her blond hair was tied back in a ponytail, revealing the tapered ears of an elf.

"Where the hell'd you come from?"

"I felt it would be better if my surveillance of Yarbanig was covert, sir. But with your arrival, there seemed to be little point in continuing to do so."

"Has he left the place?"

Aleta shook her head. "He hasn't left since I arrived here. And I did see movement up there."

"Yeah, but that could be the brother."

Again, Aleta shook her head. "No, sir, Urbanchik is doing a construction job in Barlin. He won't be back in Cliff's End until winter."

Iaian nodded, impressed despite himself. He was starting to understand why Grint sent her.

"Let's go," he said, striding toward the front door.

Within moments, they were at Urbanchik's second-floor flat. Trying the latch, Iaian saw that it was locked. Turning to Simon, the larger of the two guards, he said, "Bust it down."

Aleta said, "Excuse me, Lieutenant, but isn't it standard procedure to knock on the door and give the occupant a chance to answer?"

Iaian turned to stare incredulously at the elven woman. "This shitbrain kidnapped three kids—again—and there's no way I'm givin' him any chance to get away with it."

"Sir, if you break down the door, I'm going to have to report you to my sergeant."

The respect Iaian had felt for Aleta began to decline sharply. "You really wanna do that, kid? For someone like that?"

Aleta stood her ground. "It's not even his door, sir, it's his brother's—in fact, technically, it's the building owner's property that we'd be damaging for no reason if he'll just open the door. I thought we were supposed to *protect* the citizens of Cliff's End."

Unable to help himself, Iaian burst out laughing. "Must be nice to know how the world works. Wear that armor for a couple decades, and I might take you seriously." He turned to Simon. "Bust down the—"

Then the latch moved down and the door swung open to reveal Yarbanig. "Can I help you, Lieutenant? I heard you all talking out here. Look, I already talked to your partner. I try anything, and a whole bunch of guards—maybe these three?—will beat me into mulch. I get it. I just want to move on with my life."

"My *partner*?"

"Yeah, with his warning."

Iaian had no idea what he was talking about, nor did he ask. He could barely be bothered to care what Grovis was doing when he was actually in his presence. Instead, he just grabbed Yarbanig's arm and yanked him out of the doorway. "C'mon with me, shitbrain. You're gonna tell me where those kids are."

"What kids?"

"Don't pull that shit with me. We got you this time. You just couldn't hold back, could you? You had to take those kids this morning, didn't you?"

"Sir," Aleta said, "excuse me, but he couldn't have kidnapped anyone. He's been here since last night. If those kids were taken this morning, he couldn't have done it."

Iaian started leading Yarbanig toward the stairwell down to the street. "You must've missed him leaving."

"Come on, Lieutenant," Yarbanig said, "your own people are saying I didn't do this. And I *didn't*! I never did!"

They got out onto the street, Jared, Simon, and Aleta trailing behind. "We're headin' back to the castle, and you're goin' in the interview room, and we ain't leaving until you admit to what you did."

"Lieutenant—" Aleta started.

Stopping, Iaian whirled on the three guards. "Jared, Simon, take this piece of sputum back to the castle." He practically threw the dwarf at the two guards, who each grabbed an arm. They exchanged glances, then moved off quickly, while Iaian stared at Aleta. "Look, I don't know you, so I'm gonna assume you're not always this stupid, but let me spell it out for you. Seven years ago, a whole bunch of kids kept getting kidnapped. They all reappeared a day later, and *that* hobgoblin's bitch over there," he pointed toward where Jared and Simon had walked off with Yarbanig, "was nearby every time. The kids never talked, and the peel-backs were inconclusive because of the glamours the shitbrain used. But there was one witness who described someone of his height—and they don't make dwarves that height very often—and he didn't have an alibi for any of the kidnappings, plus he bought the type of glamour used to interfere with the peel-back. The magistrate said he was guilty and gave him seven years—and you know how I know I was right about all of it? Not because of that, but because from the time we arrested his dwarven ass, *no* kids got kidnapped like that—until today, the day *after* that shitbrain got released from prison. You *really* think that's a coincidence?"

Aleta's almond eyes had gone very wide. "I—I—"

"When you've worn this armor for two decades, talk to me again about police work. Until then, run along back to Dragon. See if Grint'll give you a cookie or something."

With that, Iaian turned to stride back to the castle. He couldn't wait to get Yarbanig to *finally* admit to what he did. There was just no way to deny it now.

Gleefully striding into the squadroom, he saw Danthres and Torin coming out of the interrogation room with Winn Avar, the serial wife-beater.

"For Wiate's sake," Iaian said, "is it something in the water they're feeding 'em on the barge? He started right back in, too, huh?"

Danthres ignored him, and led Avar out of the room, looking even more angry than usual.

Torin, however, stayed to talk to Iaian. "Actually, no. When we were interviewing the parents of the three children who were kidnapped off of Oak Way, we discovered that one of them placed a scrying pool in the play area. Boneen was able to cast a spell upon it, and it revealed that Avar was the one who kidnapped the children. He used some kind of charm to attract their attention, and another to deposit them north of where they were taken the next day. We found both charms in the Avar house."

Iaian felt his jaw drop. "What?"

"Avar was the kidnapper—not just now, but seven years ago. He confessed to all of them—and so did Yona. They worked together, and Avar started hitting her when she tried to get him to admit to it when you started investigating Yarbanig. He refused to—and then Danthres arrested him for *that* crime instead, ironically enough."

"Wait a minute. It can't— I mean—" Iaian shook his head. "What the hell is happening?"

Gently, Torin put a hand on Iaian's shoulder. "Yarbanig didn't kidnap anyone, I'm afraid. It was Avar. He didn't kidnap anyone new after he got out four years ago because he was sick for most of a year— he doesn't do well at sea. And then, when he was well, he wanted to kidnap more children, and Yona tried to stop him, and he hit her again. So Danthres arrested him again on that charge."

"I—" Iaian's mind was swimming. It didn't make any sense. Yarbanig was *guilty*, dammit!

HOURS LATER, IAIAN WAS SITTING AT HIS DESK. SCROLLS WERE PILED ON HIS desk, all the reports from the Yarbanig case seven years earlier. Ep had disgorged them shortly after Avar's arrest and Iaian very reluctantly letting Yarbanig go.

Grovis came over to stand near Iaian. "What are you doing?"

He looked up at his partner's fish-like face. "Look, I really don't want to talk right now, okay? You wanna gloat about Yarbanig, do me a favor and do it tomorrow. Today, I just can't handle it, all right?"

"In fact, I had no intention of gloating," Grovis said. "I was asking after your welfare. I was under the impression that that was the sort of things partners did for each other."

Iaian snorted. "Yeah, that and try to intimidate convicts. Did you *really* go talk to Yarbanig when he got off the barge?"

"Yes. I thought it would be foolhardy for him to attempt to cause you harm, and only make a poor situation worse. So I advised him not to pursue the course of action he'd threatened in his letters over the past seven years."

"Yeah, well, he'd have been right to." Iaian shook his head and tossed the scroll he was reading onto the pile on his desk. "I been over this ten times for the last three hours, tryin' to figure out what I did wrong."

"Why are you assuming you did anything wrong?"

At that, Iaian stared at his partner. "Of *course* I did something wrong! For Wiate's sake, Grovis, I put a man on the barge who didn't belong there! The evidence pointed to him, but it was—it was wrong! And I gotta ask myself what the hell else I screwed up." He shook his head. "I'm not sure I can make it the two years to my pension, now. Every time I take a case, I'm gonna be second guessing. Shit, I can't even figure out what I messed up seven years ago."

"And again, I ask, why are you assuming you did anything wrong?" Grovis sat down at his desk. "When I was a boy, my brothers and cousins and I used to perform in archery competitions. One time, at the Eamon Memorial Games, my brother Branik shot brilliantly, his best score ever, a fifty. You see, score is based on—"

"I know how archery works, get to it," Iaian said impatiently. Not that he had anything to go back to. If Grovis stopped talking, he'd just read those stupid scrolls some more.

Grovis continued: "Nobody had ever scored fifty in the Eamon Games before. My brother was thrilled, and we had already started congratulating him on winning the tournament." He sighed. "Unfortunately, there were two more competitors, and they each scored a sixty. Branik wound up coming in third, after shooting better than he ever had in his life — shooting better than anyone had in the history of the tournament, until a few minutes later. So afterward, our victory celebration instead became almost funereal. We all gathered in my father's sitting room, drinking wine and generally sulking — and then my father stood up and said that Branik may have lost the archery tournament, but he learned a valuable lesson that day. It is possible to do everything right and still lose."

Iaian just stared at Grovis. "That supposed to make me feel better?"

Shrugging, Grovis stood up. "Perhaps not. It certainly didn't work on Branik, as he never picked up a bow again. He could've been a champion." Grovis shrugged. "You've taught me a great deal about being a detective, Iaian. I was simply hoping to return the favor. Good night."

He left the squadroom, leaving Iaian alone.

No, not quite — Osric came in from his office. "What're you still doing here, Iaian?"

Iaian sighed. The captain was the last person he wanted to talk to. "Just getting ready to leave, Cap'n."

"Good. You're up first tomorrow. 'Cause the only way you're going to put that case behind you is to take on a new one."

Hauling himself up from his chair, and trying to ignore his knees' cracking reminder that he was getting older, Iaian wandered to the pegboard to retrieve his cloak. "Whatever. I'm gonna go home."

"It's an imperfect system, Iaian. You know that better than anyone. We don't always get the right person, and people still get away with things all the time. We try to make everyone's lives a little better, but sometimes that means making someone else's life worse."

Pulling the cloak off its peg, Iaian said, "But this was someone else who didn't deserve it. Yarbanig was on the barge for seven years, and he shouldn't have been."

"Remember that guard who was killed in a bar brawl right after I signed on as captain?"

Frowning, Iaian tried to recall the event. It was more than ten years ago . . . Then it came to him. "You mean Sunsa?"

"You and Linder found one of the people involved, but he wasn't the one who delivered the fatal blow to Sunsa — that was someone else. But he resisted being arrested, and you, Linder, and three guards beat him until he died. Afterward, I said that he didn't deserve that. You remember what you said?"

Iaian shook his head. "Yeah, I remember. 'What does deserve have to do with anything?'"

"That day, I swore I'd find a way to get you off the Guard. But I could never manage it. You never were as good a detective as you thought you were, Iaian, but you were also never as bad as I thought you were, either. Go home, get some rest, get back on the horse tomorrow."

Osric retreated to his office.

Iaian stared at the scrolls on his desk, wondering if Osric and Grovis—two people whose opinions he'd rarely appreciated—were right.

He wandered down Meerka Way, but instead of going home, he wound up at the Old Ball and Chain, the bar where members of the Castle Guard tended to congregate after their shifts ended.

After obtaining an ale from Urgoss, the tavern's owner, he retreated to a back table, giving half-hearted greetings to people he knew along the way.

By the time he was done with his flagon, and was no closer to being sure of himself than he had been before, a woman walked up to him. "May I buy you another?"

Looking up, Iaian saw Aleta, looking contrite.

Iaian didn't respond, so Aleta kept talking. "I wanted to apologize for my behavior earlier, Lieutenant. I should never have threatened you with a report like that. I've only been in the Guard for less than a year, and I obviously still have a lot to learn."

"You don't ever *stop* havin' a lot to learn," Iaian said with a sigh. "I been in the Guard for almost twenty-five years, and I just found out today I still got a ways to go in the learning area myself."

"Nonetheless, sir, I'd like to buy you a drink to make up for it."

Iaian stood up. "Nah, thanks. I think I'm just gonna go home. But listen—Yarbanig *wasn't* the guy. It was someone else. I was wrong seven years ago, and you were right this morning. So nice job. And nice job staying out of sight like that. How'd you do that, anyhow?"

She smiled. "I'd be happy to tell you—over a drink."

Staring at her suspiciously, Iaian asked, "Are you flirting with me, Aleta?"

"*No*," she said a little too emphatically. "Please, sir, don't take this the wrong way, but humans smell—weird. I mean, it's fine to be around you, but in bed? Never." She shuddered. "But—well, I'm hoping to have a long career in the Guard, and I think I could benefit from your experience." She grinned and pulled down the collar of her armor, exposing the tattoo on her neck. "And I can tell you some of the secrets I picked up when I was part of the Shranlaseth."

Iaian's eyes widened. The Shranlaseth were the special forces of the elven nation for centuries, until the Elf Queen outlawed them. Iaian had never understood that, as it just cost the Elf Queen some of her best soldiers, especially since a lot of them didn't just join the regular elven army, but scattered all across Flingaria as mercenaries and such.

Each member of the Shranlaseth had a neck tattoo with the Ra-Telvish word for their organization. At least, Iaian assumed that was what the Ra-Telvish word was. For all he knew, it said, "You will die now," which was probably an accurate piece of information for those that saw the tattoo.

Sitting back down, Iaian said, "Fine, go get us a couple of flagons, and we'll have a nice chat."

Aleta smiled. "Good."

Iaian folded his hands on the table and nodded. Maybe Grovis and Osric *were* right. And maybe Iaian himself was, too. But when you screwed up, you didn't wallow in it, you moved on to the next thing. Grovis's brother wasn't bright enough to do that, and the last thing Iaian wanted to be was just like a member of *that* stupid family.

He and Aleta sat and talked shop for the rest of the night.

FIRE IN THE HOLE

At Lieutenant Danthres Tresyllione's fifteenth uttering of that exclamation in the past hour, her partner, Lieutenant Torin ban Wyvald, sighed heavily, an action he hid from Danthres by stroking his thick red beard.

They were pacing along the wooden barricades that had been placed on either side of Meerka Way to keep the crowd from interfering with the midsummer parade. Unlike the last several years, the Cliff's End Castle Guard decided not to pay the exorbitant fee (which had gone up by twenty percent every year) to the Brotherhood of Wizards for a magickal barricade that was more effective against a teeming throng of people pushing against it than a series of long, thick blocks of wood each supported by four shorter, thinner blocks of wood. The Lumber Guild charged half of what the Brotherhood did for their barricade, and the lord and lady's chamberlain had insisted that it would do the job just as well.

Watching four muscle-bound humans, three short but sturdily built dwarves, and a tall elf all pushing against one of the barricades trying to get a better view of the flower-covered float put together by the Gardeners Guild, Torin was skeptical as to the Lumber Guild's claim.

Danthres had also noticed the eight people jockeying for position, with the elf in serious danger of stepping on two of the dwarves. The third dwarf glared up at the elf, and Torin knew that that could only spell trouble.

"Hey!" Danthres put a hand to the hilt of the standard-issue sword that dangled from her hip scabbard as she bellowed. This garnered no response, as the dwarf was too busy cursing at the elf in Ra-Telvish.

Torin's facility for the elves' native tongue was weak, but the dwarf's body language spoke volumes.

Danthres bellowed again, now standing directly on the other side of the barricade from the group. "Hey! That's enough!"

Looking down on Danthres with the disdain that only an elf could muster, he said in Common, "Who are you to speak that way to me, half-breed?"

Knowing that Danthres's likely answer to this query would be along the lines of "The person who will kill you in six seconds," Torin stepped in.

"She is a lieutenant in the Cliff's End Castle Guard, as am I, and we have the authority from the lord and lady themselves to arrest anyone we feel has the potential to disrupt this most solemn occasion."

Danthres added, "Either the elf moves, the dwarves move, or all four of you go to the hole."

One of the dwarves said, "We're not moving—it took us hours to get up to the edge of the barricade. If we change our location now, we'll never see *anything*."

The elf was still staring down his nose at Danthres. "I thought the lieutenants in the Castle Guard were tasked with solving crimes, not crowd control. Or did they realize that a person of your limited breeding was incapable of such complex tasks?"

To Torin's surprise, Danthres's response was not to take her sword all the way out of its scabbard, but to instead smile. Her face—which combined the worst elements of her dual heritage—did not allow for pleasant smiles, and this one was nasty even by her high standards. At the sight of it, the elf visibly paled.

"Thank you. I was really hoping I'd get to kill someone today."

Putting a hand on her shoulder, Torin said, "Don't, Danthres—there'll be paperwork."

The elf held up a hand. "I refuse to be treated this way! She threatened me!"

Torin stepped between Danthres and the elf and grabbed the latter's arm. "Sir, I'm afraid that, in the name of the lord and lady, I must place you under arrest. Step under the barricade and make no sudden movements, please."

By this time, they had created a spectacle, and more people were watching the tableau than were observing the parade. To be fair, the Coopers Guild float was going by. All they'd done was put a pile of barrels on a cart. Torin wasn't concerned. The crowd would find something else to distract them soon enough, especially once the float from the Prostitutes Guild came into view.

Torin led the elf up Meerka Way toward Oak Way, the official border between Unicorn and Dragon Precincts, and the separation point between the upper class and their mansions and the middle class and their more modest homes.

Oak Way itself had been a simple tree-lined pathway for many years, the land owned by the Hazlar family. The Hazlars had owned one of the two banks in Cliff's End, but a year ago, Jetan Hazlar had a falling out with the lord and lady. He agreed to a merger with the Cliff's End Bank prior to the entire family moving to Iaron.

While the Hazlar mansion at the end of Oak Way was purchased by the Grovis family—owners of the Cliff's End Bank—the rest of the thoroughfare was sold to the lord and lady, who put it up for public auction. So, where Oak Way had once been empty of habitation, it was now lined with buildings at various stages of completion.

"Where are you taking me?" the elf asked angrily as they started down Oak Way. "I know for a fact that there are no precincts here."

"Your grasp of the obvious is impressive, good sir elf," Torin said with a smile. "We have commandeered one of the new homes here as a holding area."

"You see," Danthres added, "the sheer volume of offenders such as yourself that we're forced to arrest during midsummer requires it."

The elf said nothing in reply, but did scowl at Danthres again. She just smiled back.

One of the benefits of the money saved on not using the Brotherhood's barricades was that the Guard was able to pay for the additional holding areas, which proved a boon. The holding areas in the Castle Guard's various headquarters—both the dungeons in the lord and lady's castle and the areas in the four precincts, all collectively known as "the hole"—were always filled beyond capacity within the first hour of midsummer, and the added space ameliorated the problem quite nicely.

Two guards—Manfred, from Unicorn Precinct, and Kellan, from Dragon Precinct—were standing at the doorway to the house that was being used. Though completed, it was not yet furnished or occupied, and the owner was more than willing to delay moving in for a fortnight in exchange for the Castle Guard's cash.

Kellan looked at Manfred and smiled. "That's a dozen elves. You owe me a copper."

At Torin's look, Manfred shook his head. "I figured we'd get to a dozen dwarves before we got to a dozen elves holed up here. This shitbrain means I lose."

The elf sneered. "Wagering on prisoners? Hiring half-breeds? No wonder Cliff's End is such a cesspool, if this is the brand of person tasked with maintaining the lord and lady's law."

Danthres regarded the two guards. "Don't feel any great urge to treat this one gently."

Manfred reached out to roughly grab the elf by the shoulder. "No problem at all. He just cost me a copper."

As Manfred led the elf inside, Kellan said, "How come they have you guys on crowd control?"

Torin winced. The last thing he wanted was for Danthres to get started, but answering that question would do it.

"It wasn't my idea, *believe* me." Danthres practically spat the words. "But the members of the lord and lady's court always complain about the unruly crowds during midsummer, and can't they just put more guards on Meerka Way to keep the mobs in line? So then the lord and lady complain to Osric, and he puts all the detectives on shit duty."

Attempting to change the subject, Torin regarded Kellan. "Betting on elves versus dwarves, eh? That's novel for midsummer."

Shrugging, Kellan said, "Ah, everyone bets on the dragon. It's boring. Manfred and me, we wanted to vary the routine a little, y'know?"

Torin chuckled. The entire midsummer festival was based around the yearly sighting of the dragon. A golden creature that lived somewhere deep in the Forest of Nimvale, it flew over Cliff's End every year at the summer solstice, circled the city-state once, then flew back home.

Some years, it also breathed fire. Legend had it that, if the dragon breathed fire, it would be a hot summer. If it didn't, the summer would be cooler.

"There it is!"

Torin wasn't sure who had shouted, but everyone looked up at the words. The timing of the dragon's arrival was never consistent from year to year beyond a general proximity to the solstice—which made its arrival the second-most popular subject of wagers after whether or not it would breathe fire.

"Good," Danthres said emphatically. She had been concerned that the dragon wouldn't show up until tomorrow, meaning another day of the insanity.

Smiling, Torin scanned the skies for a sign of the large, golden form. Then he spied it.

Flying so far overhead, and never with any riders, it was impossible to say how large the dragon truly was. However, Torin estimated that the creature was almost as long from the horns on its head to the pointed end of its tail as ten elves — or a dozen humans. It was covered in golden scales that reflected the sunlight, making it difficult to stare right at it. Its wings, also golden, flapped lazily, spanning the same length as the dragon's body.

Just as it had every year since Torin first arrived in Cliff's End a decade ago, the dragon circled the city-state. This year, though, Torin noticed something: the center of the circle seemed to be right over where he and Danthres were standing on Oak Way.

"I wonder if it does that every year," Danthres said.

"What, circle around this particular spot?" Torin asked. "I observed that, as well."

"Shhhh!" one of the pedestrians, a gnome, hissed. Only then did Torin realize that the entire thoroughfare had gone quiet at the sight of the dragon, excepting Torin and Danthres's own conversation.

Danthres stared angrily at the gnome. "It's not as if the dragon can *hear* us, or will react badly to our talking. It's just going to circle four times, maybe breathe fire, and then bugger off for a year so we can get back to living our lives."

"You should show respect to the dragon," the gnome said.

"Actually, *you* should show more respect to *us*." Danthres started to move toward the gnome, and Torin feared he would once again have to keep his partner from inflicting unnecessary violence on a civilian.

Before he could interpolate himself between Danthres and the gnome, though, they were both stopped short by several incoherent screams.

Looking around, Torin saw that everyone was still looking up at the dragon, but many were pointing at it.

Following their gazes upward, Torin felt his stomach turn inside out.

The dragon had stopped circling, and was now flying downward right toward Oak Way.

It only took a moment. With just two flaps of its wings, the dragon had swooped down to just a dozen or so feet above the ground.

On those occasions when the dragon did breathe fire, it created a beautiful fireball that lit up the sky even on the sunniest of days.

But that was from a safe distance in the air. Today, the dragon waited until it was right over one of the new homes on Oak Way, and breathed fire right into that house.

This fireball was loud and blinding and so hot that—even at a distance—Torin felt as if his long beard had been singed.

Then, in the time it took the dragon to flap its wings three more times, it had taken to the air again and was gone.

Leaving a burning house and a panicked populace behind.

The gnome glowered at Danthres. "I told you to show the dragon respect!"

DANTHRES WAS BEYOND EXHAUSTED WHEN SHE AND TORIN DRAGGED themselves back to the castle the following morning.

Her intention had been to go home and sleep for several days straight, but as she and Torin were about to do so, one of the youth squad came by. The girl, one of a cadre of children employed by the Castle Guard as messengers, informed them that Captain Osric wanted to see them at Guard Headquarters in the eastern wing of the lord and lady's castle immediately.

Summons from the captain were not to be ignored. Danthres came very close to doing so anyhow.

Dragging themselves to the captain's office, Danthres couldn't even be cheered by the smell of the pastries that Sergeant Jonas's wife made every morning. It didn't help that there was no sign of Jonas himself, nor of the other four detectives on their shift. Danthres hoped it was because they were still helping with the post-midsummer clean-up, because if they were allowed to rest while Danthres and Torin had to haul themselves to the captain's office, there would be hell to pay.

Osric was sitting behind his desk, facing two people in the guest chairs. Danthres was about to turn around and leave until he was done with this meeting, but Osric said, "Tresyllione, ban Wyvald, glad you're here. Come in." The captain was sharpening his dagger, which was always a bad sign.

Danthres hissed a breath out through her teeth. Not only was she denied sleep, but she had to stand during the meeting.

"Captain," she said, "we've just spent the entire night putting out a fire, getting medical care for wounded and burned people, and arresting panicking, rioting idiots. Is there any way that this meeting can wait until—"

"No, Lieutenant," said one of the people in the guest chairs, "it cannot wait. In fact, it's waited too long as it is."

The person turned around, and Danthres let out a sigh. The person in question was Lord Ythran, the wizard in charge of affairs in the Cliff's End vicinity for the Brotherhood of Wizards. Danthres had yet to have a single meeting with Ythran that was pleasant in any way, shape, or form.

Osric regarded Danthres and Torin with his right eye, the left one as ever covered with a black silk patch. "There's a double murder that you two are required to investigate."

Danthres found herself torn between anger at being asked to work a case when she was physically and mentally exhausted, and relief at being put back on the duty she was actually paid to perform. Since she was already angry, she went with the former, as it was less work.

Torin asked, "Who're the victims?"

"Ella and Gerric Fantar."

Rolling her eyes, Danthres said, "Well, that's easy. They weren't murdered, they died in a fire." Domi Fantar was the owner of the house that was in the path of the dragon's fireball; Ella and Gerric were his wife and son.

The other guest turned around, and Danthres had to resist the urge to take out her sword when she recognized Sir Rommett, the lord and lady's chamberlain, and Danthres's least favorite member of the upper class.

"The captain told us that you were both on Oak Way when the dragon arrived yesterday," Rommett said.

Torin nodded. "Yes, we were."

"Then you know better. The Fantars were murdered by the dragon."

Unable to help herself, Danthres burst out laughing. So did Torin.

No one else in the room followed suit—in fact, Osric's scowl deepened considerably, and Ythran said, "This is hardly a laughing matter, Lieutenants."

"Oh, I disagree," Danthres said. "What, do you expect us to bring the dragon in for questioning? I don't think it'll fit in the interrogation room."

"The Brotherhood will deal with the dragon," Ythran said.

Torin smiled under his thick red beard. "Really? I was under the impression that the Brotherhood generally left dragonkind alone."

"We *generally* do," Ythran said sharply, "but *generally*, dragons don't murder citizens. We need to determine what the dragon's motivations are."

"Then do so," Danthres said. "Any time a crime involves magick, you people come in and take over."

"This does not involve magick," Ythran said. "But it does concern us."

Torin grinned. "Because the reason *why* you leave dragonkind alone is because you cannot control them."

"Hardly." Ythran's denial was unconvincing. "However, that is not the point."

"What is the point?" Danthres asked. "You wish to know the dragon's motivations. What's stopping you?"

The wizard hesitated. Danthres took a perverse pleasure in seeing that, as mages rarely did so.

Finally, Ythran spoke. "The circumstances require that an investigation be performed. The lieutenants of the Castle Guard are specifically trained in such, and we feel that it will facilitate matters if the pair of you perform that investigation."

Danthres and Torin exchanged shocked looks. "Let me see if I understand you," Danthres said slowly. "*You* want *our* assistance. You, who routinely interfere in our work, who regularly ride roughshod over our investigations—now you want *us* to perform an investigation for *you*?"

"No," Rommett said with a stricken glance at Ythran, "that is not what is happening here. The lord and lady feel that this is a murder like any other, and should be investigated just like any other. It simply happens that the lord and lady's wishes coincide with those of the Brotherhood—and we are all in agreement that the pair of you are best suited to carry out the investigation."

"Really?" Danthres shot Osric a look, but the captain was focused very heavily on sharpening his dagger. "The fact that the Brotherhood is utterly incapable of performing a murder investigation has nothing to do with it?"

"Be careful, Lieutenant," Ythran said in a low voice.

"Why?" Danthres stared at the wizard. "You're the ones who need our help."

Osric finally spoke up while getting to his feet. "Threats aren't necessary, your lordship. My lieutenants are simply tired after a very long day and night protecting this city-state. They will, of course, carry out the investigation as part of their regular duties. If that's all?"

Rommett and Ythran exchanged glances of their own, then they also rose. The chamberlain said, "I believe so, yes, Captain. Good day."

While Rommett cleared out of Osric's office quickly, the wizard stayed behind. "Is there anything else, your lordship?" the captain asked.

"No," Ythran said. "But I will, of course, be accompanying the detectives."

Danthres put her head in her hands.

"Very well, then," Torin said before Danthres could comment—which was probably very wise of him, given Danthres's current mood. "Generally, the first step in a murder investigation is to examine the scene of the crime."

"There's not much to examine," Danthres said. "The place was burned to a crisp." What she didn't say aloud was that she'd spent all night on Oak Way, and was displeased at the prospect of going back with Ythran in tow.

"It's still worth looking," Torin said.

Ythran's face grew sour. "I agree with Lieutenant Tresyllione. We need to determine the dragon's reasons for targeting that house—and learn why it did so this year as opposed to years past."

Danthres shrugged—and also reconsidered her feelings on the matter, if Ythran actually agreed with her. "Apparently something changed this year."

"Well, one very obvious thing did change," Torin said. "The homes on Oak Way. All those constructions are new since last summer."

"Yes," Ythran said, "but why *that* house?"

"All the more reason to examine what's left of it," said Torin.

Danthres nodded. "Agreed—but I doubt we'll find much. When we're done there, we should bring Domi Fantar in, ask him about the construction of the house."

Ythran started to gesture carefully. "Excellent. Let us go."

The next thing Danthres knew, she was doubled over on Oak Way, disgorging the contents of her stomach. She really hated Teleport Spells.

As expected, the burned-out remains of the Fantar residence provided little of use. To Danthres's relief, Ythran stayed in the background most of the time they were there. The bulk of what they found, of course, were the burned-out husks of items that used to be in the Fantar house or used to *be* the Fantar house. The bodies of the two victims had, of course, long since been removed.

After that, the detectives had the surviving Fantar brought to the interrogation room in the eastern wing of the castle.

To Danthres's dismay, Fantar had nothing of use to say. He'd never encountered a dragon before, never had dealings with them, didn't entirely believe they were real. With a guilty look at Ythran, he admitted that he always thought the midsummer festivities to be a trick performed by the Brotherhood.

Danthres was about to tell Fantar he could leave when Torin spoke.

"Did you remove anything from the grounds before you had the house built? A tree or a rock or an object of any kind?"

Fantar squinted. "Well, there were a mess'a oak trees, yeah. Had to clear *them* out. Lumber Guild paid good money for 'em, too."

"Only oaks?" Torin asked.

"Yeah, that's it."

"And nothing else?"

"Well, there was that old trail marker. It was a rock dug deep in the ground. Cost five silver to have that thing removed, but the fella from the museum paid me three gold for it, so I came out ahead."

Danthres had been about to complain to Torin about wasting time, but this last statement made her hold that back. Instead, she stared at Fantar. "You're sure this was a trail marker?"

"S'what the fella from the museum said." Fantar shrugged. "Said it was buried so deep, it had to be from before the city was founded, and there was trail markers all over the place then, leading folks to the Garamin Sea. Why?"

"Just trying to get a complete picture of what happened, Mr. Fantar. We may have more questions." Danthres hustled the man to the door.

Ythran stared at Danthres and Torin both after Fantar left the room. "I fail to understand what a trail marker has to do with—"

"Oak Way didn't exist until long after Cliff's End was founded," Danthres said. "The members of the lord and lady's court had the oaks planted and the thoroughfare established in order to separate them from the riff-raff. The only trails — and the only places that would have old trail markers — are on Meerka Way, Sandy Brook Way, and Salmon Alley."

"I still fail to understand —"

Torin said, "If it wasn't a trail marker, it was obviously something else. Something that predates the city's founding, and therefore possibly something an ancient creature such as a dragon might know about."

Ythran rubbed his hands through his bone-white beard. "Very well. We shall proceed to the museum." The mage started to gesture.

Before Danthres could stop him, they were instantly at the Lord Kioa Museum on Galvann Hill and Danthres was dry-heaving, having nothing left to throw up after the *last* unexpected Teleport Spell.

"Don't *do* that," she said, once her wretching was under control.

But Ythran ignored her, instead demanding to see the museum manager, throwing his rank around with typical arrogance.

"Oh yes," the manager — a mousy man named Teargut — said in a whispery voice. "I recall. It turned out not to be a trail marker at all. It wasn't much of anything, really, just a rock with some markings on it. I've been meaning to get them translated, but —"

"Take me to it, *now*."

Teargut swallowed loudly, and dashed off to the back room.

When he came back with a rock the size of a person's head held in both arms, Ythran cast a quick spell, which caused the rock to rotate.

Danthres didn't recognize the lettering on it, which was unsurprising.

Ythran didn't, either, which was. "If these are sigils, they're not of a type I recognize."

"I do," Torin said quietly.

Danthres shot him a look. "You do?"

"I think so — from some ancient texts in Myverin."

Ythran regarded Torin with something resembling respect. "You're from Myverin? What brought you to such a place as *this*?"

"Free will, your lordship," Torin said with more politeness than Danthres would have in his place, especially since Torin's name indicated his Myverin heritage. Then again, Danthres was willing to bet that Ythran didn't recall either of their names.

Torin continued: "The life of a philosopher was not for me. However, I did study at the collegium, and I saw many ancient texts that used these symbols. Unfortunately, I can't tell you what they mean. I doubt anyone in Cliff's End can." Then he turned back to Danthres and Ythran and smiled. "But there is one possible way to find out."

"How's that?" Danthres asked.

"Interview the only witness we haven't spoken to yet."

Danthres frowned, then realized what he meant. "You're not serious."

"We must go to the perpetrator and the only suspect we have. The dragon has encircled the city-state every midsummer since Cliff's End's founding. This rock has also been there that long, and the first midsummer it wasn't there was when the dragon first changed its routine—and killed two people. We have to go to its lair."

Danthres turned to Ythran. "Fine. Take us there."

Ythran blinked. "Excuse me?"

"Use that be-damned Teleport Spell and take us to the dragon's lair."

Torin added, "Surely, your lordship, the Brotherhood is capable of tracking a massive creature that flies to the same location every year back to its lair."

"You wanted us to investigate," Danthres said. "This is where the investigation leads—the same place it always does, to an interview with the primary suspect."

Ythran stared at them as if they were mad, for which Danthres couldn't entirely blame him. "You wish to interview a creature that is thousands of years old, refuses to have any congress with any other races, and could kill you with a simple exhalation?"

Nodding, Torin said, "That sums it up, yes. I assume you can cast a Translation Spell, that we may understand it?"

"Of course." Ythran sighed. "You're both quite mad."

Danthres found that being prepared for the Teleport Spell did nothing to hold down the nausea.

Clutching her pained belly, Danthres glanced around at her new surroundings. Expecting a cave, she was surprised to find herself in a giant clearing in the midst of the Forest of Nimvale.

What fascinated her was what the clearing was made of: the ground on which she stood was like ash. Most of the clearing's space was taken up by the dragon itself. Ythran had brought them proximate to the dragon's head; the body was sprawled out on the ashen ground as far as even Danthres's sharp eyes could see.

The dragon's eyes were shut, but then Ythran said something in what Danthres presumed to be the dragon's own tongue.

A single eye—which by itself was about the size of Danthres's torso—opened at Ythran's words. The dragon said something that was sufficiently loud that Danthres and Torin both had to cover their ears.

Ythran then made a quick gesture and muttered an incantation. A flash of light from something in his bag later, and the dragon's words became comprehensible.

"You be humans, are you not? I cannot recall the last time these eyes beheld a human. What brings you to my lair?"

Danthres stepped back to the edge of the clearing in the hope that it would help the assault on her ears. In addition, each time the dragon spoke, the temperature of the air around them rose, and there was only so much she could stand inside her leather armor.

Not bothering to correct the dragon on her own heritage, about which he was only half right, she said, "We wish to know why you killed two people in Cliff's End yesterday."

"What be Cliff's End?"

Torin said helpfully, "The city-state over which you fly every midsummer."

"That be a city-state? I was not aware. Fascinating."

Danthres couldn't believe this. "You killed two people in that city-state!"

"Did I? I do not recall. What brings you to my lair?"

"We wish to know," Torin said, "why you burned down a building in Cliff's End yesterday."

"There be a city-state there? I just be looking for the marker."

Ythran quickly muttered an incantation, and then an image of the rock from the museum appeared before the dragon. "Is this the marker you refer to?"

"That be the marker near the sea. Every midsummer I check that marker like Gamtar instructed. Midsummer be soon, be it not?"

Ythran actually gaped, an expression Danthres had never seen on a wizard before. "Gamtar? You knew Gamtar?"

"Of *course* I knew Gamtar. 'Twas my rider. Until he died. Then he stopped."

"So," Danthres said slowly, "you encircle Cliff's End every midsummer just for this marker?"

"The marker? That be what Gamtar charged me with checking until the end of my days. Each of the Sorfar be so charged."

Torin asked, "What happens now that the marker is gone?"

"The marker be gone?"

Danthres threw up her hands. "You just told us—"

Ythran interrupted. "What would you do if the marker was not present?"

"Why would the marker not be present?"

Ythran held up a hand before Danthres could explode in frustration. "Enough," the mage said. "We apologize for taking up so much of your time."

"Wait—" Danthres started before her stomach was again turned inside out, and she found herself back at the castle, standing next to her desk.

While she was doubled over in agony, Torin whirled on Ythran. "We were not finished with the interview!"

"Yes, you were," Ythran said. "Did you notice the color of the scales on the dragon's neck?"

In a weak voice, Danthres replied, "They were ochre. So what?"

"What in the name of the lord and lady is going on?" That was Osric, who had come from his office at the sudden noise of people arguing.

Ythran ignored the captain and answered Danthres's question. "A golden dragon's neck scales turn that color after it's passed its three thousandth year. That particular type of dragon rarely lives past *two* thousand. Also? Gamtar was a dragonrider during the reign of Syleen the Weary. It's likely that the marker was one of the cornerstones of the spell the dragonriders used to banish Helsek Gam a thousand years ago."

Torin frowned. "But Helsek Gam returned from banishment and was killed."

Danthres raised a hand. "I haven't the foggiest idea who any of those people are."

Osric regarded Ythran with something like amazement. "You mean that rock that Fantar dug up was one of the runestones that banished Helsek Gam?"

"Quite likely, yes," Torin said. "Which means that it is *also* quite likely that the dragon came out every midsummer to check on a marker that maintained a spell that is no longer running."

"Why would it do *that*, ban Wyvald?" asked Osric testily.

Danthres answered. "Because the dragon is three thousand years old and hasn't got much of a brain left."

"This case is completed," Ythran said dismissively. "The Brotherhood will handle it from here. We will ensure that the museum returns the marker to its proper place for the time being."

With that, he uttered the Teleport Spell and disappeared from the castle.

"Finally. I thought we'd never be rid of him."

Torin asked Sergeant Jonas, who had come dashing in, for some tea for Danthres, for which she was grateful. Sitting at her desk, she said, "So that's that, then. The entire ridiculous midsummer ritual—the parades, the bets, the celebrations, the rioting, the drunken idiocy—all of it was because a dragon was too dim to realize he shouldn't keep doing what he'd been told to do by a rider who's a thousand years dead."

Osric scowled. "Midsummer isn't 'ridiculous,' Tresyllione, it's the most popular festival of the year. Do you know how much coin is made during midsummer?"

"Including by us, thanks to all the overtime," Torin added with a smile.

"Perhaps. But I'll still take sleep over this nonsense, again."

"It may not matter." Torin was now scratching his thick beard. "The dragon will die soon."

"So?" Osric said. "People will still expect it, and it'll give them something new to bet on. Besides, who cares *why* it started? It's tradition, so it will continue."

"Joy," Danthres muttered. "I *hate* midsummer!"

HOUSE ARREST

THE HOUSE FAERIE HAD BEEN SITTING IN THE SMALL, DRAB ROOM IN THE eastern wing of the castle for over half an hour before somebody finally walked in. The home of the lord and lady who ruled the city-state of Cliff's End, the castle was also the workplace of many of the nobility and others who served the demesne. This wing housed the headquarters of the Cliff's End Castle Guard, who were tasked with maintaining law and order in the port city. This was the first time the faerie had entered the lord and lady's seat.

But then, as a house faerie, he had reason to stay inside his own home.

Being confined to this room, however, was frustrating for the faerie, as there wasn't enough room to fly about, and there wasn't anything in the room to hold his interest. The décor was rather pedestrian: a table surrounded by three chairs, two on one side, one on the other; a lantern that cast odd shadows; and nothing else. The house faerie had been brought here by two large members of the Guard "for questioning," along with the humans who lived in the house for which he was responsible.

Well, all but one of the humans. The one they didn't bring was also the reason why they had been brought to the castle: Alvin, the middle son, was dead.

The house faerie regarded his new visitor, a tall man with long red hair and a thick red beard that obscured virtually all of his face, save an aquiline nose and probing green eyes. He wore an earth-colored cloak, indicating his rank of lieutenant, which also meant that he was tasked with the solving of the more elaborate crimes—such as murder. The cloak covered leather armor was decorated with the gryphon crest of the lord and lady.

"Good afternoon," he said, closing the door to the small, drab room behind him as he entered. "My name is Lieutenant Torin ban Wyvald."

The faerie had been pacing. "It's about time somebody showed up. I was going barking mad in here."

"My apologies. I'm afraid that this case is rather complex."

"I can't even sit, thanks to those blessed backed chairs, and the place is too small for flying. These wings ain't for show, I'll have you know, Lieutenant."

"Again, my apologies. I'm afraid we don't have any stools. Feel free to sit on the table."

With a loud groan of annoyance, the faerie did so, crossing his green legs and folding his green arms. Indeed, the faerie was entirely green, save for his wings, which were more of a teal color.

Torin would normally have sat in one of the two chairs with their backs to the door, facing the person being questioned, who was in the chair on the other side of the table, but the faerie's position on the table's edge made that awkward, so Torin remained standing. "Now then, you are the house faerie of the Grabodlik residence, yes?"

"Right."

"I'm afraid I was never able to get a name for you — what are you called?"

Smiling sardonically, the faerie said, "The house faerie of the Gra-bodlik residence'll do the trick, thanks. 'Fraid you couldn't pronounce my name."

"You'd be surprised what I could pronounce, good, ah — good sir."

"Not properly." The faerie sighed. He went through this every time a non-fae tried to call him by his name. "See, us fae, our language don't just use the throat — the vibration of our wings're a part of it, too. Like I said, they ain't just for show. So you're not physically capable of pronouncing my name, and if you try it, it'll sound wrong."

"Very well, good sir faerie." Torin nodded and leaned up against the wall. "I assume you know why we've brought you here?"

"I'm guessing it's got to do with poor Alvin's death?"

"Correct."

"Well, at least it got me out of the house. Honestly, I almost never leave. Don't have much call to, really — I mean, as a house faerie, I got a job to do, and it ties me to the place most of the time, y'know?"

"Understandable."

"The castle's nice—not so sure about this room, though. Rather drab. I thought you lot had a whole troupe of fae working here."

Torin half-smiled. "The lord and lady do employ a swarm of house faeries, yes."

"Obviously, they forgot this room the last time they swept through." The faerie didn't even try to keep the disdain out of his voice.

Seeing no need to explain that the room was kept drab on purpose, Torin pressed on. "We're here to talk about young Alvin Grabodlik."

"Right. How'd he die, anyhow?"

"That, in fact, is what we are trying to determine. My partner and I have been interviewing the members of the Grabodlik family."

The faerie shook his head. "You have my sympathies, Lieutenant."

"Oh?" Torin said with a bushy red eyebrow raised.

"Look, I don't mean to speak ill of the folks or anything, really," the faerie said, unfolding his arms to hold up his hands in a gesture of reassurance. "I mean, they're decent enough, for humans. But—well, I've been the house faerie of that place since the lord and lady founded Cliff's End, and it has seen better owners. Seen worse, too, really, but these guys ain't hardly the best I've seen."

Now Torin did sit in one of the chairs, taking care to pull it away from the table. The faerie winced when the wooden legs dragged on the stone floor. "I'm afraid we haven't been able to determine the provenance of the house. Who were the prior inhabitants?"

Looking up, as if the ceiling would aid in remembering, the faerie let out a breath before speaking. "Well, it started out belonging to a fishing family, the Tosbrats. They were nice—always gave me a saucer of fresh milk in exchange for cleaning the house. Then the last of them died, and it went to some rich sod at the estate sale—one of the Cynnis boys. He rented it to a young fellow who was getting married. Everything was fine at first, until they had a kid. Then it all went to hell. They kept forgetting to put out milk, let the kid knock over the charms—well, I can't work under those conditions." Again folding his arms, the faerie shook his head. "I refused to keep the place clean unless they performed the rituals right—they didn't, so I stopped."

"How did that get resolved?"

"The place was such a pigsty that the kid got sick and died. The wife committed suicide after that, and the man—don't know what happened to him. Then the Cynnis boy rented to a healer, who lived alone with her cat. She was great, real nice, but the cat was a little monster—kept drinking my milk." Smirking, the faerie added, "Not that little, really. That was one fat old moggy. When the cat up and died, she moved to Iaron, and next up was another couple, the Forgrins." The faerie shuddered. "Never forget those two—didn't even acknowledge my existence." At Torin's questioning gaze, the faerie explained: "Temisans."

"Ah, yes," Torin said with a nod. "If I have my theology correct, Temisa frowns on the fae, does She not?"

"Temisa can go hang, for all I care." The faerie pointed a green finger at Torin. "I'm just trying to make an honest living here, I don't need some goddess sticking Her nose into my business. Okay? So after they left—"

Holding up a hand, Torin interrupted. "Wait a moment, please— why did the Forgrins depart?"

"It's all well and good to disbelieve in house faeries, but then you need to pick up the slack, don't you? Mrs. Forgrin was the world's worst housekeeper, and Mr. Forgrin was allergic to dust. So they left, and Cynnis couldn't find anyone, so *he* moved in. Used to entertain his lady friends every once in a while."

"Which Cynnis was this?"

"Jared."

Torin blinked. "Isn't he married?"

Grinning widely, the faerie said, "That's why it was only every once in a while." The grin dropped quickly. "Was kind of frustrating, too, 'cause the only time he'd leave out milk for me was when he was entertaining. Mind you, he'd leave a huge bowl of the stuff, so I'd make the place cleaner than the lord and lady's china—but then the place'd go to pot between trysts. I remember one time his wife caught him at it—I didn't see him for months. I swear, I was this close to sucking on a cow."

His face scrunched up in mild disgust, Torin said, "It never came to *that*, I hope."

The faerie shook his head. "No, Jared couldn't keep it in his tights that long. Anyhow, it wasn't long after that that his investments all went bad on him and he had to sell the place. This was about ten years ago."

"Ah, yes, right after the crash." At that, Torin got up and started pacing the room. "That was shortly after I began working for the Castle Guard."

"Yes, well, it was great for me. I got the best family since the Tosbrats: the Melkins. They were the best of all possible worlds—neat freaks who didn't drink milk, so everything they bought went to me."

"I can see how that would be appealing to you."

"Oh, it was great. One speck of dust, and they were putting up charms and putting out the big bowls of milk. Now to be honest, I don't care *that* much about the charms. It's just cheap symbolism, really. But the milk—I *live* for the milk!"

The faerie got a bit of a faraway look, until Torin cleared his throat and said: "According to what Mr. Grabodlik told us, he bought the house from Mr. Melkin after the latter's wife died, yes?"

"Yeah, it was some dinner party or other. The cook made something with a 'secret ingredient,' which turned out to be milk. She up and died right there."

Torin scratched his thick beard. "So what happened after that?"

"The Grabodliks came in. Nice enough folks, I suppose, but a little odd. I mean, Mr. Grabodlik spends all his time in the library. Won't let me in there at all—put up wards, even."

"Were you closed off from any other part of the house?"

"No, just there. The old sod *loves* to read, I guess." The faerie folded his arms again. "Didn't matter to me none. Mrs. Grabodlik was the laziest woman who ever lived, and she was more than happy to let me do all the work. Lazy women are the best thing for a house faerie, that's a fact."

"And I daresay active women are the best thing for lazy house fae?"

The faerie glanced over at Torin, as if never having considered that before. "I suppose so, but I wouldn't know. Don't matter to me none, I'm just in it for the milk."

"Of course. What of the rest of the family?"

Shrugging, the faerie said, "The children're all nice enough. Especially Alvin. Very good boy, he is. A shame he had to go and die like that. How'd you say he died again?"

"I didn't." Torin stopped pacing and walked over to the table. The faerie's small size meant that he towered over the creature. "If I may ask, how often did the Grabodliks require your services?"

Again, the faerie shrugged. "About like usual. Not as often as the Melkins, but enough. I'd say twice a week, maybe three times if the children got rowdy."

"Or if there is a rash of accidents."

"I'm sorry?" The faerie squinted.

Torin walked toward the door and leaned against it. "According to what Mrs. Grabodlik told my partner, there have been a rash of strange accidents lately. The looking-glass on her vanity broken, the kitchen utensils all on the floor, the kerosene draining out of the lanterns."

"I remember cleaning up that kerosene. Foul stuff, let me tell you. I almost held out for more milk for that one."

"That would have been a bit of a hardship."

"Whaddaya mean?"

Now Torin started walking slowly back toward the faerie—who, for his part, was shifting on the table. "Well, you are, of course, aware of the bovine malady that has struck Cliff's End?"

"What's a bovine malady?" the faerie asked, sounding genuinely confused.

"A sickness among the cow population. Approximately a quarter of all of the cows used by Cliff's End for food and dairy had to be slaughtered and destroyed due to an illness." By now, Torin was again face to face—or, rather, face to neck—with the faerie. "I'm surprised you were unaware of that."

"Look, I told you, I'm in the house all day. That's my *job*. The comings and goings of cows are hardly my lookout, is it?"

"Perhaps, but since your payment comes in the form of milk, it would perhaps behoove you to be cognizant of it."

Now, the faerie stood up on the table so he was nose to nose with the detective. "Look, I feel bad for those poor cows and all, but what's this got to do with poor Alvin? You've yet to tell me how he died. Don't you lot have a wizard on staff to do a peel-back spell on crime scenes?"

"Yes, we do." Torin folded his arms. "The problem is our magickal examiner was unable to determine the specifics. We know only that he died in the living room of the house, apparently of a broken neck."

Again, the faerie's voice was tinged with surprised. "You couldn't tell what he slipped on?"

"No, that was obscured in the peel-back—which indicates that there is some minor magick at work."

"Minor?" The faerie sounded almost offended by that.

"There are types of magick that can be unseen by a peel-back, but this type of obscurity—according to our M.E., at least—indicates actions by a magickal creature."

"Really? You mean to tell me there's some *other* magickal creature I don't know about wandering the house?"

Torin smirked. "That is *one* possibility, yes. Tell me, were you upset when the Grabodliks cut back to only requiring your services once a fortnight instead of once or twice a week?"

"What're you talking about?"

"Just what I asked. You see, my partner and I, we asked the Grabodliks what had changed recently to account for the accidents. They told us that the price of milk had gotten so high, thanks to the cows being sick, that they were forced to cut back on their use of your fine services. Mr. Grabodlik's job at the book dealer does not pay especially well, you see."

In a subdued voice, the faerie said, "'Fine services'? That was what they said?"

Torin nodded.

"Huh. Nice of them to say." The faerie flapped his wings, which filled the room with a mild buzz, and started levitating and moving toward the door. "Well, look, Lieutenant, I'm getting very tired, and I'd like to fly on home, so if there isn't anything else?"

Torin moved to stand between the faerie and the exit. "There's quite a bit else, good sir faerie. You see, what I think happened was that you had become dependent on a regular source of milk. After being so horribly rationed by the irregular schedule of Jared Cynnis, you positively gorged under the care of the Melkin family. So when the Grabodliks cut you back to only once or twice a week, and then to twice a *month*, you were livid. You started arranging accidents in the house to make your displeasure known."

"That's a fine story, Lieutenant, but—"

"How did you know that Alvin slipped on something?"

That brought the faerie up short. The buzz dimmed as his wings flapped more slowly and he descended a bit. "What?"

"You asked me a minute ago if we couldn't tell what it was that Alvin slipped on. I never said he slipped on anything—merely that he broke his neck in the living room."

Turning his back on Torin, the faerie flew back to the table, alighting on the chair, but not sitting. "Well, it stands to reason, doesn't it? I mean, how else does a boy break his neck in the middle of a living room?"

"Quite a number of ways, actually. That you were so sure it was slipping on something indicates to me that you were the cause."

"And what if I was?" the faerie angrily snapped. "I need dairy, don't I? I'm a *house faerie*—milk is what we *live* on! And I got—well, let's just say I was accustomed to more than I was getting from the Grabodliks. They should have—"

"They had no *choice*. They could not afford—"

"How was *I* to know that?"

"So you killed young Alvin to show your displeasure?"

"No!" In but a moment, the faerie's anger and outrage burned to ashes. "I mean—hell, Lieutenant, I didn't *mean* to kill him! I just used some elbow grease."

Torin squinted in confusion. "I beg your pardon?"

"Elbow grease—the stuff we secrete from our elbows?" The faerie talked slowly, as if to a not-very-bright child. "How you think we get things so clean?"

After hesitating a moment, Torin smiled. "I must admit I hadn't thought about it that closely."

"Well, that's where it comes from. I squirted out an extra bit on the floor when I knew the kid was walking through. I just wanted him to fall down and look stupid, that's all. I didn't think he'd break his neck."

"So you confess to the crime?"

The faerie let out a long breath. Now that he'd told the truth, it was as if a weight had been lifted from his wings. Fae are creatures of truth, after all—while misdirection and being overly literal was part and parcel of their lives, out-and-out deception was not an easy thing for them. It had just been a matter of time before Torin outlasted him. "I suppose I am. Dammit." Staring up at the lieutenant's green eyes, the faerie started pleading. "Look, I just wanted my milk. Is that really so wrong?"

Torin walked over to the door and opened it. "It is when a person is killed. Guards?"

"Yeah."

Two guards—the same two who had brought the faerie and the Grabodliks to the castle—came in. "You'll be taken to the hole," Torin said, "until the magistrate is ready to see you."

"The hole" was the colloquial name for the holding dungeon in the basement of the castle. One remained there until the magistrate decided on your sentence. If you were lucky, it was to return to the hole. The faerie was unlikely to be so lucky.

The faerie let out a long sigh. "I'm really sorry about all this, Lieutenant, you must believe that. He was a good kid."

"Yes, I'm sure he was. Take him away."

The guards nodded and each of them grabbed one of the faerie's small arms.

As they carried him out, the faerie's legs dangling in the air beneath him, the creature called out, "Lieutenant?"

"Yes?"

"They have any dairy in the hole?"

Torin considered, realized he wasn't sure. "Perhaps."

"I hope so. I've been without for almost a week now—I'm getting the milk shakes."

BROTHERLY LOVE

"About time someone came in here! I've been going crazy waiting here for— Honestly, I haven't heard the timechimes, so I guess it hasn't been an hour, but it *feels* like longer. I'm sorry, I'm babbling, I'm just so stunned by what's happened."

"Sorry, Mr. Mathe. I'm Lieutenant Danthres Tresyllione. We just need to ask you a few questions about your sister."

"I—I guess so. I have arrangements that need to be made, and I need to get to them—but I suppose this is to help you find out who killed her?"

"What arrangements might those be?"

"Are you at all familiar with the teachings of Ghandurha, Lieutenant?"

"One of my fellow detectives worships Ghandurha, but I'm afraid I haven't paid close attention to the nuances of your faith."

"We have to bury Gertha within two days of her death."

"Why is that?"

"Excuse me?"

"I assume there's a reason why Ghandurha worshippers such as yourselves bury the body within such a specific time frame."

"Oh. Well, you see, after two days, the body starts to—to decay. It no longer is recognizable as a person. It is best to bury your loved ones while they still look like themselves."

"It is my experience, Mr. Mathe, that dead bodies look nothing like living ones more or less from the moment they die. But it doesn't matter. At the moment, your sister's corpse is with our magickal examiner, and it's being kept in stasis by a spell. Until he releases it from that spell, it won't decompose. We can't release the body until our investigation into her death is complete, at which point you will be able to bury her."

"I—I don't—I mean, that's not what the texts say."

"You just said that the rule was so that the person could be buried before they decompose. I assume those texts were written more than nine years ago?"

"Yes, of course."

"That explains it. The Preservation Spell didn't exist, then—our M.E., Boneen, first developed it shortly after he started working with us."

"But the texts say—"

"So slavishly following the words of the texts is more important than actually fulfilling the wishes of your god?"

"I—"

"I shouldn't be surprised, given what Grovis has told us about Ghandurha."

"You know the Grovis family?"

"I'm sorry, Mr. Mathe, but we're getting away from the point of this interview, and I believe you said you were in a hurry."

"Yes, of course, I'm sorry, I'm just beside myself. But I believe I know who might well have done it."

"And who is that?"

"His name's Elgin. He's been working as a clerk at our store, and Gertha took up with him not that long ago. To be honest, Lieutenant, I never really liked him. He always struck me as—well, suspicious. I tried to warn Gertha about him, but she wouldn't listen to me. People in love tend to be stubborn, I've noticed."

"Let's back up a moment, Mr. Mathe. Now you and your sister both run the Mathe Tailor Shop on Stone Path?"

"Yes, we opened the place six years ago. It's been very profitable, too, most of the finest outfits worn by the lord and lady's court came from our shop."

"I'm sure. Did you last see your sister at the store?"

"No, we had a large meeting of our congregation at the Cliff's End Church of Ghandurha on Galvann Hill. In fact, come to think of it, I believe the Grovis family was there."

"Yes, Lieutenant Grovis did mention it, and my partner and I have spoken with the other attendees. They verify your story."

"My—my 'story'? I'm confused, Lieutenant. If you already knew I was there, why did you ask if I last saw my sister at the store? Oh—oh, no. You're—oh, for Ghandurha's sake, you're treating *me* like—I can't even say it out loud."

"In the early stages of a death investigation, Mr. Mathe, I've found it's simpler to just assume that everyone is a suspect until I'm given reason to think otherwise. So you had this church meeting. At what time did that break up?"

"Let me think—the timechimes had just rung twenty-three when we left the church. I said good-night to Gertha, and she went to her home, and I to mine."

"Did anyone see you go to your home?"

"Everyone did."

"And you went straight home?"

"Of course."

"To your house on Maple Path?"

"Yes."

"That would be, what, half-an-hour's walk?"

"I suppose so, yes."

"In fact, your house faerie said that you were home half an hour before midnight."

"Ah, of course. I hadn't even thought of checking with the house faerie. I very rarely see her, just set out the milk and charms and let her do her work. Still, I didn't even consider that she could be a witness to my arrival home. That's very clever, Lieutenant."

"I'm actually surprised, Mr. Mathe. In general, Ghandurha worshippers don't employ house faeries."

"There's no proscription against it—we're not Temisans, you know—but I've found that she keeps the place neat. Besides, she came with the house."

"I see. What was your relationship with your sister?"

"Quite excellent. We've been running a successful business for years. I mean, yes, there were arguments, and there've been some financial difficulties. I mean, it's one of those—well, slumps that one goes through, I suppose."

"My partner spoke to one of your clerks, and he said something that surprised me. He said that you used to have a wizard in your employ?"

"Yes, we did."

"Why didn't you mention this wizard?"

"Well, because he is not in our employ any longer."

"And because your store isn't licensed by the Brotherhood of Wizards."

"There's nothing for them to license, Lieutenant. Truly, we investigated it quite thoroughly, and such a license was not required, because we don't actually sell any magick or magickal items."

"But this wizard did enhance the goods?"

"Not—not exactly. You see, the process by which we make our clothing hasn't changed, but what Fenrik did was speed up the process considerably. We were able to fulfill orders much faster. Then . . ."

"Then what?"

"Look, I don't wish to speak ill of Gertha now that she's—she's gone, but—well, she broke his heart."

"I'm sorry?"

"Before she got involved with Elgin, she was—well, she was seeing Fenrik. The wizard."

"What does 'seeing' him mean, exactly, in this context?"

"They were romantically involved. Mind you, they only kissed—Ghandurha looks poorly upon premarital fornicating."

"And the Brotherhood of Wizards looks poorly upon their mages getting romantically involved."

"Yes, I know. That was the excuse Gertha gave for why she didn't stay with him, but the thing is, after she ended the relationship, he left the store, and then we weren't able to deliver as quickly, and . . ."

"You lost customers."

"Well, yes, we did. And that was a source of tension, yes, and of that slump I mentioned, but—"

"Do you think that Fenrik might have killed your sister?"

"I suppose it's possible, but—well, he's a wizard. I saw Gertha's body, she was hit very hard with a shovel. Wizards don't generally hit people with shovels, in my experience."

"In *my* experience, Mr. Mathe, they don't generally get intimate with non-mages, either. So you don't find Fenrik to be a credible suspect?"

"I'm afraid not. No, I still think it had to be Elgin. She was with him after she left the church meeting, you know."

"Was she? That's interesting."

"He *is* a suspect, isn't he?"

"As I said, Mr. Mathe, in the early stages, everyone is."

"Well, this might help you out, then—they were arguing."

"What about?"

"I'm afraid I only caught a few bits and pieces here and there, but one thing I remember very clearly. Elgin said, 'I can't believe you'd do this to me after all I've sacrificed to be with you.' I have to admit, I found that rather—well, odd."

"Why is that, Mr. Mathe?"

"He's just a clerk—a broke one, at that. He's worked some odd jobs all over Cliff's End. When we interviewed him, he told us that he had no family. I just don't understand what someone like him could possibly have given up? Oh, and another thing—part of his job is to clean the area around the store, and he generally uses a shovel for that."

"And why is that relevant, Mr. Mathe?"

"Uhm—well, you said before that Gertha was killed with a shovel."

"Actually, Mr. Mathe, I said no such thing."

"Excuse me?"

"*You* said that Gertha was killed with a shovel. And that's actually rather fascinating, because you said you knew that based on seeing the body."

"No, I didn't. You told me."

"I most certainly did not. Now, I saw the body, and while it's obvious that your sister was hit very hard on the side of the head with *something*, it was impossible to tell just from seeing her body what that something was. Yet here you are, definitively saying that it was a shovel."

"I—"

"Plus, there's also the matter of your house faerie."

"What about her?"

"Initially, yes, she did say that you got home *before* midnight—until she changed her story, and told us that you arrived home shortly *after* the timechimes rang midnight and that you gave her extra milk to tell anyone who asked that you arrived home at twenty-three and a half."

"I—I—"

"The fae are tricksters, Mr. Mathe, but direct falsehoods tend to disquiet them. You never should've told her to tell a lie."

"All right, all right, I'm sorry, truly, I—I didn't go straight home, and I—I did follow Gertha, but from a distance. I know that she was hit with a shovel, and I'm so sure that Elgin's the murderer because I saw him do it."

"Did you now?"

"Yes."

"And why didn't you say that in the first place?"

"Because—because if I told you that I was there, you'd assume I did it."

"And yet, you didn't tell me that and I assumed it anyhow."

"I'm telling you now, please, Lieutenant, this is very difficult—don't you understand? I watched my sister get killed! It was—it was horrible."

"Please, Mr. Mathe, tell me what you saw when you followed your sister home."

"I kept my distance, since I didn't want them to know I was following. That's why I only caught snatches of conversation, like that bit about sacrificing. Gertha has a porch behind her house that's one story up from the ground, and after she and Elgin went inside, they went out onto it. I came around and listened from under the porch. I heard them argue, and then I heard just an *awful* sound. I ran out from under the porch to see him standing over her, holding—holding a shovel in his hand. Then he turned and ran away."

"Why didn't you stay to help your sister?"

"Honestly, Lieutenant, my only thought was to wring Elgin's neck. I ran after him—chased him all the way to Meerka Way, but then I lost him in the crowds. Even around midnight, Meerka's fairly well packed."

"What did you do after you lost him?"

"By the time I got back to Gertha's house, several guardsmen were already present, and I—I panicked. I thought people would think I killed her, so I went home, bribed the house faerie, and then your people came to talk to me."

"I see. It's an interesting story you tell, Mr. Mathe, and very enlightening."

"It's not a story, Lieutenant, it's the truth."

"Is it? You see, your sister was killed at twenty-three and a half—exactly the time you told your house faerie to say you were home. And there are two dozen witnesses who can place Elgin at the Dog and Duck from a quarter past twenty-three all the way until they closed at three."

"That—that can't be right. Those people must be lying."

"I suppose it is possible that twenty-three drunkards and one sober bartender might all be lying, but it's been my experience that it's more likely that one person is lying. Especially when that person has already committed bribery to create an alibi."

"It had to be Elgin! I saw it! I would never kill Gertha! Not ever! She's my sister! Yes, I wanted her to stop seeing that idiot clerk and try to patch things up with Fenrik, but that's just because I wanted her to be happy—and, all right, yes, because business would pick up, but—but— Oh, dammit."

"Actually, Mr. Mathe, you've already given me a very good reason why it can't be Elgin."

"What—what do you mean?"

"You said it yourself—a wizard would never hit somebody with a shovel."

"I'm sorry?"

"You see, Mr. Mathe, your sister didn't end her relationship with Fenrik—exactly. The Brotherhood of Wizards has very strict guidelines regarding what you Ghandurha worshippers so quaintly refer to as fornication. They gave Fenrik a choice: end his relationship with Gertha Mathe or continue it, but renounce his magick. He chose the second option."

"W-what?"

"Elgin is Fenrik. The sacrifice you heard him talking about was giving up his life as a mage in order to be with her."

"That—that can't be. It—it can't—just—just can't."

"Yes, actually, it can."

"I—I just wanted her to be happy."

"She *was* happy. Until you killed her. And now you're going to spend the rest of your life in the hole—which should only be a week or two until the magistrate condemns you to death."

"I—why didn't they *tell* me?"

"Perhaps they didn't imagine you'd do something so insane as kill your sister."

"I didn't mean to, but she kept telling me that she'd found true love with that stupid clerk, and suddenly I had the shovel, and—"

"And then you ran home, bribed your house faerie, and concocted your idiotic story about Elgin. And now you're going to die."

"Why are you enjoying this so much, Lieutenant?"

"Because today I've done my job. I speak for people who can't speak for themselves. And right now, your sister is speaking out for justice—which I'm delivering. Guard! Take this shitbrain to the hole."

BLOOD IN THE WATER

He wasn't sure when it had stopped being the case, but the fact that he no longer did so made him both happy and sad. The latter because it used to be that he couldn't sleep without Zan curled up next to him, and now it seemed he could.

The former because Zan got up an hour before sunup every damn day.

He understood why, of course. While Dru toiled for the Cliff's End Castle Guard, Zan used the basement of their house as a haven for small children who needed to be taken care of during the day, and she needed to get up that early to get everything prepared. In particular, she had to be ready for the twin infants whose parents and older sister had been on Saptor Isle since the spring.

It paid well, and it fulfilled the maternal urges that Zan had had since she was a little girl helping her mother raise her siblings. Handy, since Zan, it turned out, was barren, a pronouncement from the healer that would have turned a weaker soul into a quivering mess — and, indeed, it did do that for Dru, who had always wanted children and was devastated by the news. Zan, however, found another way to care for children. If it couldn't be her own, it'd be other people's.

When the timechimes rang six times, Dru clambered out of the half-empty bed. His shift started at seven, and he only needed an hour to get ready and walk to the castle. Their house was located on Tyran's Way, in Dragon Precinct, the middle-class district of Cliff's End, but close to Unicorn Precinct, the upper-class district where about half of Zan's clients lived.

"Can you do me a favor?" Zan asked as he got up.

Dryly, Dru said, "G'morning, sweetness, how are you this morning?"

She rolled her eyes. "I'm fine, love. Look, I need a favor. I got a message this morning that Kari's sick, so she won't be able to go down to the docks for me."

"Why do you need Kari to go to the docks?" Dru asked incredulously. Kari was a young girl who helped Zan out most days. "That's really a shit place for a little girl to go."

"Please watch your language, Dru."

This time Dru rolled his eyes. "You didn't answer my question."

"You know the twins, Elva and Lonn?"

Dru nodded. "The ones with the family on Saptor?"

"Yes, them. The family in question is due back today on the *Bela's Bones*. They sent a message that they wanted someone to meet them at the docks when they arrived. I was going to have Kari do it, but—"

"But she's sick." Dru walked up to Zan and put a hand on her shoulder. "I can do it."

"Are you sure? I don't want Osric yelling at you again."

Chuckling, Dru said, "The captain'll yell at me no matter what. Nah, it'll be okay. Me and Hawk are next up, so we get the next case. If we do, we'll be wanderin' all over the city-state, and I can sneak off at noon to the docks. If we don't, we'll be sittin' on our asses all day, and I can go out to meet the boat at midday. Either way, Hawk'll cover for me."

Zan breathed a sigh of relief. "You know I wouldn't ask, but they *are* clients, and honestly they paid more than I quoted them, and the twins've just been *darlings*, and I don't want to let them down."

"Don't worry about it, sweetness." He kissed the top of her head. "I gotta get to work."

She looked up at him with her almond eyes and almost smiled. "Thank you, love."

One of these days, Dru thought with a sigh as climbed into his leather armor, she was going to smile at him again. He was sure of it.

He ambled slowly up Meerka Way through Unicorn Precinct, the early-morning sun dappling through the trees that lined the street, which also served to conceal the mansions from the riffraff that passed along Cliff's End's main thoroughfare.

When he arrived, about ten minutes before the shift started, his first stop was, as always, the pantry. He didn't even bother to take his cloak off, first. Jonas's wife made the best pastries, and for some reason he was particularly hungry for them. Maybe because Zan had recently stopped making breakfast for him, busy as she was with getting the house ready for the day's infestation of children.

His partner, Lieutenant Hawk, was already there, his dreadlocks hanging over his cloak, which he also hadn't bothered to remove upon entry. "Whasamatta?" he asked with his mouth full.

Dru shrugged. "Just—nothing. Really. Same shit, y'know?"

Danthres, Grovis, and Iaian each arrived in turn, and Jonas provided some quick updates on things—including confirmation that Dru and Hawk were back in the rotation.

Frowning, Danthres said, "Wait, those idiots from Mermaid were your guys?"

Hawk nodded. "Yeah, we talked to 'em down in Mermaid's hole yesterday, an' they came right out an' said they hit Felspan's, too."

Grinning, Dru added, "Maybe next time they'll know better than to hit a fish place when three Guards from Mermaid are having lunch there. So now we got 'em on *two* robberies, and the Felspan's case is finally closed."

"I'm really hopin' nobody commits no crimes today," Hawk said with a sigh.

"Me, too. Listen, Hawk, can you do me a favor and cover for me around noon? I need to run an errand for Zan at the docks."

Hawk looked annoyed right up until he mentioned his wife. "Yeah, okay, if it's somethin' for Zan, sure."

"So, what, you weren't gonna when it was just a favor for me?"

"Your wife, I like. Your wife, she didn't crap out on me when I needed someone to help me with Dad."

Dru put his head in his hands. "You don't need any 'help' with your father. Your father ain't crippled, and he ain't—"

"'Scuse me!"

Turning, Dru saw a young girl with a rat's nest of blond curls and a pointed nose. She was one of the youth squad, children who per-formed errands for the Castle Guard, usually carrying messages.

"Sergeant Mannit said t'find s'm detectives. Says there's a boat floatin' out in the Garamin that's s'posed t'be dockin', but it ain't movin'. Sent a dinghy out, 'n ain't nobody alive onna boat. They're towin' it in now, but the sarge figgers they'll need detectives."

Jonas nodded and looked at Dru and Hawk. "You two are up, so I guess this is yours." He smiled. "And this'll make it easy for you to run your errand, huh, Dru?"

"Guess so." Dru turned to the girl as he fished a copper out of his money pouch. "Which boat is it?"

"*Bela's Bones.*"

Dru dropped the copper piece on the floor. "Shit."

BY THE TIME DRU AND HAWK MADE IT DOWN TO THE DOCKS, *BELA'S BONES* had been towed in by the dinghy that Mermaid Precinct had sent out.

They were met there by an elderly guard in a green cloak emblazoned with a mermaid medallion that matched the one on his leather armor.

Shaking his head as they approached, Dru said, "I still can't believe Osric got your sorry ass back in leather."

Mannit uttered a croaking laugh. "Well, retirement wasn't really engaging me all that much. Besides, who else was gonna take this shit job?" Mermaid Precinct had been rocked by scandal, exposed by Iaian and Grovis just before midsummer, with Sergeant Gaffni forced to resign. Mannit was a Castle Guard lifer who had hit his twenty-five-year mark and retired; Osric had talked him out of retirement in order to run Mermaid.

"Anybody but you." Dru had come up with Mannit as his training officer in Dragon Precinct. "Weren't you the one who told me never to let them promote you, 'cause bein' a guard was the only good job in town?"

"Yeah, and we both didn't listen." Mannit pointed at the boat, which two of Mermaid's guards were mooring. "There's your crime scene."

Dru nodded, Hawk following him.

Hawk was an expert sailor, having spent much of his youth on the water with his boat captain grandfather, so he went up first, hopping onto the boat's deck with the ease of long practice. Dru, who tended to throw up when on a ship at sea, climbed in a bit more gingerly.

Expecting Hawk to move about the deck, Dru was surprised to settle onto the deck and find his partner not having moved. "What's goi—"

Then he saw it. The deck was stained with blood, and there were corpses *everywhere*. Some were obviously sailors, others well-dressed passengers.

Most of them had their necks ripped open, and the few that didn't had wounds in their upper thighs. Glancing about, Dru saw no other obvious wounds. He also saw surprisingly little blood given how many wounds there were.

Or, rather, not surprising at all, given that they *were* neck and thigh wounds.

"Shit," he said. "We've got a new nest'a vampires."

"I thought all the vampires were wiped out five years ago." Captain Osric sat behind the desk in his office, sharpening his dagger.

"Yeah, me too," Hawk said from one of the guest chairs across from him. "In fact, I knew me a vamp hunter who retired after the Brotherhood made that there pronouncement about wipin' vamps out."

"I have to admit," Osric said, "I was dubious about that pronouncement, but we also haven't had a single vamp attack in those five years. Should've known better. Pity I can't berate Boneen on the subject."

The Castle Guard's magickal examiner, a wizard on loan from the Brotherhood of Wizards to aid in investigations, was away at a conference, along with the local Brotherhood representative, Gunderson. Not that Boneen would be of much use here. Vampires disrupted magick, so his peel-back spell to ascertain what happened on *Bela's Bones* would be useless.

Then again, Dru thought as he sat in the seat next to Hawk's, they hardly needed a spell to tell them that vampires killed those people. Vamps were the only creatures who feasted on blood like that, and neck and upper thigh wounds were the ones that bled the most profusely.

"Is this vampire hunter in Cliff's End?" Osric asked Hawk.

He nodded. "Last I heard, he was livin' in the place over Minar's."

"Good. Go find him — we'll need all the help we can get on this."

"Oh, he'll be helpin'. Corvin's got himself a serious mad-on for vamps." Hawk got to his feet. "You comin', partner?"

"Hm?" Dru looked up. "Sorry, was just thinkin' about how I'm gonna have to tell Zan that the twins' parents and sister are dead. I dunno what we're gonna do with 'em."

HAWK WAS STARTING TO GET WORRIED ABOUT HIS PARTNER. DRU HAD BEEN unusually quiet the entire walk down Meerka Way into Dragon Precinct. When they turned onto Auburn Way, Hawk finally asked him, "What's wrong?"

"I told you back at the cap'n's office." Dru shook his head. "Bad enough we gotta deal with these kids during the day, and these twins? An aunt's supposed to take 'em at night, but half the time, she don't even show, and we're stuck with 'em overnight."

"Well, maybe the aunt'll take 'em permanent now?"

Before Dru could answer, Minar came lumbering out of the shop's front door. "Lieutenants, gladjer here." He pointed above his shop toward the apartment there with one massive arm. "There might be somethin' up with Corvin. Heard all kindsa nasty-ass noises up 'ere early last evenin'."

"That ain't good," Hawk said.

Dru asked, "You check on him?"

Minar shook his head. "Nah, the noise stopped after a while, an' then I had a shit-ton'a customers t'deal with, so I didn't get the chance to check. But I ain't seen him come down from 'ere, and he usually stops in on his way to breakfast in the mornin'."

"Where does he have breakfast?" Dru asked.

Hawk answered before Minar could. "The Dog an' Duck, yeah? He always has that nasty stew for breakfast."

Minar nodded his large head. "Yeah, he's still goin' there ev'ry mornin'. But I ain't seen him today."

"We'll check it out," Dru said, and Hawk followed his partner around to the side door that led to the staircase up to the flat.

When they got to the top, Hawk knocked on the door and started to say, "It's Hawk from the Castle Guard, open up!" But he only got as far as "It's" when the first knock pushed the door open with a slow creak.

Hawk put his hand to his sword hilt as he pushed the door open the rest of the way.

"Corvin?" he called out as he walked into the disaster area of an apartment. It was only one room, but it was a mess. All the furniture was overturned and/or damaged, one of the windows (looking out the rear of the building) was cracked, and the floor was littered with jagged-edged pieces of wood, glass, and ceramic.

The two detectives slowly moved through the apartment, which didn't take long. Hawk saw no bodies, and very little blood.

He looked at his partner. "This is the worst kinda bad."

Dru threw up his hands. "Who *is* this guy, anyhow?"

"The best damned vamp hunter in Flingaria, that's who he is. And we got the same lack'a blood we had on the boat."

"That could just mean he wasn't here, and the drops we *are* seein' are from the guy who trashed the place."

"Or a vamp got him." Hawk shrugged. "Bound to be happenin' eventually, 'specially since he ain't fought one in five years."

"Something's wrong, though," Dru said, looking around the place.

"What is?"

"Couple things. For starters, Minar said he didn't see Corvin leave. So where is he?"

Hawk hadn't thought of that. "Maybe he snuck out to the Dog an' Duck without Minar noticin'?"

"It's worth asking."

"What's the other thing?" Hawk asked as they headed out of the apartment.

Shaking his head, Dru said, "Not sure. Something feels wrong about that place — beyond the obvious, I mean."

They went back outside and looked around before finding a member of the youth squad. Dru talked to her while Hawk went to Minar. "We're gonna be gettin' a guard from Dragon here to keep an eye on things. Don't be lettin' anybody up to Corvin's place, an' if you see someone tryin', call a guard."

"Absolutely," Minar said with a nod.

Hawk walked back to Dru, who dropped a copper in the youth squadder's hands. "Hey, that's two of the little brats I tipped today. You either get the next two, or you buy lunch."

"Yeah, yeah." Hawk considered pointing out that Dru and his wife both made money, while Hawk was single and had to take care of Dad, but he didn't feel like having the argument again.

As they walked back down Auburn toward Meerka Way, Dru asked, "So why's this Corvin guy such hot shit? I mean, if I remember right, the whole thing about vampires is that they prefer to come out at night, they mess up magick, they drink blood, they're strong and fast, and the only way to kill 'em is by beheading."

"Right. But Corvin? He bagged himself hundreds'a vamps. When they had that infestation of 'em in Barlin back after the war? He's the one that cleaned the town up. Him and Gan Brightblade, they killed those vamps that had taken over Saptor Isle. And I heard that he saved King Marcus his own damn self from a vamp in Velessa."

Dru snorted. "If he saved the king's life and was a friend'a Brightblade's, why's he livin' in that shithole over Minar's?"

"'Cause I ain't toldja the other part yet. Reason I know Corvin is 'cause we had us a vamp murder in Mermaid back inna day. Just like this one, boat floatin' out on the Garamin, we towed it in, an' there was nothin' but dead bodies and not nearly enough blood for all the neck and thigh wounds. Then we got two more just like it, and I kept noticin' this one guy always bein' there."

Six years earlier, Hawk stood on the docks and approached Lieutenant Linder. "'Scuse me, Lieutenant, but I been noticin' somethin'."

Linder had just finished talking to the dockmaster. "What's that, Hawk?"

"That man over there, he's been lurkin' at each'a the scenes."

"So've half a dozen sailors. Don't worry about it."

Hawk had more to say, but Linder wandered off. And dammit, there was *something* off about this guy. He wasn't just watching like all the other sailors and dock rats and such, who just wanted to see a pile of dead bodies. This guy was *observing*. When he'd been on duty when Lieutenants ban Wyvald and Tresyllione were on a case, he'd noticed that they observed like that. But Linder, and his partner Iaian, they weren't like that.

Hawk needed to find out who this guy was. So he went over to him —

— except, all of a sudden, he was gone. He searched the docks up and down and couldn't find him.

The next day, there was another murder, just a single dead body with a neck wound in the Dancing Seagull. Except this one had blood pooling around the body. Hawk and another guard from Mermaid, Gaffni, were on the scene, and Gaffni said, "We'd better get the Cloaks down 'ere. Looks like another vamp."

But Hawk was noticing the guy from the docks sitting in a booth. Walking over to him, Hawk said, "I need to be talkin' to you."

"Your partner is a fool. That person was not murdered by a vampire."

Hawk nodded. "Too much blood, yeah. I figured, but last time I was disagreein' with Gaffni, he yelled at me and did what he wanted anyhow. So now I just let him go an' let someone else yell at *him*."

The man sipped his drink. "You are wise."

"You been at all the vamp murders. You know somethin'. You gotta be tellin' us so we can stop this."

"Believe me, you cannot stop this. These are the remnants from vampires I assisted in exterminating on Saptor. I beheaded one last night, and I have tracked the other one."

"So what you doin' here?" Hawk asked accusingly.

"When I heard about the cut throat, I believed it might be the vampire I sought. It was not — which I should have known. Vampires are creatures of habit, and this one has never been one to kill but once, nor kill in a tavern. However, you and that other guard will not permit anyone to depart, so I have remained. I prefer not to have issue with the Castle Guard."

"You're gonna be havin' a lot more 'issue' if you don't be talkin' to the lieutenants when they get here. If you know who did this—"

The man set his drink down and grabbed Hawk's wrist in a tight grip. "You are not equipped."

"Ow! Hey, let go'a me!"

He acquiesced, letting go. "The Castle Guard *cannot* deal with this. My name is Corvin. Vampires killed my wife and my children, and since that horrible day, I have dedicated my life to hunting down these monsters and destroying them."

"Yeah, well, the Castle Guard's *job* is to hunt down folks that kill other folks, an' we've gotten pretty good at it. And folks who stop us from doin' that get themselves arrested, which is what we'll be doin' to you if you don't talk to the lieutenants when they get here."

Corvin took a sip of his drink, then said, "What if I deliver the decapitated corpse of the guilty party to you?"

"Like I said, if you talk to the lieutenants—"

"No, not the lieutenants. You." For the first time, Corvin came close to almost smiling. "You noticed my presence at the other scenes. I have what some call a gift for not being noticed. I even snuck up on my good friend Gan Brightblade once."

Hawk was impressed. The legendary hero was known for being impossible to catch unawares.

"But you observed me, which is a rare gift. Meet me underneath the old port at an hour before sunset."

The door to the Dancing Seagull opened, then, and Hawk turned to see Linder and Iaian walking in. Gaffni told them they had a dead body and led them to it.

"Lord and Lady, Gaffni," Linder said, "what kind of shitbrain are you, anyhow?"

"Excuse me?" Gaffni sounded indignant.

"We're lookin' for a *vampire*. You know, big scary monster that *drinks blood*? If a vampire killed this poor bastard, there wouldn't be any blood around, because the vampire would've *drunk it all* because that's what vampires *do*. Now since you're too stupid to do your job right, me and Iaian will walk *all the way back* to the castle and send two *other* lieutenants who don't actually *have* a case to solve this murder."

Shaking his head, Linder left, Iaian following. Hawk turned back to ask Corvin more questions—

—but he was gone.

"Wait a minute," Dru said as they approached the Dog and Duck. "You mean the informant you said helped you find that vampire was this Corvin guy?"

Hawk nodded.

Dru shook his head. He'd heard this story plenty of times before, from Hawk and from others who served with him in Mermaid at the time, since it was his finding that vampire that led to Hawk being promoted when Lieutenant Nael died. "Unbelievable. Why didn't you say who it was?"

"He was askin' me not to. 'Sides, you know what he did when I met up with him at the old port? Took out this huge curved sword—ain't seen nothin' like it before or since. He cut right through the planks with it, exposed the vamp and cut its head off with one slice."

Dru's eyes widened. "Seriously?" He'd never seen a sword that could behead someone cleanly. Hell, most axes couldn't even get it done that neatly.

They walked into the Dog and Duck. The proprietor, Olaf, came waddling out from behind the inn's front desk, the light from the window reflecting off his bald pate. "Hello to you, Lieutenants! What can Olaf be doing for you this fine day!"

Rolling his eyes at Olaf's broken Common—he'd moved to Cliff's End from the islands to the east almost two decades ago, now, and he didn't need to affect the silly accent—Dru said, "We're wondering if Corvin came by for his breakfast this morning."

"Funny is that you should be asking this. On the yesterday, Corvin, he comes for to break his fast, but to go is how he takes it, as he cannot stay to eat."

"Is that unusual?" Dru asked.

"Very, yes, unusual, yes. Always in the inn does he eat. But he says he has appointment with swordmaster. And today, he does not come at all."

"Did he say which swordmaster?"

Olaf shook his bald head, but Hawk answered the question. "I'm knowin' which swordmaster. C'mon."

"Stay, will you not, Lieutenants, and have a drink? Perhaps some stew? We are having the extra today."

"We need to be findin' Corvin," Hawk said, grabbing Dru's arm and practically dragging him out of the inn.

As they went out of the front door, Dru said, "Y'know, it's gettin' to be lunch time, and you still owe me a meal."

"Later. We need to be findin' Corvin. We find him, we'll find the killer."

"Why you so sure? This guy isn't even a lead on the case, he's—"

Hawk stopped in the middle of the street and turned to stare at Dru. "Only swordmaster he used was Molano—she's the only one can handle that curved blade'a his. And if he went t'her yesterday, it means he's re-sharpenin' the sword, which means he knows there's a vamp in town. We gotta be findin' him, and his sword."

Dru wasn't entirely sure his partner was right, but Hawk knew this Corvin guy, and while he may not have been a real lead, they didn't have any actual leads, so it couldn't hurt to play this one out.

They walked over to Alfar's Way. Dru's stomach was growling now, and he really wished that they'd taken Olaf up on his offer of food.

Dru had met Molano once or twice before. He remembered being surprised that she was an elf, given that her name was human, but she claimed to have been raised by humans. She was as tall and ethereal, though her hair was darker than most elves. Currently it was tied back into a ponytail as she was polishing a short sword while sitting in a big easy chair on the side of her small shop, the walls of which were lined with swords. No other weapons were on display—Molano was a specialist.

She bounded up from her seated position, then gently set the sword and polishing rag down on the table next to the chair. "Hello, Lieutenant Dru, Lieutenant Hawk. Been a few years. *Please* tell me that the Castle Guard is finally upgrading its weaponry!"

Chuckling, Dru said, "That's way over our pay grade."

"Damn." Molano shook her head, her ponytail waving back and forth. "I'll have to talk to Sir Rommett when he comes in to get his saber cleaned."

Hawk winced. "Sir Rommett uses a saber?"

"Sir Rommett owns a saber. I wouldn't bet any coin on his ever having used it." She let out a very musical laugh, then asked, "So, if you're not here to enact the upgrade that I've been begging for—seriously, those longswords you use? Pitiful."

"T'be fair," Hawk said, "we don't hardly ever use 'em. I ain't rememberin' the last time I took it out for anythin' 'cept to clean it."

"Yeah, me either," Dru added.

"Well, in any event, how may I help you gentlemen today?"

Dru nodded. "We heard tell that Corvin brought his sword in to be serviced yesterday."

"He did." Molano practically bounced over to the far wall. The woman was bursting with energy, but she still was gentle as she gingerly removed a curved blade that was at once thin and thick. She held it almost reverently. "And he was supposed to pick it up this morning."

"He ain't come to get it yet?" Hawk sounded almost panicked.

"If he doesn't, I can find a thousand buyers for this—including me. The craft of this blade is like nothing I've seen before that wasn't magicked—it's three layers of metal fused together. It's incredibly sharp, too. This thing could probably cut down an entire stone building and only dull a little bit."

"Somethin's wrong," Hawk said. "He wouldn't be leavin' this unless somethin' happened. We gotta be gettin' back to his place."

Hawk practically ran out of Molano's. After shooting an apologetic look at the swordmaster, Dru chased him, wondering if he was ever going to eat today.

HAWK TORE THROUGH THE MESS OF CORVIN'S APARTMENT, TRYING TO FIND something that would give him a hint. As he tossed aside a chair to see if there was anything under it—there wasn't, aside from some shards of glass—he muttered, "I'm really wishin' Boneen was back from his damn conference so we could get us a peel-back."

"Wouldn't matter, remember?" Dru said from across the room, going through some scrolls that had been dumped on the floor. "Vampires mess up the spell."

"I know, but—" In frustration, Hawk threw a broken piece of pottery against the wall.

Dru watched as it hit the far wall—and then, finally, he figured out what had been bothering him since they first got here earlier. "That wall—no way that's the far wall of the building. I been in Minar's dozens'a times."

"Yeah, an' this is bein' the same size as his shop," Hawk said, not clear as to what his partner was getting at.

Pointing at the far wall, Dru said, "Yeah, the *shop*—but what about the storage room in the back? That's gotta be another dozen handslengths or so. Hallway and staircase're on this side, so what's over there?"

Frowning, Hawk looked around the room—and realized that his partner was right. This flat should have been larger.

Without another word, they started searching the far wall for some kind of hidden doorway—but found nothing.

"Maybe we should be tryin' the skeleton key?" Hawk asked.

But Dru shook his head. "That only works on regular locked doors, not magicked walls. We need Boneen."

"Yeah, well, we ain't got him." Then, suddenly, Hawk remembered something, snapping his fingers. "Wait, remember the Janzen case from, like three years ago?"

Dru frowned. Then he brightened. "Yeah, the guy who had bodies hidden in his wall?"

"Right, an' he was havin' some kinda charm to 'open' the wall so's he could be puttin' more bodies in."

"And Boneen confiscated it. We need another one of those charms. Minar prob'ly has one downstairs."

Hawk shook his head emphatically, his dreadlocks shaking with the gesture. "An' who's gonna be payin' for that?"

That brought Dru up short, and Hawk could see that his partner had come to the same realization as he had: charms of that sort weren't cheap, and the paperwork to requisition the funds to pay for such out of the Guard's budget was a nightmare. "Okay," Dru said, "so we get the charm from the Janzen case. It's gotta be in Boneen's lair, right?"

Hawk let out a sigh. "Yeah, it prob'ly is."

By the time they got back to Corvin's place, Dru was shuddering. "I swear to Mitre, Xinf, Wiate, Temisa, Ghandurha, and whatever other god you care to name that I'm gonna have nightmares tonight. It's gonna be that damn gryphon's voice comin' out of that damn sprite's body, and she's gonna torture me all night."

Hawk chuckled, which earned him a fierce gaze from his partner. Entering Boneen's laboratory in the basement of the castle was problematic at the best of times, as the door was guarded by a magickal gryphon with a screechy voice. But with Boneen away at that Brotherhood of Wizards conference, he left a sprite behind to keep an eye on things. She led them to the charm eventually, but it took a lot of explaining before she got around to it, and kept asking over and over again if they'd be returning it when they were done.

"Long's we're returnin' it when we're done," Hawk said, "we'll be okay. I don't wanna be thinkin' about what happens if we don't."

"Let's get this over with," Dru said and pointed the charm at the far wall.

Moments later, the wall faded away, revealing another section of the apartment—except this space was filled with an elaborate bench. There were levered bars at ankle and wrist level, which had shackles on the end of them. This meant whoever was on the bench could be compressed or stretched out via his or her limbs. The bench itself was stained with blood, as well as something purple, though all of it was long since dried. Littered all over the floor were containers with the logo of Kardy's Butcher Shop.

Looking closely at the bench, Dru pointed at the shackles. "These have been busted open."

"What the hell was he doin' back here?" Hawk asked. "Relivin' the days of Chalmraik the Foul?"

Dru shook his head slowly. That wizard had menaced Flingaria in the past, and he was said to have tortured his prisoners. This device that Corvin had been hiding behind a magicked wall just had to be an instrument of torture. Bending over, Dru picked up one of the butcher shop's containers. "I know this place — it's on the River Walk. Let's see what they have to say."

"Yeah."

Dru didn't like the sound of his partner's voice. "What's wrong, Hawk?"

"Let's just be goin'." Hawk exited the apartment.

Following him, Dru said, "Dammit, what's the matter?"

"Ain't none'a this makin' any sense," Hawk said. He and Dru both nodded to Manfred, the guard from Dragon Precinct who was keeping an eye on the place. They continued out toward Meerka Way, which would take them to the River Walk — that being the border between Goblin and Mermaid Precincts.

"Look, we're doin' what we always do — we follow the leads."

"Yeah, but they ain't makin' sense." Hawk let out a long breath.

"You said that already, but —"

Stopping short, Hawk looked at Dru. "He was savin' my life, okay?"

Dru frowned. "What?"

"When we was meetin' up at the old port, Corvin cut down some'a the old planks so we could get at where the vamp was hidin' — but I barged right on in, and the damn thing jumped me. I was tryin' to take my sword out, but it was all over me. An' then Corvin, he impaled the bastard on his curved blade, an' I was able to get away. But if he'd acted just a little slower? I'd'a been the vamp's last meal."

DRU HAD EXPECTED CORVIN TO LOOK MORE IMPRESSIVE.

When they arrived at the old port, Hawk led them straight to the spot under the rotted planks of Cliff's End's original dock. The location was a more natural port than the current docklands, which were constructed after Cliff's End grew too large for the original spot to be practical. The old port had fallen into disrepair.

Pushing aside a pile of pitted wood, Hawk revealed a small, dank, humid cubbyhole.

Dru had to admit, he hadn't been sure what they would find here. He wasn't even sure why he went along with Hawk's crazy notion to come here after they talked to the butcher.

But then, they found Corvin tied to two of the planks with a thick rope. At least, Dru assumed it was Corvin, mostly based on Hawk calling him by name when they entered. His neck was smeared with blood, his clothes filthy and torn, and he seemed unusually pale.

"Hawk?" Corvin said weakly. "In—in Mitre's name, I n-never expected to—to see you, or—or anyone ever ag-g-gain. P-please, you m-must release me from these b-bonds."

As Hawk unsheathed his sword in order to slice the ropes, Dru asked, "When's the vampire due back, you think?"

"Ex-excuse me?"

"Don't be playin' dumb," Hawk said as he cut one rope. Corvin then moved to untie the other knot himself.

"I—I am not p-playing anything, L-Lieutenants. B-but I—"

Dru interrupted. "You had a vamp shackled to your little torture device—the one you hid behind the wall? You kept him there for, what, six years?"

"I'm guessin' he's the one you told me you decapitated back at the Dancin' Seagull. 'Cept you didn't cut his head off, you captured him so you could torture him."

"You fed him just enough blood to keep him alive—you had a butcher in Goblin give you animal blood. And before you try to deny it, the butcher already confirmed it."

Corvin rubbed his wrists, the skin of which was raw from his bonds. "You are v-very clever. Yes, indeed, I d-did capture one of those—those monsters. The sp-spell I purchased to hide it from sight app-apparently also protected it f-from the spell that the B-Brotherhood of Wizards c-cast five years ago to wipe out all living vam-vampires." He took a deep breath and swallowed. "They are f-foul c-creatures of m-magick. They kill without m-mercy or remorse or r-reason."

"Actually, that's the funny thing," Dru said. "They do kill for a reason. To feed. Except he didn't feed off you. He brought you here, instead."

"Not too surprisin'," Hawk said. "Like you was sayin' to me back in the day, vamps is creatures'a habit. This is where they were holed up last time, when they was killin' folks on boats. When your prisoner got loose, he trashed your place, and started doin' the same thing over again. Even brought your sorry ass to the same place he holed up in then."

"But why?" Dru asked.

Corvin's hands balled into fists. "You interrogate me as if I were one of your prisoners."

"Our 'prisoners' are criminals," Dru said. "Of course, torture is a crime. So's harboring a fugitive, and so's letting a murder suspect run loose."

"Torture of people is a crime, Lieutenant," Corvin snapped. Dru noticed that he ignored the other parts. "That—that foul *thing* does not have the same rights as you or I, any more than—than a dog does."

"A dog wouldn't go to the trouble of bringing you here, though." Dru stepped forward. Corvin was half a head taller than Dru—indeed, he was taller than Torin, who towered over everyone in the squadroom—and his breath smelled like something had died in his mouth, but Dru didn't care. If they were right—and it was looking increasingly like they were—the only reason this vampire got loose to kill the people on *Bela's Bones* was because this guy *let* it loose. "So why'd he let you live?"

A papery voice sounded from behind Dru. "Revenge."

Whirling around, Dru put his hand to his sword hilt. Standing in the corner of the cubbyhole beneath the erstwhile dock was a pale, hairless creature with watery, yellow eyes, and a dry-lipped mouth filled with sharp teeth. The vampire was hunched over, holding bent, taloned hands in front of his body.

The vampire continued to speak, though the words sounded odd coming from a mouth filled with such long, sharp teeth. "To kill is not enough. This monster must pay for what he did to me."

"*I* am the monster? Your kind killed my family!"

Hissing, the vampire then said, "And you killed mine!"

Hawk then asked the question that was on Dru's mind. "Since when do vamps be speakin'?"

"The night creatures have always spoken, human," the vampire said with a sneer. "But we never felt the need to learn your gutter tongue. However, listening to this monster for six years enabled me to speak as you do. Having to wrap my lips around your idiotic language is the final torture this creature has visited upon me."

Corvin moved slowly forward. "Then these words shall be your last."

Then the vampire hissed and slashed at the air in front of him with his hands. Corvin backed off, perhaps suddenly remembering that he was unarmed, his best weapon still at Molano's.

"I'm sorry, friend," Dru said slowly, hand still on sword hilt, "but we're gonna have to arrest you in the name of the lord and lady for the murder of two dozen people on the *Bela's Bones*."

"Pfagh! Do you arrest a dwarf who eats meat? A human who consumes a stew?"

"You have a problem with it," Dru said, "you can take it up with the magistra—"

And then the vampire leapt and attacked him.

Dru tried to pull his sword out, but the monster was too fast, leaping atop him and knocking him to the ground, the pair of them rolling on the rocky, uneven ground beneath the wood.

Hawk immediately yanked his sword out and went for the vampire, but he slashed at Hawk, his talons cutting through the leather armor right at the gryphon medallion on his chest, drawing blood.

The vampire was now kneeling on Dru's chest and snarling down at him, baring the two rows of sharp teeth. He was suddenly very sorry that he left the house annoyed with Zan this morning, because he really wanted the last thing he would ever say to his wife to be that he loved her.

Then Corvin took a jagged plank of wood and shoved it into the vampire's neck.

A purple ichor spurted forth, and Dru suddenly realized that the purple stains on the bench in Corvin's apartment were the vampire version of blood.

Screaming, the vampire—the plank still embedded in the side of his neck—jumped at Corvin, the two of them smashing through the wood and onto the rocky coast. Clambering to his feet, Dru limped out, unable to put his full weight on his right ankle, to see the vampire's sharpened teeth biting fiercely into Corvin's neck, while the latter was trying to shove the hunk of wood deeper.

Hawk stumbled out right behind him, right hand gripping his sword, left arm cradling his chest trying to keep the blood from the scratches in.

Both bodies went limp at roughly the same time. Dru glanced at Hawk, and the pair of them cautiously approached the vampire and the vampire hunter from two different sides.

After a moment, though, it was obvious that they both were dead, having succeeded in killing each other.

Quietly, Dru said, "I guess they each got their revenge, huh?"

HAWK WATCHED AS THE HEALER—HAVING ALREADY DEALT WITH HAWK'S scratches, which turned out to be superficial—gave Dru a potion that would heal his ankle within a day. Also present were several guards from Mermaid Precinct, as well as Sergeant Mannit, who had personally escorted Zan. She ran straight to Dru, sitting on one of the rocks near the old port.

"Oh, love, I thought you were dead." She practically fell on him with her embrace.

"It's just my ankle, sweetness."

"It was a *vampire*. When that guard came to the house . . ."

"I'm *fine*. But I got bad news about the twins."

She nodded quickly. "I heard. I've already talked to their aunt, and she promises to take custody of them, but only on the condition that I continue to care for them during the day as I have been."

Hawk shook his head as he walked over to the pair of them.

Dru grimaced. "And when she doesn't show up again?"

"Then we will deal with it."

"Yeah, but—"

"How are you doing, Hawk?" Zan asked over Dru's objection, sounding genuinely concerned.

"I'm not bein' as lucky as my partner," he said with a small smile, "'cause I ain't got me a great wife."

She put a hand on his. It was warm and comforting. "Some day, you shall." She looked around. "Though I'm surprised that your father isn't around."

"He ain't gettin' around that good, on account'a he's all crippled, and—"

Dru rolled his eyes. "Lord and Lady, Hawk, your father is not crippled! He's just a lazy-ass shitbrain!"

Before Hawk could reply, Zan said, "You'll have to excuse my foul-mouthed husband, Hawk, the potion obviously made him delirious."

Hawk just shook his head. "Me, I'm wonderin' what was with Corvin. Thought he was glad to be ridda vamps. Instead, he kept hangin' onto the hate, keepin' that thing in his *home* for all these years."

"S'what happens when you get obsessed, I suppose." Dru sighed. "Me, I'm just glad this case is closed and the bastard's dead."

Unable to believe his ears, Hawk whirled on his partner. "He saved our lives, Dru."

"They only needed savin' 'cause'a him!"

"Yeah, but . . ." Hawk trailed off, having nothing to say to that.

"Look," Zan said after a moment, "why don't you come over to our house, Hawk? I'm making a nice dinner for the children, and you can join us—and continue your argument over a meal."

Dru smiled, a peace gesture. "What do you say, partner? Now that we killed the big monster, we can deal with some tiny monsters?"

After a moment, Hawk returned the smile. "Yeah, okay."

But he wondered as they walked away from the old port, which of the two beings who died today was the bigger monster.

A CLEAN GETAWAY

Lieutenant Danthres Tresyllione was already in a bad mood when she arrived at the house in Unicorn Precinct, and finding herself being yelled at by one of the guards did not improve it. Looking down, she saw that the floor of the house was covered in some kind of dark muck.

Her superiors were generally amenable to paying for a Laundry Spell to get blood stains out of her boots and earth-colored cloak. This whatever-it-was, on the other hand, would be a harder sell, and Danthres was in no mood to fight that particular battle with whatever functionary in the lord and lady's court oversaw the appropriations for such things.

"I'll stay out here, then," she said, stopping in the threshold.

"Not a problem," said a familiar voice from inside. It was her partner, Lieutenant Torin ban Wyvald. "I've already been soiled, so I'll provide the gory details."

Danthres peered inside to see a large sitting room that under normal circumstances would have been considered fancy and high-class, but for the fact that it was covered in a truly impressive amount of dirt and grime and muck. Tramping around in it were the guard who had cautioned her against stepping lightly—whom she recognized as Manfred, one of the few grunts in the Cliff's End Castle Guard who had anything approaching a brain—and Torin. Hovering about a handslength above the floor was the M.E., Boneen. Typically, the magickal examiner refused to degrade himself, so he used his wizardly abilities to levitate; just as typically, the cranky old bastard didn't offer the same to the others.

"I'm surprised to see you here already, Boneen," Danthres said. "It usually requires a team of dragons to get you to a crime scene with any dispatch."

Glaring witheringly at Danthres from his position over the floor, Boneen said, "Does it disturb you, Tresyllione, to make so many attempts at wit and yet fall short of the mark?"

"Not in the least." Danthres turned to Torin. "So what happened?"

Torin cleared his throat before speaking. "This house is owned by the Jaros family. The actual owner is the family patriarch, Millar Jaros, and his son, daughter-in-law, and four grandchildren all live here as well. This morning, the daughter-in-law, Abbi, came downstairs to prepare breakfast, and discovered this."

While Torin was talking, Danthres had been looking at the muck and noticing something. "All right, this is odd—there's a pattern to the gunk. Like it all exploded outward." She'd seen similar patterns in blood when someone was struck with a heavy object, especially in the head, but it wasn't something she ever expected to see with dirt.

"Yes, it did." Torin was now pointing at a closet door. "It seems to have come out from there."

Crankily, Boneen said, "No 'seems' about it. I did the peel-back, and it showed this garbage literally exploding outward from the closet." On loan from the Brotherhood of Wizards, the magickal examiner's primary purpose was to cast an Inanimate Residue Spell, commonly called a "peel-back," which allowed him to see what recently happened in a particular place. "And once I did that, I had this young man call you two in."

That, at least, explained why Boneen's arrival preceded theirs. She looked at Manfred. "You summoned the M.E., Manfred?"

"Yes, ma'am." The guard sounded pleased that she remembered his name. "And he had me bring you in, like he said, ma'am."

Danthres's mood grew darker by the second. "Pardon me, Boneen, but I was under the impression that the function of lieutenants in the Castle Guard like myself and Torin was to investigate crimes that occur within the lord and lady's demesne."

"What are you driving at, Tresyllione?"

Angrily, Danthres said, "What I'm driving at is that what I see here is an accident, not a crime—unless there's a dead body I'm missing under all this?"

Torin's long red hair and thick red beard obscured all of his face save for his humorous eyes and aquiline nose—except when he smiled broadly, as he did now. "No, but there is a bit of a wrinkle."

She sighed. "Of course there is."

Manfred said, "I talked to Abbi Jaros, and then her husband, father-in-law, and children, and they all say the same thing: until this morning, there was no closet there, just a blank wall."

"So there's magick afoot." She fixed her irritated gaze upon Boneen. "Isn't magick the Brotherhood's concern?"

"Licensed magick is, yes. This is unlicensed magick." Sniffing, he added, "The Brotherhood does not consort in magicks that cast dirt about."

"What, your desire to keep from getting your hands dirty extends to the rest of the world, too?"

"Something like that, yes. In any case, I've already communicated with Lord Ythran, the local Brotherhood representative, and he and I agreed that this is an unlicensed commercial spell, and therefore not within the Brotherhood's purview. So have at it."

With that, Boneen gestured, muttered something, and disappeared in a flash of light.

After blinking the spots from her eyes—Danthres was half-elf, which made her more sensitive to the bright light that accompanied Boneen's Teleport Spell—she said, "This doesn't answer my question."

"What question is that, Danthres?" Torin asked as he slogged through the muck toward the front door.

"What crime has been committed?"

Torin looked down, smiled, then looked back at Danthres. "Well, vandalism at the very least."

"A crime easily solved even by the pea-brained idiots of the guard rank." Turning to Manfred, she said, "Nothing personal, Manfred."

Manfred grinned. "Honestly, ma'am, most guards' brains aren't that large."

Danthres found herself laughing against her better judgment, then quickly grew serious again. The last thing she wanted to do was get chummy with one of the guards. "So why are we handling this?"

Torin walked slowly to the closet door. "I said vandalism was the very least this could be. I've examined the closet door—it doesn't match the design of the rest of the house, and the space it takes up can't be accounted for by the shape of the house. It's definitely something magickal. It might be some sort of attack on the Jaros family. Since we haven't actually spoken to them yet, now might be the time to do that, and see if this is part of something larger."

Rolling her eyes, Danthres said, "Somehow I doubt that very much." She sighed far louder than perhaps she should have, and asked Manfred, "Where are they?"

"Next door, ma'am—they said they didn't want to stay in here until it was cleaned up."

Torin gingerly walked across the sitting-room floor toward Danthres. "Perhaps you can recommend that cleaning service of yours?"

Her face darkening even more, Danthres said, "Not likely. I spent half the morning trying to find where they *put* everything." At the behest of a rather aggrieved landlady, Danthres had hired a cleaning service for her rooms. Said landlady had rented Danthres the two rooms on the upper floor of her house in Dragon Precinct on the condition that Danthres keep the place clean and neat. However, Danthres had not been keeping up that part of the bargain especially well, thanks to the long hours she put in as a detective for the Castle Guard as well as her own inherent laziness when it came to matters of housekeeping. Since the landlady was threatening to toss Danthres out on her ear if she didn't comply, she hired a cleaning service.

They'd done a thorough job of making the place neat and shiny and clean. It was far more thorough than Danthres would have believed possible—so much so, in fact, that Danthres couldn't find a single thing she was looking for this morning. It was what had set her on her bad mood in the first place.

As Torin did his best to wipe his feet on the welcome mat, he said to Manfred, "Seal off the house for the time being, and get Sergeant Arron to send someone to guard both the front and back doors."

Danthres rolled her eyes. "Waste of time."

"Perhaps, but I'd rather have guards there and not need them than the other way 'round."

"Fair enough. If you're done, let's go talk to the family."

THE FAMILY, TO DANTHRES'S LACK OF SURPRISE, WAS SINGULARLY UNHELPful. That lack of surprise was due to the way her day had been going. First there was the scavenger hunt for her every personal item. Then she arrived at the east wing of the castle, where the sergeant informed her that the magistrate had returned a not-guilty ruling on her and Torin's most recent murder case, which did nothing to improve either her mood or her opinion of the magistrate. She couldn't complain to Torin about it because he was late as usual—only he wasn't coming in at all, because he'd been summoned to the crime scene in Unicorn.

To add to the annoyance, none of the Jaros family seemed to be in any way insincere about their confusion over what had happened. Danthres had been a detective in the Castle Guard for a decade now, and she had developed a good ear for when people were lying. While Millar Jaros did lie about his monetary worth and Abbi Jaros lied about how she was a good and faithful wife, and the children lied about any number of things, they all seemed quite sincere to her trained ear when they discussed the suddenly appearing closet.

Just as Torin and Danthres were about to leave the neighbor's house, Abbi asked, "Excuse me, Lieutenants, but, well, I mean—" She threw up her hands. "What are we supposed to *do* about that?"

"Hire a cleaning service, I would expect," Danthres said dismissively.

"I'm a good housewife," Abbi said stubbornly. "I don't believe in cleaning services."

"Have at it, then," Danthres said with a wicked grin. "But if you decide you'd rather not get on hands and knees and muck out your own house, I can recommend a service to avoid. They're called Forak's Perfect Clean, and they've made a mess of my own place."

Abbi frowned. "What kind of cleaning service leaves a place a mess?"

"That's kind of my point." With that, Danthres left.

DANTHRES'S MOOD WAS EVEN WORSE WHEN SHE CAME IN THE NEXT MORNING. After spending the morning wasting their time interviewing the Jaros family, they spent the afternoon wasting their time interviewing Alfrek Jaros's coworkers. Alfrek, Abbi's husband and Millar's son, worked in the lord and lady's castle, as a deputy to the transport minister, Sir Lio. That, at least, made tracking them down easy, as they were in the same building where Danthres and Torin worked.

They were no more helpful in revealing why someone would mess up the Jaros sitting room from a hidden closet.

Sergeant Jonas came dashing in from the kitchen, shuffling parchments, his green cloak billowing behind him. He scowled at Danthres as she approached her desk. "You're late. And where's your—"

"Jonas, so help me, if you ask me where my cloak is, I will ram my sword so far up your ass the point will stick out your left ear. Just fetch me another one, will you?"

The sergeant twisted his lips as if considering saying something, then thinking better of it, and zipped off to fetch a fresh cloak. All members of the Castle Guard wore leather armor, with a crest emblazoned on the chest to indicate posting: a gryphon for the castle, and a unicorn, dragon, goblin, or mermaid to indicate the precinct with the same name in the city-state proper. Those above the level of guard had a cloak to indicate rank: lieutenants wore brown.

Danthres saw, to her shock, that Torin was already at his desk, which abutted against hers. True she was later than usual, but for Torin, late was usual. He was also holding some parchments in his hands. "Paperwork," he said dismissively as he set them aside. "What happened to your cloak?"

"Forak's. I'm guessing one of their cleaning people made off with it when they cleaned the place. That's why I'm late, I had to go over there to complain. They promised to search and get back to me." She sat down at her desk. "What have you been doing?"

"I was thinking about what other avenues we could explore, and I thought we might try the architectural angle."

Danthres frowned. "Excuse me?"

"Millar, Abbi, and Alfrek all said that the closet wasn't part of the original design of the house, that it was a blank wall until yesterday morning."

"Right. Whatever magick cast the muck also created the closet."

"Perhaps. But this house dates back to when the city-state was first being built. Lord Galmar, Lord Albin's late grandfather, insisted that all constructions have their blueprints filed in the castle. Neither Albin's father nor the lord himself continued that practice—the city-state grew too large for it to be practical to keep track of every single building—but back in the old days it was a requirement." One of Torin's smaller smiles peeked out through his beard. "So I've requested the blueprints."

Instinctively, Danthres wanted to object. In her experience, the best way to find out what happened was to figure out who was most likely to have committed the crime and interrogate them until they confessed.

But they'd tried that, and hadn't turned anything up. Torin's notion was as good a one as any.

"What's wrong?" Torin asked.

"Hm?" Danthres looked up. "What do you mean what's wrong?"

Torin smirked. "I expected at least a grouse about what a pain it is to paw through records when we should be questioning people."

"What would be the point?" Danthres said with a dramatic sigh. "Besides, I used up most of my invective this morning with those shitbrains at Forak's." Waving off the platitude Torin was likely to espouse, she said, "It's fine, don't worry about it. Let's get to work."

"Well, we can't until—"

One of the castle page boys came in, laden with massive rolled-up parchments, and looking nervously from side to side. "Lieutenant bin Givald?"

Chuckling, Torin got up. "Close enough. Over here, lad."

The page boy dashed over to Torin's desk, dropped the parchments unceremoniously on its surface, then dashed out of the squad room as fast as his spindly legs would carry him.

"No doubt concerned about overexposure to the thugs," Danthres said irritably, using the word far too many of the aristocrats in the castle used when speaking of the Castle Guard.

Torin grinned. "No doubt." He unrolled the dried-up old parchments, one for each floor of the house.

Danthres got up and walked around to Torin's desk. As she started to peer down at the blueprints, she noticed that Torin was wearing new boots. "What happened to your boots?"

Shrugging, Torin said, "I couldn't get that muck off, so I sent them to be cleaned, and they issued me a new pair."

"I should mark this day down," she said dryly. "In ten years, I think that's the first time you've changed boots without being threatened with bodily harm." She was also impressed that Torin had managed to convince the service to do the job in the first place.

"It takes forever to break them in," Torin said testily. "I have wide feet."

She shook her head. "They're *boots*, Torin, not pets." Not wanting to get into this argument *again*, she looked down at the ragged material.

"I'm amazed these things haven't fallen to pieces. Aren't they over a hundred years old?"

"Magick, probably," Torin said, "cast when it was realized that they were, in fact, falling to pieces." He studied the first floor. "Interesting. There isn't a design for a closet—but there is a space there." He put his index finger on the spot where the closet was now. "That's odd."

"What is?"

"Feel that."

Looking at her partner like he was crazy, she said, "What?"

"The parchment, on the spot where the closet is now, feel it."

Shrugging, Danthres did so—and was surprised to feel something etched into the parchment. "It feels like a character of some kind."

Torin looked up just as Jonas came zooming in, a cloak in his hand. "Sergeant, could you fetch Boneen, please?"

Jonas handed Danthres her cloak in the manner one would give a diseased rat to a waste disposer. After Danthres snatched it out of his hands, the sergeant said to Torin, "He's on a call right now—Dru and Hawk found that invisible robber's house, and he needs to do a peel-back on it."

Nodding, Torin said, "Fine, when he gets back, could you ask him to tell us what the sigil is on this section of the parchment?"

Jonas looked at where Torin was pointing and nodded. "Oh, by the way," he said as he turned to leave, "they couldn't do anything for your boots. The Laundry Spell didn't work, for some reason." With that, the sergeant left the squad room again.

"You know, it might not even *be* a sigil," Danthres said, "though I agree that's the most likely thing."

"Either way, best to sound sure with Boneen—otherwise he'll yell at us for wasting his time."

Danthres snorted. "Like he won't anyhow."

"Fair point. I wonder what the problem was with the boots."

Shrugging, Danthres said, "They probably got a cheap Laundry Spell that doesn't actually work."

"Probably."

"Lieutenant?"

Since no name was given, both Torin and Danthres turned at the sound of the voice, which came from one of the guards assigned to the castle. Danthres couldn't remember his name, so she just thought of him the way she did most of the guards: he was the stupid one.

"Yes?" she said.

"There's someone here to see you both—she says it has to do with the Jaros case."

"Who is she?" Danthres asked.

The guard said, "Her name's Amaralla, and she says she—"

Suddenly, a very short, dark-haired woman barreled past the guard and said, "Enough of this, I'm *busy*, dammit, don't have time for this. Are you two Trestle and bag Wyverin?"

"I'm Lieutenant ban Wyvald," Torin said slowly, to make sure the woman realized just how badly she'd mangled their names, "and this is my partner—"

"Yes, yes, yes, you're the ones investigating what happened to the Jaros house, right?"

"We are," Torin said. "How may we—"

"You can do your damn jobs, that's what you can do. You're supposed to be able to stop this kinda thing, right?"

"Actually, no," Danthres said with as insincere a smile as she could manage—which was pretty insincere indeed. "Our job is to find who did it and stop *them* from doing it again."

"Well, then who's responsible for stopping it?"

"I'm sorry, who are you again?"

Sighing dramatically, the woman said, "As I told this mouth-breather with the mite-sized brain—" She indicated the guard, who took the insult with aplomb. "—my name is Thea Amaralla, and I represent the Amaralla Cleaning Service."

That's two cleaning services in Cliff's End I despise, Danthres somehow managed not to say out loud. "And what is your connection to the Jaros case?"

"If you'd just *listen,* I'd tell you. They hired us to clean up the mess in their place."

"In that case," Danthres said, "the answer to your question is you."

"I beg your pardon?"

"You wanted to know who's responsible for stopping it. It's a mess, you're a cleaning service—I would think the answer would be obvious?"

Turning to Torin, Amaralla asked, "Is she always like this?"

"No," Torin said cheerily, "usually she's belligerent. Madam, I'm afraid my partner is correct, cleaning up the mess is your job. We simply need to find out who did this and—"

"Not *did*."

"I'm sorry?" Torin frowned in confusion.

"Not *did*. *Is* doing. The mess is getting worse. And every attempt we've made to clean it up has met with failure. Nothing will make it go away—and now it's growing." She stomped her foot. "So will you *please* figure it out? The Jaroses are demanding their money back!"

Just as Danthres was about to speak, Torin cut her off. "I'm afraid that issues of payment must be worked out between you and the Jaros family, madam. However, you can rest assured that we will be looking into this new development." He looked over at the guard. "Will you please escort the lady out?"

Smiling nastily, the guard said, "Gladly, Lieutenant." He grabbed Amaralla by the arm and yanked her toward the door.

"I will not be treated this way! Let go of me! This is an outrage! This is—"

Whatever else it was was lost in her rapid, guard-aided retreat. Danthres made a mental note to be less nasty to that guard in the future.

Torin looked at her. "There would appear to be more to this than we thought. I suggest we go back."

Danthres desperately wanted to argue the point, but she found she couldn't. And that only made her mood worse.

Before they could even make it to the door of the Jaros house, Millar Jaros intercepted them, screaming a blue streak.

"What the hell's wrong with you people? You see the *mess* in there? Well? Didja? It's a *mess*! How're we supposed t'live in there if it's such a *mess*?"

Next to him was Abbi, who put a hand on his shoulder. "Father, take it easy, they can't—"

Whirling on his daughter-in-law, Millar said, "How'm I supposed t'take it easy when there's such a *mess* in there!"

"I know, Father, but—"

Torin finally said, "May we please take a look?"

Throwing up his hands, Millar said, "Sure, take a look, but all you're gonna see is a *mess*!"

Danthres shot Torin a look, as if to say, *What else were we supposed to see?* Torin shrugged back, and the two of them then walked past the

Jaroses to the guard who'd been assigned by Dragon Precinct to stand at the front door.

"Open it," Torin said.

Nodding, the guard opened the front door.

The smell was the first thing to hit Danthres. On their previous visit, the place had smelled bad, but no worse than the thoroughfares of Goblin Precinct during midsummer, or the docks of Mermaid Precinct in the afternoon after the fish came in.

Now, though, the Jaros house made the docks seem like an orchard by comparison. Danthres's nose wrinkled up immediately, and pretty much stayed that way as she surveyed the sitting room.

Not that there was much of the sitting room to survey—it was covered, wall to ceiling, in the same dark muck. She could make out small shapes under the muck that she assumed to be the furniture, and also saw other bits and pieces jutting out from it.

"Lord and Lady," Torin muttered.

"Close the door," Danthres said to the guard. "We need to get Boneen in here."

It took the better part of an hour for the magickal examiner to make his appearance. During that time, Danthres tried to ignore Millar Jaros's complaints, mostly by coming up with entertaining ways of flaying the old man alive.

When Boneen did arive via Teleport Spell, he looked even more perturbed than usual. "I've already *been* here."

"Yes," Danthres said, "and all you told us was that it was unlicensed magick. What *kind* of magick was it?"

Boneen sneered. "The unlicensed kind. Why am I wasting my time with this?"

Torin asked, "Boneen, did you identify the sigil on the blueprints on my desk?"

"Yes, right before I was told to come here. It's the symbol for hiding something."

Looking at Danthres, Torin said, "Like a closet."

Millar stepped forward. "What do you mean?"

"The blueprints for your house have a mark on the spot where the closet is now," Torin said. "It would seem that the hidden closet was part of the building's original plans."

"Excuse me," Boneen said before Millar could go off on another rant about messes, thus marking the first time Danthres had ever been grateful for Boneen's crankiness, "but why am I here?"

Steeling herself, Danthres told the guard to reopen the door to the Jaros house.

Boneen seemed unperturbed by the stench. He simply looked inside and said, "Oh, dear."

"Well put," Danthres muttered.

Shaking his head, the magickal examiner looked away from the muck-covered sitting room. "I had assumed this to be a one-time event—someone using the Duality Spell once for whatever arcane reason—but it looks like it's been used for some time, and still is being cast on a regular basis." He regarded Torin and pointed at the closet in the back of the sitting room. "That sigil I was translating—it was on the spot where that closet is?"

Torin nodded.

"Can we please close the door before I die?" Danthres asked plaintively. The elven half of her heritage came with sharper senses than that of humans, and the smell that irritated them was going to kill her ere long.

Waving his hand dismissively, Boneen said, "It won't do any good, but go ahead." The guard did so, to Danthres's relief.

Millar drew himself up to full height. "What do you mean it won't do any good? And who's going to clean up that *mess*?"

"And what exactly," Danthres asked, "is a Duality Spell?" As a rule, Danthres preferred to avoid magick, but reality didn't allow for that, and ten years in the Castle Guard made her painfully aware of the most common spells—particularly the ones that were commercially available. This one, however, rang no bells.

"To answer your earlier question, Tresyllione," Boneen said, folding his spindly arms across his chest, "this magick is of a type devised by a wizard named Ivano the Misguided. He pioneered an entire system of magick that involved checks and balances—every time you cast a spell, there was a concomitant reaction elsewhere. This way there'd be no effort on the part of the spellcaster, and allowed anyone to wield magick."

"Anyone *can* use magick," Danthres said impatiently. "All they have to do is buy a spell—"

"—that's already been cast." Boneen sounded just as impatient. "A wizard casts the spell into the scroll, which then goes on the market. The purchaser then uses it, but the energy of the spellcaster has already been spent. With Ivano's magick, one didn't need any kind of training to cast a spell, nor did one need to purchase a spell—you simply needed to incant it."

Torin nodded. "That explains why that Amaralla woman's people couldn't clean the place—and why my boots resisted the Laundry Spell."

Seeing an out, Danthres said with a smile. "So that means this *would* be a case for the Brotherhood, wouldn't it?"

"If I bring this to the Brotherhood, the first thing they'll ask is why I didn't bring this to them sooner." Boneen for once sounded abashed. "If it's all the same to you, I'd rather not bring that to their attention."

"Oh no," Danthres said angrily, pointing an accusatory finger at Boneen, "you're not getting out of it that easily. I've had far too many murders and assaults shitcanned because it's 'Brotherhood business,' and everything gets swept under the rug. Now, the one time where they'd actually be a *help*, which only happens once every third blue moon, and you're telling me you won't *inform* them?"

"I'll help you," Boneen said.

That brought Danthres up short. The M.E. had never used those three words in sequence before that Danthres was aware of. Boneen considered the work he did for the Castle Guard to be a waste of his precious time and energy, and he begrudged every second of it. For him to volunteer . . .

Boneen went on. "Give me a minute to gather myself up and let me examine the house more closely. I might be able to trace where the spell's being cast."

"Uhm, excuse me?" That was Abbi Jaros, whom Danthres had briefly forgotten, having focused most of her ire on either her father-in-law or the M.E. "What kind of spell *is* this exactly? What's happening to our house?"

Boneen started waving his arms about. "Ivano's magick always has a secondary effect. Someone is doing something pleasant, and that requires that somewhere else there be something awful. However, the awful can be directed, and in this case, it was to the closet that was hidden in your house when it was built." He cast a glance at the shut door. "But they've obviously been casting this spell for some time. The muck in your closet has become too big to fit therein, and has spilled out into the house." Now he looked at Danthres and Torin. "We need to find out who's doing this. At this rate, it will expand to take over and destroy this house. In a week, it will have consumed the entire block."

Danthres blinked. Perhaps she didn't want the Brotherhood involved, after all—not if she wanted this solved properly. "All right, then, what do we do?"

"First, I examine this house." Boneen slowly got down onto the floor and sat in a lotus position; Danthres could hear his bones creak and crack as he did so. The aged wizard muttered something, waved his right hand about, and then started to float upward.

About a minute later, he unfolded his legs, while still floating, and placed them on the ground. "This is worse than I thought. It's been going on for at least a decade, possibly longer. I can't tell for sure—there are magickally enhanced items in there interfering." That last was said with an accusatory look at Abbi and Millar.

"That's impossible!" Abbi said. "We don't keep anything magickal in the house."

"That's right," Millar said. "Got rid of it all. Filthy stuff, magick."

Noting that was the first thing Millar had said that hadn't made Danthres want to punch him, she asked Boneen, "Is there any way to extract those items? If they don't belong to the family, they might belong to whoever cast the spell."

"It's possible, but I'm already rather tired, and—"

"Fine, then." Danthres turned to Torin. "What's the name of the Brotherhood representative?"

"Ythran," Torin said. "I'm sure he'd be overjoyed to hear all about Boneen misreading the peel-back."

"I didn't misread it!" Boneen was almost pouting. "All right, all right, I'll cast the blessed spell."

This time, Boneen didn't bother with the lotus position, but the muttering took longer, and he gesticulated with both hands.

Danthres had to blink away the spots in front of her eyes that the resultant flash of light caused, but when they did, she looked down at the ground in front of Boneen to see seven objects, all encrusted in the muck that had taken over the Jaros house, all looking like articles of clothing.

Boneen pointed at one of two items that looked like cloaks. "That looks like a Protector Cloak—a low-level one, it'd just keep the shit off you walking around Goblin—but that explains the magickal interference."

However, Danthres was more interested in the other cloak.

Breathing through her mouth to avoid the stench—which, while not as bad as the room had been, was still pretty awful—Danthres bent over to grab it. Grateful that her uniform included gloves, she picked it up by one end with her right hand, wiping the center of the cloak off with her left glove.

Then she smiled grimly. "I know who did this."

FORAK'S PERFECT CLEAN HAD OFFICES IN DRAGON PRECINCT, ONLY A SHORT walk from Danthres's rooms, which was why she had chosen them in the first place. That evening, she entered their waiting area, accompanied by Torin. As had been the case when she had gone there to make the appointment, and again when she filed the complaint about her missing cloak, the waiting area consisted solely of a bench, a desk behind which sat a prim young woman, and a door leading to the back.

The prim woman—whose name, Danthres recalled, was Emanuela—looked up at their entrance. "Ah, Lieutenant Trellis, isn't it?"

"Tresyllione, actually," Danthres corrected automatically.

"Of course. I'm afraid we haven't found your cloak yet, but I can assure you that it will turn up. We here at Forak's guarantee customer satisfaction—it is our watchword, after all." Emanuela said all that without once changing her inflection.

"Well, I'm afraid that isn't good enough," Danthres said, trying to sound like an outraged customer—which wasn't too difficult an act for her just at the moment. "I want to speak to your supervisor immediately."

"I'm afraid Mr. Forak isn't available right now, Lieutenant, but if you wish to make an appointment—"

"*I'm* afraid that I must see Mr. Forak right now, or I will shut this place down."

Emanuela opened her tiny mouth into an O, then closed it. She didn't have a prepared response to that, it seemed, and it took a few moments for her brain to actually function. "Can you *do* that?"

Torin smiled his most pleasant smile. "We are lieutenants in the Castle Guard, madam. The lord and lady have granted us considerable leeway in such matters, and all we would have to do is pronounce this place a menace to the well-being of Cliff's End and its inhabitants, and it would be shut down. Mr. Forak could, of course, appeal to the magistrate, but that might take days."

"Weeks, even," Danthres added. "And you would not be permitted to conduct business until that—"

"Mr. Forak!" Emanuela cried out in a tone very much like a mouse's squeak, apparently unable to handle any more disruptions to her world. "Some people here to see you!"

A short man with thin hair and a thick mustache came out through the door to the rear. "What? What? Dammit, Emanuela, I told you not to bother me, I'm trying to— Oh!" That last word was spoken upon sighting two people in leather armor and earth-colored cloaks, symbolizing that they were detectives in the Guard. "Dammit, Emanuela, why didn't you tell me that the good people of the Cliff's End Castle Guard were here?"

"But—" Emanuela tried to protest, but Forak didn't give her the chance, bounding forward with a broad smile peeking out from under his mustache.

"You're Mr. Forak?"

"Yes, Lieutenant, yes, I am most definitely him, yes, I am. Now then, who might you be, and what service can Forak's Perfect Clean do for you on this lovely day?"

"I'm Lieutenant Tresyllione, this is my partner, Lieutenant ban Wyvald. I'm one of your customers, actually."

"Ah, yes, well, of course," Forak said, sounding relieved. "Are you satisfied with our service, Lieutenant Tresilon?"

"Tresyllione, and I mostly am, yes, although an item has gone missing. A cloak—just like the one I'm wearing now. I told your girl about it there—"

"Right, of course, yes, we're getting right on that. My best people are searching for the cloak even as we speak."

"Your best people?"

"Of course."

Danthres nodded. "Fascinating."

"Mr. Forak, I apologize," Torin said, "but I'm a bit befuddled. You see, before coming here, we went to the castle and examined your tax records. They say that you only have one employee." He nodded his head at Emanuela. "I have to wonder — who does the actual cleaning?"

"And who's looking for my cloak?" Danthres added.

Forak started to shuffle from foot to foot, and twisted the end of his mustache with his right hand. "Yes, well, ahm, you see, I mean, that is to say, uh—"

"Let me save you the trouble of lying, Mr. Forak. You don't have any employees, do you? You charge one gold per room cleaned, which, when I first came here, you said was to cover cleaning supplies and labor costs. Other cleaning services usually charge two gold, but they also give the option of providing your own supplies — which you don't do."

"Erm, yes, you see, I—"

"This is because you don't actually have a staff, do you, Mr. Forak?" Danthres started moving slowly closer to Forak, who backed up until he bumped into Emanuela's desk. "Instead, you cast a spell to clean the room, and send the dirt to a closet hidden in a house in Unicorn, where no one will ever find it. There are only two problems, Mr. Forak."

"Oh, ah, yes? What's, er, what's that, then?"

"First of all, the closet filled up, and exploded. The dirt from all the homes you've cleaned has now taken over the house, and soon will encompass an entire block. Do you know who owns that house, Mr. Forak?"

"Er, well, no, actually, I—"

"Alfrek Jaros. He works for Sir Lio, the transport minister. Do you know what Sir Lio will think about someone doing this to one of his deputies?"

"Uhm—"

"The second problem is that it isn't just dirt that goes to the Jaros closet. According to our magickal examiner, the spell requires sending the items from one closet to another, and some items in the closets of your clients got mixed in with the dirt. They included two pairs of boots, a Protection Cloak, three tunics — and *my* cloak."

"Ah, yes, well, you see, I can, er, that is to say, I—"

Torin grabbed Forak's arms. "I would reserve comment until you've seen the magistrate."

Puffing himself up, Forak said, "Hang on, you can't arrest me! I've done nothing wrong!"

Danthres snarled. "You've done quite a bit wrong, Mr. Forak. Fraud, for one thing."

"I didn't defraud no one, I didn't! I said I'd clean your place, and I *did!*"

Torin glanced at Danthres. "He has a point."

"True. But there's also littering. And vandalism to the Jaros house." She smiled a most unpleasant smile, then. "And, of course, there's the Brotherhood."

Forak went white. "Th—the Brotherhood? You mean, that is to say—of Wizards?"

"Yes, that Brotherhood. They don't take kindly to people using unlicensed magick."

That deflated him, and he took Torin's advice and refrained from further comment. They led him out the door and handed him off to one of the four guards from Dragon they had left waiting outside. That guard would take him to the castle for imprisonment until the magistrate—and the Brotherhood—could deal with him. Torin instructed the other three to escort Emanuela to Dragon for questioning, and to close up the offices of Forak's Perfect Clean.

Danthres looked up at the sky, seeing the sun starting to set into the horizon, and she realized that she was in a good mood. Justice had been done, she'd found her cloak, and she didn't even have to deal directly with the Brotherhood.

Then Torin said, "You realize that when this is all over, he's going to have to reverse the spell in order to salvage the Jaros house. That means all the dirt will probably have to go back."

"Actually, I hadn't realized it." Danthres snarled, her foul mood back full force.

"Yes," Torin said with a smile. "You've been left with quite a mess."

Somehow, Danthres managed not to kill him.

HEROES WELCOME

THE PARTY APPROACHED THE ABANDONED CASTLE CAUTIOUSLY. THE ROAD TO *the edifice was overgrown, and Gan Brightblade – who, of course, took the lead – had to hack through branches and bushes that impeded their forward movement.*

From right behind him, Olthar lothSirhans muttered, "You do know that I can magickally clear a path, yes?"

"No," Brightblade said emphatically. "We cannot risk that Mitos will detect your spells. Then all would be lost."

Olthar testily replied, "Assuming, of course, that Mitos is there."

He glanced back at Brother Genero, who – along with the halfling twins Mari and Nari – was in the center of the group.

From behind Genero, Ubàrlig the dwarf grinned. "Do you doubt our Temisan priest's vision, lothSirhans?"

"I would no sooner doubt that he had a vision, dwarf, than I would doubt that you have never bathed a day in your life. It is the contents of the vision that I call into question, as it was, as is typical of Genero's goddess, somewhat vague."

Genero shrugged in his battered red robes, making him look far shabbier than the average Temisan priest. But then, he was hardly an average priest. "I cannot control the visions that Temisa sends me. I can but interpret them – "

From the rear, Bogg the Barbarian finished the priest's words in a singsong voice. " – to the best of my ability, babble babble babble. We heard it all before, Genero, and we don't give a shit. Leastaways, I don't. Let's just get there so I can bust some heads." Bogg smiled, displaying a mouth that had very few teeth in it. "I ain't beat somebody up in days."

"You're not bloody likely to beat anybody up here, neither," Mari said.

Nari added, "It ain't like there's nobody 'round here. Place's obviously been abandoned for decades."

"Why couldn't we just stay in Treemark?" Mari asked.

"Yeah, there was lotsa people there," Nari said. "Betcha Bogg coulda found lotsa folks to beat up."

Genero gave the twins a sidelong glance. "And found some innocents to fleece?"

Mari grinned. "Hey, look, if they're dim enough to fall for our grifts, they ain't innocent'a nothin'!"

"Silence!" Brightblade snapped, coming to a sudden halt. Olthar, Genero, Mari, Nari, Ubàrlig, and Bogg all did likewise. Everyone either unsheathed their weapons or held up the ones they'd already had out.

The party had arrived at the drawbridge that led to the ancient castle, as expected. The drawbridge was down, but rotted and pitted, also as expected.

However, there was a sentinel guarding the bridge, which was most assuredly not expected. Especially since this sentinel was a troll.

Brightblade had to at least try to talk to the troll first. As he walked forward, Olthar hissed. "What are you doing? I can get rid of this beast with but a gesture."

"No." Brightblade held up one hand to stay Olthar. "Let me solve this with words — or steel. We must not alert Mitos that we have a mage of your strength with us."

Olthar snorted. If Mitos really was in this castle, which he seriously doubted, either he already knew exactly who was approaching or didn't care all that much. Either way, if he'd placed the troll here, the minute they defeated the monster, Mitos would know that he was beaten by Gan Brightblade. And everyone in Flingaria knew that the Elf Queen's cousin the wizard often travelled with Brightblade.

As Brightblade approached the troll, who stood ramrod straight at the edge of the drawbridge, great sword point down in the ground in front of him with two massive hands on the jeweled hilt, the creature said in a deep monotone, "None may cross this drawbridge. Any who attempt to do so will be killed where they stand."

Ubàrlig frowned. "Strangely eloquent for a troll. Now do you believe that Mitos is behind this, lothSirhans?"

"Hardly," Olthar said dismissively, "since the troll's words are coming, not from the troll himself, but rather from a charm embedded in that jewel in the hilt. Any idiot can purchase such a charm."

"Any well-to-do idiot," Mari said.

Nari added, "Those charms ain't cheap, y'know."

"Either way," Olthar said, "the eloquent troll doesn't prove that — "

Whatever it didn't prove would never be known, as Olthar's rant was interrupted by the troll's sudden movement. Brightblade had been slowly moving forward in a guarded position, and apparently he crossed some manner of threshold, as after taking one particular step, the troll moved to attack.

Brightblade parried the blow easily. The troll and the hero exchanged several sword blows before Bogg pushed past the others and moved to join the fray.

"Enough'a this shit," he said, "time to kick some troll — ARRRRRGH!"

Bogg screamed that last when he was suddenly thrown backward when he reached the same spot that Brightblade had crossed to make the troll attack him. The barbarian went careening into Genero and the halfling twins, knocking all four of them to the ground in a heap of arms and legs and cries of pain.

"Get this big lug offa me!" Mari cried, even as Ubàrlig moved forward gingerly.

"Don't be an ass, dwarf," Olthar said even as Brightblade continued to trade sword blows with the troll, "there's nothing you can do."

"We cannot simply allow Gan to fight that troll alone!" Ubàrlig cried angrily.

Olthar smiled derisively. "Of course we can't. I said there's nothing you can do. There is quite a bit that I can do."

And then the elf gestured and suddenly the troll was lifted off the ground as if from a mighty wind, which then tossed the creature and his great sword into the moat that surrounded the castle. A spark of light followed that made the very air in front of where Ubàrlig stood glow for a moment.

"Now we may proceed."

Brightblade whirled angrily on Olthar. "I would have defeated him!"

"Possibly — I chose not to take the risk for a surprise that no longer exists."

"Olthar — " Brightblade started, but the wizard cut him off.

"The moment that troll spoke and the barricade between you and the rest of us was erected, whoever is in that castle knew exactly what is happening out here. Preventing me from using my magick from this point forward will serve only to cripple us to no good end. Now let us proceed across this bridge and see what, precisely, that troll was guarding against."

BROTHER GENERO OF VELESSA WALKED INTO THE DINING AREA OF THE DOG and Duck Inn in Cliff's End with the same feeling of discontent that had been present since he arrived in this city-state.

He had come to Cliff's End with a purpose, alongside his dearest comrades, prepared to take on the evil wizard known as Chalmraik the Foul, whom Temisa had told him had resurrected himself. But an incident on the road to Cliff's End had far-reaching consequences, as a young man who tried to rob them went on to study chronotic magick, and then travelled to his own past to enact revenge, killing Gan Brightblade, Olthar lothSirhans, and Mari and Nari before the Cliff's End Castle Guard had found and incarcerated him.

To make matters worse, they had been assured by the Brotherhood of Wizards that Chalmraik was not a threat and their trip had been for naught.

The three survivors—Genero, Bogg, and Ubàrlig—had remained in Cliff's End through midsummer and beyond, the owner of the Dog and Duck allowing them to stay as long as they liked, free of charge. Lord Albin and Lady Meerka had offered to let them stay in the castle, but Brother Genero did not wish to abuse their hospitality. Besides, Bogg was chafing in so much comfort . . .

Speaking of the barbarian, he sat at their usual table in the far corner of the inn's dining room, Ubàrlig alongside him. Along the way, the priest nodded to those he knew, some old acquaintances like Corvin, the former vampire hunter, who always ate breakfast at the Dog and Duck, others new friends made here at the inn where the trio had spent their evenings telling stories of their adventures (one of the conditions of their free room and board).

"You're looking haggard, old friend," Ubàrlig said without preamble as Genero sat next to him at the round table. A mug of tea was already on the table, as it had been every morning.

The priest nodded. "I prayed to Temisa again this morning, and she remained silent."

"Gods are fickle bastards," Bogg said. "I 'member you tellin' me once how you'd go years without hearin' from her."

Nodding, Genero said, "I know, Bogg, I know, but—" He let out a long sigh and then took a sip of his tea before continuing. It was bitter and scalding, matching his mood. "I sometimes feel as if she has forsaken me. She sent us on this fool's errand to stop Chalmraik, and instead she led us to our doom. Had it not been for her instructions to me, Gan, Mari, Nari, and Olthar would still be alive."

"I keep tellin' ya," Bogg said, "you're better off ignorin' the gods. Shit, that's why my people killed our gods."

Ubàrlig rolled his eyes. "Oh for Xinf's sake, not the we-killed-our-gods story, *please*, Bogg. I'm trying to *eat*."

The barbarian pointed a meaty finger at the dwarf. "Look, gods're more trouble'n they're worth. That Temisa bitch proved that pretty damned thoroughly."

Wincing, Ubàrlig started, "Bogg, show some respect!"

But Genero held up a hand. "No, it's all right, Ubàrlig. Bogg has a point. Temisa may well have led me astray. Perhaps, we . . ." Genero trailed off, as he noticed a strange look on the dwarf's face. "Ubàrlig, what is it?"

"Those two men who just sat down at the table across the way. They look very familiar."

"I don't recognize 'em," Bogg said.

Turning, Genero followed Ubàrlig's gaze. Then his eyes widened and he turned back so as not to be openly gaping.

Ubàrlig was staring intently at the priest. "So I'm not imagining it, right?"

"No." Genero shook his head and slowly sipped his tea.

Impatiently, Bogg asked, "Who the hell is it?"

"That's Thorn and his brother Kail."

Bogg just stared at him blankly.

With a snarl, Ubàrlig said, "The castle outside Treemark!"

Now Bogg blinked. "*Those* shitsuckers?"

"Yes—those shitsuckers who nearly killed all seven of us," Ubàrlig muttered.

ONCE THEY CROSSED THE DRAWBRIDGE, OLTHAR AND THE TWINS TOOK POINT, *the former to find any magickal traps, the latter the more mundane ones.*

Sure enough, when they were about to pass through a castle corridor that had a shaft of light shining through a small window across the way, the twins stopped them, Mari holding up his left hand and Nari holding up her right.

"Hang on." Mari knelt down by one of the bricks in the wall, Nari by his side.

"Will you look at that?"

"That's a great one, that is."

Impatiently, Bogg started walking forward. "I dunno why you two halfwits're lookin' at that brick, bu—"

"Don't move!" Mari snapped.

Nari added, "You cross that shaft'a light, and that panel over there — " She pointed at an odd-shaped brick in the wall. " — will open right up and shoot atcha."

Bogg frowned. "What'll it shoot?"

Shrugging, Mari said, "Hell if we know."

"Arrows, maybe."

"Or daggers."

"Or maybe mud."

Olthar had had enough. "Can you keep the trap from springing?"

Mari was offended. "Of course we can!"

Nari touched a few spots on the brick on the floor, and then smiled. The party all heard a very loud clicking sound. Mari rose, took off his hat, and threw it across the shaft of light. Nothing happened.

Nari stood up next to her brother, and the twins held out both hands. "Ta-da!"

Brightblade strode forward. "Let us continue. That makes two snares in this allegedly abandoned castle. We must learn who dwells here."

"Slow down, Gan," Olthar said testily. "As the halflings have proven, there are traps aplenty here. Let us proceed carefully, that we may confront our foe in one piece."

Nodding, Brightblade put a hand on the elf's shoulder. "You're right, of course, my friend. Please — go ahead and blaze a path."

As they proceeded down the corridor, though, it was Bogg who saw the next trap. It was a hatch in the ceiling that caught the barbarian's eye, and he noticed it open right over Olthar.

"Watch it, Olthar!" Bogg cried as he pushed the elf bodily out of the way.

A cube made of some kind of clear gelatinous substance fell from the ceiling and surrounded Bogg completely, rendering the huge barbarian immobile.

"Oh, Xinf, no. Bogg!" Ubàrlig cried. "We have to get him out of there — he won't be able to breathe inside a minute or two! Don't bother!"

That last was said to Brightblade, who nonetheless swiped at the cube with his sword. It embedded itself in the cube.

"Damnation." Brightblade tugged at his sword's hilt, but it would not move.

Ubàrlig was shaking his head. "There's nothing we can do, physically. Only magick can destroy this thing. That's why it attacked lothSirhans."

He gave Olthar a look, but the elf just scowled at him. "Sadly, any attack I make upon it will also harm the barbarian."

"So?" Mari said. "You don't even like him."

"Yes, well, I was raised to believe that it's tacky to kill the person who just saved your life."

The cube started oozing toward Olthar, Bogg and Brightblade's sword both still trapped inside it.

Brightblade shook his head. "We must do something!"

Genero spoke, then. "Can you do a Freezing Spell?"

"Of course," Olthar said, "but — "

"Do it. Bogg is from the north, he can survive in the cold long enough for Gan and Ubàrlig to remove the sword from the frozen cube, thus shattering it."

"Are you sure that's — " the dwarf started, but the priest interrupted him.

"Bogg will die in a minute unless we do something, and if magick is all that may affect this thing . . ..."

That was good enough for Olthar, who gestured, spoke the words of the Freeze Spell, and moments later, the cube stopped its forward motion and was now a large block of ice.

Shivering at the sudden drop in temperature in the corridor, Brightblade grabbed the hilt of his sword and tugged hard on it. With a mighty crack that echoed throughout the corridor, the ice shattered, and Bogg fell to the floor amidst the shards of ice, shivering and barely breathing.

Genero walked up to him, whispering a soft prayer to Temisa. In response, the goddess granted him some small healing magick that enabled his very touch to restore Bogg.

Still shivering, but now breathing normally, Bogg clambered to his feet, rubbing his arms with his hands. "Sh-sh-sh-shit, that was c-c-c-cold."

"That's why you shouldn't wear just a loincloth," Nari said.

"P-p-p-piss off."

At the end of the corridor was a double door, and Brightblade strode toward it. "Enough of these foolish games."

Nari winced, and Mari said, "Gan, don't just storm into a pair of doors without — "

Ignoring the halflings, Brightblade threw open the doors, which slammed loudly against the walls. The others exchanged glances and shrugs and followed, seeing that the doors opened to a huge, empty room that was probably a receiving room or dining room when the castle was in regular use.

The room had a balcony all around it, and two men wearing chainmail and horned helmets stood on it, laughing as they looked down at the party. One said, "So, you made it this far."

The other said, "Mitos will be disappointed that at least one or two of you didn't die from the troll or the spears —"

Mari and Nari exchanged glances. "Spears! Why didn't we think of spears?" Nari asked.

" — or the cube. We were hoping that there'd only be three or four of you idiots to face Ana, Unu, and Ono."

Three harpies flew in from the window and started encircling the room. They had wings and legs of an eagle, but the torsos and heads of sickly human women, breasts sagging from their misshapen chests, teeth rotted and pointed, eyes yellow and watery.

Brightblade held up his sword. "Who are you that mocks us so?"

"We are but thralls, Gan Brightblade," one said. "I am Thorn, and this my brother Kail. We are minions of the great Mitos, and he instructed us to kill you and your friends after he lured you here."

"It seems," Genero said with a sigh, "that Temisa was both right and wrong."

"No matter," Ubàrlig said, brandishing his Fjorm axe. "These harpies will be dead soon enough. Attack!"

"I am being sorry," Olaf said in his deliberately broken Common to Genero, "but never before have I seen those two men before this morning they are coming in. The names they check in under are being Kail and Thorn."

Genero nodded and placed his hands on the front desk of the Dog and Duck. "Thank you, Olaf."

"Of course! I am happy to anything be doing for the great heroes who at my inn they stay! If anything there is I can to be doing to make *more* comfortable, just please to be telling me soonest, yes?"

"We will." Genero smiled, and started to turn away. "Again, Olaf, thank you."

As Genero walked away from the desk, Olaf called out, "For example, for the barbarian I could be giving to an actual *room* . . ."

Chuckling Genero turned back around. "Thank you, but no. The best way to make Bogg comfortable is to allow him to continue sleeping in the stables. The only way to improve it would be to make snow fall upon him, at which point he'll feel just like home."

Olaf shook his bald head. "I am not understanding the peoples from the northern place."

"If it makes you feel any better, they don't understand us much, either."

With that, the priest went out to the aforementioned stables, where Ubàrlig was already waiting. Bogg arrived a moment after Genero.

"I talked t'everybody," Bogg said. "Ain't nobody knows who these guys are or what they're doin' here."

"Likewise," the dwarf said. "Which means they are probably up to some kind of mischief."

"Olaf is unfamiliar with them, as well, though they did check into the inn under their own names."

Bogg said, "I also saw a coupla guards wanderin' around lookin' squirrelly."

Genero frowned. "What crest did they wear on their chests?"

"Whaddaya mean?"

"The symbols on their chests," Ubàrlig said. "They indicate what precinct they're from."

"Who gives a shit?"

The priest sighed. That question was Bogg's way of saying he didn't notice. "It does not matter. If the thralls of Mitos are in Cliff's End, it cannot be anything other than ill for the people of this fine city-state. We will observe them until such a time as they are somewhere far from other people."

Ubàrlig stared at Genero. "We're in the middle of the most populous city-state in Flingaria. There is no place far from other people."

Tilting his head to concede the point, Genero said, "As isolated as we can be, at the very least."

For the next several hours, the trio kept an eye on the brothers, who seemed to spend most of their time sitting and eating and talking. Eventually, around midday, they met with two elves. The four of them shared a meal. Genero was unable to get close enough to overhear their conversation, especially given how loud the dining area of the Dog and Duck got at midday. The place was packed with a wide assortment, from natives, to tourists, to people who wanted a look at Genero, Bogg, and Ubàrlig. There was even someone from the Castle Guard, a Mermaid Precinct officer, based on the crest of his uniform. That last part was odd, since Mermaid covered the docklands, but maybe the guard was here for lunch.

But he did notice one thing: both elves had neck tattoos that indicated that they were former members of the Shranlaseth, the special forces of the elven nation. It had been his dear late comrade, Olthar lothSirhans, who had placed a (completely false) seed of doubt into his cousin the Elf Queen's mind about the trustworthinesss of the Shranlaseth, tricking the tyrant into disbanding one of her most powerful weapons.

After lunch was done, the four shook hands, and the elven soldiers went upstairs, presumably to their rooms. Thorn and Kail proceeded outside.

It was when they turned down Sandy Brook Way—probably to take advantage of one of that thoroughfare's many brothels—that they moved in. Bogg came down from the west side of the street, blocking their way forward, and when they turned around, they saw Ubàrlig and Genero. Bogg was holding his broadsword with both hands, and Ubàrlig held his Fjorm axe in a similar manner.

"Uhm, look," Thorn said, "we don't want any trouble."

"You wanted plenty of trouble fifteen years ago," the dwarf said. "I made a promise, then, and I intend to fulfill it."

Kail winced. "Oh for Wiate's sake, you're not still pissed about *that*, are you?"

"Not still *pissed*?" Bogg bellowed. "I got stuck in a damn gunky cube and then got frozed! Not to mention those harpies . . ."

"All right, that's enough."

Whirling around, Genero saw five members of the Castle Guard, all wearing the crest of Dragon Precinct, the section of town where the Dog and Duck was located.

Five more guards came from behind Bogg. One looked familiar to Genero.

One of the guards stepped forward. "In the name'a the lord and lady, we gotta bring all five'a you to the castle."

Bogg smiled. "You an' what army?"

The guard looked at Bogg. "You're outnumbered two to one, sir."

Thorn and Kail held up both hands quickly, and the former spoke even faster. "That's ten to three, Mr. Guard, sir. My brother and I, we ain't resisting at all, no sir."

Ignoring Thorn, the guard continued. "Those odds'll get worse inna next few minutes when our reinforcements show up."

Genero frowned, finally placing the familiar guard, who was also the only one present whose crest was from Mermaid rather than Dragon. "You were at the Dog and Duck."

The Mermaid guard smirked. "What of it?"

Bogg held up his sword. "We ain't goin' nowhere we don't wanna go!"

Genero held up a hand. "Bogg, please, lower your sword."

"You kiddin' me, Genero? We can take these guys."

Ubàrlig lowered his axe. "And then what? I don't fancy the notion of being a fugitive from the largest law-enforcement organization in Flingaria."

"Nor I," Genero said. "Lower your weapon, Bogg."

Snarling, Bogg did as Genero asked, to the priest's great relief. Looking at the guard, Genero said, "We will accompany you."

"Thanks, Brother Genero. We kinda prefer to avoid violence if we can."

They began walking together, a huge group of ten guards and five—prisoners? Genero wasn't sure if that was the right term, as they weren't actually arrested—walking down Sandy Brook toward Meerka Way. "Unfortunately, Bogg does not share that preference. Be grateful that I was able to calm him, because he was right—he would have easily taken all ten of you, as well as whatever reinforcements you had coming. But Ubàrlig was correct as well—the consequences would have been deleterious to us."

The guard chuckled at that.

"Did I say something amusing, Guard?"

"The name's Jared, and yeah—trust me, Brother, there're plenty'a deleterious consequences waitin' for you guys."

Jared did not explain his words, and Genero didn't bother to ask. Instead, they walked in silence toward the castle, through Dragon and Unicorn Precincts. Everywhere they went, people parted and stared and pointed. The priest caught snatches of exclamations here and there.

"It's Gan Brightblade's friends!"

"I thought they left town after the Castle Guard found who killed the others."

"Nah, they ain't leavin' town till the real killer's found. Castle Guard ain't found shit, buncha idjits."

"I love you, Ubàrlig!"

"Why's the Guard escortin' 'em?"

"To keep shitbrains like you from askin' for their autograph."

By the time they reached the mansions of Unicorn Precinct, the number of onlookers had decreased significantly. And eventually they went through the large, open portcullis and were escorted to the eastern wing of the castle — but not before their weapons were confiscated. Bogg was even less happy about that than he was about going in the first place, but Genero reminded him that that happened the last time they were in the castle, and they got their weapons back when they left.

Bogg, Ubàrlig, and Genero were placed in one of the interview rooms, with the brothers in the other.

And then they waited.

"They pulled this shit last time." Bogg grumbled as he paced the dark room, lit as it was only by a small lantern. "Kept us in these damned rooms for hours on end."

"True, but last time," Genero said, "they also kept us separated. At least we're together now."

"I just hope it's not that ugly half-elf bitch and her stupid red-bearded partner like last time. Those two *really* pissed me off."

Ubàrlig frowned. "They're the ones who found the killer."

"Yes," Genero said in a faraway voice.

"What's wrong, Genero?" the dwarf asked.

"Lieutenants Tresyllione and ban Wyvald accused us of withholding information. Mari and Nari might still be alive if we'd been honest with them."

"Stop that." Ubàrlig got up from the stool he'd been sitting on. "We thought we were facing Chalmraik. Under the circumstances —"

"Under the circumstances, General Ubàrlig," came a deep voice from the doorway, "you still should have confided in us."

The voice belonged to Lieutenant Torin ban Wyvald, the "stupid redbearded partner" Bogg had referred to. He was entering the room, alongside "the ugly half-elf bitch," Lieutenant Danthres Tresyllione.

"Were you anyone else," Tresyllione said, "we would have arrested you for impeding an official investigation."

"Were we anyone else," Genero said with a small smile, "we would never have been in a position to impede it."

"True."

"May I ask why we've been detained in this manner?"

"To keep you from getting into a fight that would damage Sandy Brook Way."

Bogg pointed at the door. "You know who them two *are*?"

"We do now, yes," ban Wyvald said. "Former thralls of Mitos the Mage."

"Then whyn't you let us kick their asses?"

Smiling, and showing the excellent teeth that one would expect from a native of Myverin, ban Wyvald said, "Because they are *former* thralls of Mitos. The wizard is dead, and the brothers served a term of seven years in prison."

Ubàrlig threw up his hands. "C'mon, Lieutenant, they're plotting *something*. We saw them meet with two former Shranlaseth. Probably muscle for their next job."

"Not exactly," ban Wyvald said as he leaned against the wall. "You see, we actually *investigated* Thorn and Kail the moment their boat came into the docks."

"Boat?" Genero parroted.

Tresyllione said, "Yes. It turns out that, after your little gaggle killed Mitos, the two brothers managed to make off with quite a bit of gold that the wizard no longer had much use for. They purchased a cargo boat called *Wikker's Fury*, and have been sailing cargo all over the Garamin for six years now."

"We know this," ban Wyvald added, "because the moment the *Wikker's Fury* docked, Mermaid Precinct assigned a guard to tail those two — precisely because they used to work for Mitos."

"You see," Tresyllione said, "there's a guard from Mermaid named Fran Lavian. He was one of Mitos's slaves. In fact, he remembers clearly the day you three and lothSirhans and Brightblade liberated him and Mitos's other slaves at Storm's Pass."

"Waitasec," Bogg said, "you made one'a those mindless shit-suckers a *guard*?"

Ubàrlig looked to the ceiling in supplication. "Did you *never* listen to Olthar?"

Bogg grinned. "Not if I could help it."

That prompted a burst of laughter from ban Wyvald, even as Ubàrlig said, "He told us that it was a spell that enslaved them. Once he cast the counterspell, they were perfectly normal."

"In any case," Tresyllione interrupted before Bogg could reply, "Lavian recognized Thorn and Kail as soon as they got off their boat, and he tagged them to make sure they weren't up to anything illegal."

Tightly, Genero said, "As were we."

"Yes," Tresyllione said witheringly, "but the difference is that Lavian is an actual member of the Castle Guard whose *job* it is to deal with illegal behavior within the lord and lady's demesne."

"And he's also much better at it than you," ban Wyvald put in. "You see, he was able to determine that Thorn and Kail are legitimate sailors with a legitimate cargo business."

Genero couldn't believe that they were so wrong. Again. "But I spoke with Olaf—he said he never saw them before."

Shrugging, ban Wyvald said, "It was their first time at the Dog and Duck. In truth, they haven't spent much time within Cliff's End's walls at all, preferring to stay on their boat."

Grumpily, Ubàrlig asked, "And what of the Shranlaseth they met with?"

"Former Shranlaseth," Tresyllione said, "as, indeed, they all are now. As it happens, we learned of them from Jared."

"The guard who brought us in?" Genero asked.

Tresyllione smiled most unpleasantly. "The guard who was assigned to follow you."

Bogg slammed a fist into the wall. "You had someone *followin'* us?"

"Since you moved out of the castle," Tresyllione said.

Genero shook his head. They hadn't even noticed. It was Gan or the twins who usually picked up on such surveillance, noticing when some mendicant or other spied on them. Neither he nor the other two survivors were trained for that sort of thing.

Meanwhile, Ubàrlig asked, "And did this Jared person determine who the Shranlaseth are?"

Stepping away from the wall, ban Wyvald replied, "He didn't need to. You see, one of Jared's fellow guards in Dragon is another former Shranlaseth, a woman named Aleta. She vouched for the pair that Thorn and Kail met with—they're leather workers who sell a great deal of their work to the Ber-Gan Islands, and recently lost their cargo carrier."

"What you saw," Tresyllione said, "was them negotiating with Mitos's ex-minions for shipping rates on *Wikker's Fury*."

Bogg hit the wall again. "Shit."

"*Please* stop doing that!" Tresyllione snapped.

"Yeah? Make me, bitch!"

"Bogg!" Genero cried, which stopped the barbarian.

But it didn't stop Tresyllione who stood right up to Bogg. "Trust me, barbarian, I could *very easily* make you. You raise a hand to anyone in this room, and the wards will restrain your ass and bring you to the hole, where I'd be more than happy to let you rot for the rest of your days. See, the lord and lady would throw a fit if we put either of these two in, but you? Nobody cares about the idiot from the north."

"That's enough, Lieutenant," Genero said. "I wish to ask a question. I know you've said that you don't answer questions in this room, but I'd like you to make an exception. I think we've earned it."

Tresyllione looked away from Bogg and stared at Genero with an intense gaze. "You haven't, actually, but you're not under arrest, either, nor are you suspects in anything except being stupid, so sure, go ahead and ask."

"Why did you have us under surveillance?"

That prompted guffaws of laughter from Tresyllione, and a small smile from ban Wyvald, though Genero suspected it was more at his partner's reaction.

"The question amuses you?" Genero asked testily.

Through her laughter, Tresyllione said, "That you — you have to *ask* it — does."

"You see," ban Wyvald said, giving Tresyllione a chance to catch her breath, "we anticipated that you might try to do something idiotic. So we kept an eye on you."

"And when Jared and Lavian realized their respective targets had come together, they immediately summoned reinforcements," Tresyllione added, "and sent a message to us."

Bogg was shaking his head. "I don't believe this shit. We wasn't doin' nothin' wrong!"

"Yet," Tresyllione added pointedly.

"Had Jared, Lavian, and the others not arrived at Sandy Brook Way when they did," ban Wyvald said, "you would have assaulted two innocent men."

"They ain't innocent by a *damn* sight!" Bogg yelled, pointing at the wall this time.

"Maybe not," Tresyllione said, "but they've served their time, and now they're citizens of Flingaria, whom you were about to assault. If you *had* gone through with it, you three would be in the hole right now."

"However," Genero said, "we did not assault anyone. In fact, we have committed no crime, and cooperated with your questions — a cooperation that has now ended. Unless you intend to arrest us, I believe that, by the lord and lady's laws, we're free to go, yes?"

Tresyllione stepped aside so the trio could easily exit. "By all means, Brother Genero, get the hell out of the castle. And try to stay out of trouble *this* time."

UBÀRLIG TRIED TO KEEP FIGHTING, BUT THE HARPY'S CLAWS HAD TORN INTO *his leg and he could no longer stand upright. Genero tried to keep the one harpy at bay with his short sword, but he was fighting a losing battle, especially since Brightblade, Olthar, Bogg, and the twins were fully occupied by the other two. He needed to get to the dwarf and heal him so he could get back in the fight.*

But the harpies were smart. The other two traded off going after Olthar, keeping the mage from having a moment to formulate a spell.

Then, finally Brightblade and Bogg managed to coordinate an attack, with the barbarian swinging high and the warrior swinging low, and they cut through the harpy's wings, sending her careening into the ground for Mari and Nari to stab multiple times with their daggers until she was dead.

Bogg ran to aid Genero while Brightblade went after the other one to distract her while Olthar prepared a spell.

Then fortune finally favored them — or Temisa smiled upon them, if you asked Genero. Mari and Nari both had throwing knives, and they were both expert at hitting their targets — but less so when the target flew about the large room the way the harpies did. As a result, the floor was littered with throwing knives.

But then Nari threw one that struck the harpy directly in her right eye. On virtually any creature, the eye is the most vulnerable spot, and the harpy died the instant Nari's blade embedded itself there.

Even as the harpy crashed to the floor, Bogg and Brightblade went after the final one, Olthar gestured and muttered the language of mages, and Genero ran to Ubàrlig.

"You will be fine, my friend."

A massive lightburst interrupted whatever response the dwarf might have supplied, and a moment later, the last harpy lay dead on the cracked marble floor.

Of Thorn and Kail, there was no sign.

Brightblade, who now clutched his ribs in pain that he'd been stoically ignoring during the fight, said, "Mari, Nari, see if you can find Mitos's minions!"

Genero moved to heal Brightblade, and then Bogg, though it took the priest some cajoling to finally allow him to aid the latter. The barbarian always viewed Temisa's healing touch as a sign of weakness.

A few minutes later, the twins came back. "Nothin'. Whole place is empty," Mari said.

Nari added, "Thorn and Kail must've scarpered once they realized we were gonna take care'a them harpies."

Bogg slammed a fist into a wall. "So this whole damn thing was a trap from Mitos? Bastard wasn't even here."

"Worry not, my friend," Brightblade said, "we will find him."

"And we'll find those two brothers," Ubàrlig added. "The next time we see them, I promise to lodge my Fjorm right up their asses."

GENERO STARED DESULTORILY AT HIS SALAD. HE, BOGG, AND UBÀRLIG WERE at their usual table in the Dog and Duck.

"Can I ask a question, Genero?" the dwarf said after swallowing his mutton.

"Hm?" Genero shook himself out of his reverie. "What is it, Ubàrlig?"

"Why are we still here? If Chalmraik did resurrect himself, the Brotherhood took care of it. Gan, Olthar, and the twins are dead. The Castle Guard is so enamored of our presence that they've stuck a guard to keep an eye on us." He snorted. "If it were up to Lieutenant Tresyllione, we'd all be in the hole by now. I suppose I just don't see the value of remaining in Cliff's End, beyond the storytelling service we've been providing."

With a heavy sigh, Genero pulled a battered scroll out of the folds of his robe. He handed it over to the dwarf. "This came by messenger during midsummer."

Ubàrlig unrolled it and read it. Though he was illiterate, Bogg leaned over to look at the scroll as well.

After perusing it, the dwarf handed it back. "Has the bishopric ever held a hearing on you before?"

"Once, but that was when Mitos was mentally controlling the entire bishopric and used the hearing to lure me back to Velessa." Genero took the scroll back. "I suppose I'm avoiding returning home."

"Excuse us."

Looking up, Genero saw Thorn and Kail standing by their table, looking contrite.

Bogg started to stand, but Thorn held up both hands. "Look, we don't want any trouble!"

Kail said, "Seriously, as Wiate is our witness, we're straight now! We did our time, and we'd be just as happy to forget we ever even *met* Mitos!"

Harshly, Genero said, "You allied yourself with evil. Such actions have dire consequences."

"We weren't 'allies.'" Thorn shook his head. "We were *employees*. We didn't give a shit what Mitos wanted to accomplish, we just liked getting a hundred gold a week."

Ubàrlig's eyes widened. "A *week*?"

"Oh yeah," Kail said. "'Course, there were all kindsa conditions, like wearing those stupid helmets."

"And that chainmail chafed like you wouldn't believe," Thorn added.

Bogg snorted. "Armor's for sissies, anyhow."

Genero looked away from the two brothers in shame. He had judged these two solely on the basis of who they were employed by. He had rushed to ambush them without giving any consideration to how much things might have changed in a decade and a half.

Or, indeed, not changed much. Like all those in Flingaria who were not wealthy, these two were simply trying to find a way to survive. He certainly couldn't blame an ordinary person for jumping at the chance to make a hundred gold pieces per week, especially when the person paying it was a powerful wizard who likely used coercive measures to ensure employee loyalty.

"Why don't you join us?" Genero said.

"Say *what*?" Bogg asked.

"That's a great idea," Ubàrlig said. "Hell, I always wondered what it was like workin' for a lunatic like that."

"We'd love to," Kail said, and Thorn went to grab two stools to place at the table.

As he sat, Thorn said, "For starters, Mitos always wanted us to speak a certain way. That whole, 'We are minions of the great Mitos' nonsense? That was all him. If we didn't talk like that, he docked our pay—*and* threatened to turn us into newts."

"That's why we don't have bosses," Bogg said. "I'm my own damn boss."

"Easy for you to say, being the size of a house and all," Kail muttered.

"Bogg," Genero said quickly before the barbarian could respond to that.

"Look," Kail went on, "we were two orphans with no skills and no prospects. Mitos hired us, paid us more money than we'd ever seen."

"And we actually learned some skills. We learned sailin' thanks to workin' for him." Thorn smiled. "'Course, took us a while to get the hang of it."

"Yeah, we spent seven years in stir, but we still had our money when we got out, so we bought *Wikker's Fury.*"

"And it's been great." Thorn's smile widened. "Honestly, life of a sailor's the best ever. On the sea, everything makes sense, y'know?"

Genero had always hated sailing, and so said nothing. Ubàrlig asked, "So you traversed the Garamin to and from the Ber-Gan Islands?"

Thorn nodded. "Yeah, we scouted out the place, and we set it all up. Took *months.* Especially after Andear."

Frowning, Genero said, "That was the Ber-Gan island that sunk, wasn't it?"

Thorn nodded. "It didn't sink, Mitos sunk it. It was right after you guys fought him in the Forest of Nimvale."

Shuddering, Genero said, "Don't remind us of that, please. It took *weeks* to get the smell of hobgoblin out of my robes."

Bogg shrugged. "I didn't think it was that bad."

Laughing, Ubàrlig said, "Because it was competing against all the other odors that linger on your person."

To Genero's relief, Bogg actually returned the laugh.

The conversation continued into the evening, with others gathering 'round to hear stories of Gan Brightblade and his friends' adventures, as usual, but focusing more on when they battled the evil Mitos the Mage, with the added bonus of how things went from Mitos's side.

As the stories went on into the night, for the first time since Gan Brightblade died in his room in this very inn, Brother Genero of Velessa's feeling of discontent dissipated. He felt good.

WHEN THE MAGICK
GOES AWAY

Dedicated to the fond memory of
Rabbi David M. Honigsberg for a lot of reasons,
but mostly for Track #4 on Blues Spoken Here.

ACKNOWLEDGMENTS

Flipping great wodges of thanks to the following, without whom this story would not have been possible:

JD Adams, Ben Adler, Lorraine Anderson, Lance Roger Axt, Tom B., Em Baisch, Mark Beaulieu, Bonnie Beck, Diane Bellomo, Mo Blaner, Jeremy Bottroff, Buzzy Multimedia, Karen Mitchell Carothers, Danny Chamberlain, Joseph Charpak, Mike Crate, Jim Crider, Alan Danziger, Dwight Davis, John S. Drew, Michael Dougherty, Cormac Dullaghan, Heather Eberhardt, Michael & Rosalyn Falkner, Richard Fine, Dave Finnerty, "Finny", Lydia Fithian, Will Frank, Tony & Becky Glinka, Rich Gonzalez, Robert Greenberger, Elektra Hammond, Julie Harris, Shael Hawman, Solomon Jones, Andrew Kaplan, David "Handlebar" Kingsley, William Leisner, Jeff Linder, Shira Lipkin, Stephanie Lucas, Maryjean Lugo, Siannan MacDuff, Ken Mars, Kelsey Mayer, Ian Mond, Tiffany Newell, Meg Nuge, Mitch Obrecht, Julio Angel Ortiz, Thomas Pesso, Kalley Powell, Zan Rosin, "Scantrontb", Jeff Schultz, Tina Sorrentino, Mark Squire, Ann Stolinsky, Scott Thede, Ronnie Virga, Ariel Vitali, Josh Ward, Audrey Zarr, and Mike Zipser.

You guys are the absolute best!

KORT

NO MATTER HOW MANY DECADES HE LIVED AS A WIZARD, AND HE'D LIVED plenty by this point, Tam Kort never grew tired of drinking ale in a tavern.

Of late, his preferred drinking hole of choice was the Stone Kobold, located on Axe Lane in the port town of Cliff's End. One of Kort's magick shops was located in Cliff's End, and his employees had spoken highly of the place. Kort had been coming here for a few years now, ever since the people of the northern city-state of Iaron, where another of his shops was located, learned he was a wizard. That took all the fun out of it. When people knew you were a magick-user, they bowed, they scraped, they sucked up, and they generally stopped treating you like a person. Kort came to a bar so he could listen to stories and enjoy the company of people.

Wizards weren't people. Kort had spent enough time as a member of the Brotherhood of Wizards to understand that to be a fact. Indeed, he'd figured *that* little truism out after spending about an hour with the mage he was apprenticed to, the old bastard.

But, as he hoisted his third — or was it fourth? — ale, Kort didn't think about being a wizard, he just thought about having a good time.

"And then, and *then*," said a dwarf, who was sitting on the stool next to Kort, his legs swinging in the air even as he gesticulated in the energetic telling of his tale, "the stupid bastard starts *playing* the lute! Of course, it sounds like utter shit, and I finally had to grab the thing and smash it against the wall. That's when all the coins came pouring out of it and onto the floor."

A brown-haired human woman on the other side of the dwarf asked, "He thought you were paying him with a lute?"

"T'be fair," a bald, thick-bearded human next to Kort said, "in th'hands'f a great bard, a lute's of tr'mendous value."

Gava, the tall, beautiful human woman behind the bar, laughed and said, "That leaves Sam's lute out, then."

Kort also laughed. "I'll drink to that." Sam was the bard who performed at the Stone Kobold thrice weekly, and Kort endeavored mightily to make sure that his trips to the Kobold were on one of the other four days.

His imbibing in honor of Sam's awful bardistry was enough to finish his current flagon, and he placed it down on the bar and asked Gava for another. She held the flagon under the spigot of the ale barrel, then handed it back saying, "This one's on the house."

Eyes widening, Kort asked, "To what do I owe the privilege?"

"You're just about the only gentleman in here," Gava said with a bright smile. "Certainly the only regular. You always tip well, and you're the only person who's never tried to get me to sleep with them."

Were they not in Kort's current favorite bar, he might have told Gava that wizards were encouraged to tamp down their sexuality in order to focus on the magick. Strong emotions like lust and love played merry hell with spells. Not that all wizards lived up to that notion, as Kort had learned the hard way . . .

"Actually, lutes can be of even greater value than gold," said a deep-voiced man from the other side of the bar. He had long red hair and he either had become too lazy to shave or was in the midst of growing a beard.

The dwarf spit his ale in surprise. "Are you mad? Nothing's of more value than gold."

"Value is circumstantial," the red-haired man said. "During the war, I spent a winter in the Nemerian Wastes. Gold would, at that point, been of far less use than a lute, as a lute can be used for kindling."

Everyone chuckled at that one.

Another dwarf, who sat at a table near the bar, stared at the red-haired man. "You fought for the king and queen against the elf bitch, didja?"

He nodded. "I served under General Osric in the 17th Company for three years until the Elf Queen finally abdicated her throne."

The dwarf grinned. "Hah! I served in the Elmgren Regiment of the dwarven army. You must've fought at Hobgoblin's Run."

"Indeed, I did. Torin ban Wyvald." He held up his flagon.

"Zorbanig," the dwarf replied, doing likewise. "A pleasure."

"Y'know," the bearded man next to Kort said, "Osric's here'n Cliff's End now. He's runnin' th'Castle Guard."

"So I've heard," ban Wyvald said with a smile.

The other dwarf, who'd told the story about the lute, asked, "What happened at Hobgoblin's Run?"

Kort sighed. He hated war stories, but they were becoming increasingly common, as more and more ex-soldiers started pouring into Cliff's End. Some came here due to lack of work, others used Cliff's End the way so many did, as a waystation. The city-state had the busiest port in all of Flingaria.

And all of them had stories to tell about the elven wars. It grew tiresome.

Still, Kort gulped down his ale while trying to at least pretend to be interested in the story that ban Wyvald and Zorbanig told about their battle—thought Kort noticed that the former did most of the talking.

"You tell your story well, Torin ban Wyvald," the brunette two stools down from Kort said after he got to the part where the elves retreated. "Perhaps Gava should hire you as the new bard."

Gava shook her head. "Sadly, that's not my choice, and we're still stuck with the old bard."

"Of course," Zorbanig said, "you lot were lucky we showed up, otherwise your sorry asses would've been routed by those pointy-eared bastards."

"That is certainly possible," ban Wyvald said before sipping some more ale.

Zorbanig slammed his flagon down onto the table and stood up. "You callin' me a liar, human?"

"Not at all. As I said, it's possible you're right, and we might have lost the day without your arrival. Since you *did* show up, we shall never know."

Kort was impressed with ban Wyvald's deft but gentle attempt to defuse the situation.

Sadly, the attempt failed, as Zorbanig then stomped toward ban Wyvald angrily, elbowing the bearded human next to Kort as he strode by.

"'Ey, watchit, shorty!" The human took a clumsy swing that cleared Zorbanig's head by two handslengths, then stumbled forward into another table, spilling half a dozen drinks while doing so.

The four burly humans sitting there did not look pleased. One grabbed the human by the head.

Zorbanig yelled, "Fight! Fight!"

Kort had very little memory of what happened after that, beyond a flail of arms, legs, and ale, both within and without its containers. For his part, he muttered a Shield Spell that kept him safe from harm.

Within a minute, the melee was over, as most of the Kobold's patrons were lying on the floor, breathing heavily, crying in pain, or moaning softly. The exceptions were ban Wyvald—who appeared to have comported himself well in the fight, standing over two of the large humans from the table next to Zorbanig's—and Kort himself.

Turning to the bar, Kort said, "Gava, you'd better—"

But of Gava, he saw no sign.

Ban Wyvald was peering over the bar. "I'm afraid she is unlikely to answer, sir."

Looking over, Kort saw that Gava lay prone on the floor, blood trickling from her mouth and from the wound formed by the ornate dagger lodged in her chest.

QUANE

Lieutenant Quane struggled to throw the cloak on over his neck and in very short order found himself tangled in it. The brown cloak with the gryphon crest emblazoned on the back that symbolized his new rank as a lieutenant in the Cliff's End Castle Guard now covered his entire face. That, at least, spared him the indignity of watching his fellow detectives laugh hysterically, not to mention whatever dire look his new partner was giving him.

He could *hear* the laughter, though. Plus Nael saying, "Bravo! Well done, Quane, well done!"

Once he finally managed to disentangle himself from the cloak and place it properly, he looked over at his partner.

"Are you *quite* finished?" she asked. She stared dolefully at him. Her bizarrely constructed face was the result of a human-elven pairing, but she was much uglier than the half-elf prostitute in that place on Sandy Brook Way that he visited last year.

"Yes, Lieutenant Treslin," he said quickly.

She winced. "It's 'Tresyllione,' and will you just call me 'Danthres' and have done with it, you stupid shitbrain?"

"Sorry, Lieutenant—I mean, Danthres!" He followed her toward the exit from the squadroom, leaving the snickering of the other four detectives, as well as Sergeant Newcastle.

Quane had to follow Danthres as he hadn't yet learned his way around the castle. In fact, when she made a left out of the squadroom, Quane cried, "Left?" a bit louder than he should have.

Danthres stopped, closed her eyes, and turned on her partner. "Oh, Lord and Lady, Quane, will you just follow me? You don't need to express surprise at everything that doesn't go as you planned. You're a detective now, and I guarantee that *nothing* will go as planned and you'll just exhaust yourself from all that shock. Don't worry, you'll learn your way around the castle eventually."

"I—I know, Lieut—I mean, Danthres." Quane shook his head. "I'm sorry, but I was assigned to Unicorn and Mermaid, and I never really got up here to the castle much, except for that ceremony, and that other—"

"Quane!"

Recoiling as if slapped, Quane stammered, "I'm—I'm sorry, I just—"

She held up a hand. "Stop talking. Now."

Quane stopped talking.

With that, Danthres turned and continued out of the castle.

They walked in silence out of the portcullis and onto Meerka Way. Exiting the castle, which was deemed Gryphon Precinct, they traversed into the city proper. Quane had always found Lord Albin and Lady Meerka's method of dividing up the city-state to be genius.

He tried to remember the borders of each precinct. From the castle to—was it Pine Path? Anyhow, that was Unicorn Precinct, where the wealthiest citizens of Cliff's End resided. That was where Quane had served as a rookie in the Guard, taking complaints from annoying rich people. Between there and Axe Way was the middle-class district of Dragon Precinct, with the slums between Axe Way and the docks serving as Goblin Precinct. The docklands themselves were Mermaid Precinct, and it was Quane's cleverness in helping figure out who hijacked the *Fool's Gold* that led to his promotion when Lieutenant Bergin quit the Guard rather suddenly.

It wasn't until his third day on the job as a lieutenant that Sergeant Newcastle informed him that Bergin had quit rather than continue to be partnered with Danthres. And that Quane was now her sixth partner since her own promotion almost half a year earlier.

As they passed Oak Way, Quane cursed himself. "Pine Path," indeed. It was Oak Way that served as the demarcation between Unicorn and Dragon. He should have remembered that.

They reached Axe Lane—not Way, dammit—and turned left until they reached the Stone Kobold.

Forbin was on guard outside the tavern. Quane nodded at him.

"Ho there, Quane," Forbin said, then said more formally to Danthres, "Ma'am."

Danthres looked back and forth from Forbin to Quane. "You two know each other?"

Nodding, Quane said, "We came up in Unicorn together. Remember that gnome that kept trying to peek into Lady Murvane's bedchamber?"

That got a chuckle out of Forbin. "Indeed. No matter how many times we cast his tiny form into the hole . . ."

Quane grinned. He wasn't entirely sure why the dungeons beneath the castle and the holding cells in the precincts were collectively called "the hole," but that name had been part of the Guard's lexicon since he joined, so he called them that, too, so he wouldn't look like an idiot. At least not like more of an idiot than he had been since being promoted.

Danthres snarled. "If you two are done with your hilarious reminiscing about your soft duty in Unicorn, we have a case."

"With respect, ma'am, that's why they put rookies there — because it is, as you say, soft."

"I wouldn't know," Danthres said. "When I first joined up, I was assigned to Goblin."

Quane watched Forbin's eyes go wide, which was the way he himself had reacted when Danthres had informed him of the same thing. That was not standard procedure for the Castle Guard.

Danthres stared at Forbin intently. "What have we got?"

"A bar brawl, much like any other bar brawl. I have not questioned any of the participants, though I overheard one person mention that a dwarf started it. There are a couple of dwarves inside, by the way. In the end, the bartender was found with a knife in her chest."

Danthres folded her arms. "I'm impressed. That's more than I usually get out of a guard. Please tell me you haven't let anyone leave."

Shaking his head so fast Quane wondered if it would turn all the way around, Forbin said, "No, ma'am. Everyone's still present and accounted for — at least, since I arrived shortly after I received word of the fight. I can't guarantee that someone didn't depart the premises before my arrival."

"Good enough." She stormed past Forbin and went into the Stone Kobold.

Forbin glanced sidelong at Quane. "She's a fun one, isn't she?"

Quane just shuddered and went inside as well.

As soon as they entered the bar itself, everyone started speaking at once. The bar was mostly populated with humans, as well as a smattering of dwarves. No elves or gnomes or halflings or any other species that Quane could see.

"Quiet!" Danthres yelled, her voice echoing off the Kobold's wooden walls.

Everyone shut up. Quane wondered if they put her on crowd control when she was a guard in Goblin.

"Everyone stay where you are. We need to look at the victim, then we will be questioning you one by one. Where's the body?"

Several of the patrons pointed to the other side of the bar, located against the back wall. Danthres walked to it, moving past the tables that were shoved haphazardly about the floor.

Quane followed, then stumbled as he kept crashing into tables that Danthres, somehow, nimbly avoided.

They got around to the other side of the bar. Looking down, Quane saw a blond-haired human woman. Her tunic was darkened by blood, pooling beneath her from around the dagger jutting out of her chest. Her eyes just stared upward without blinking, and the blood looked like it was everywhere, and . . .

Suddenly, Quane's entire being was focused on the nausea that welled up from his belly into his throat. Turning, he ran toward the front door and barely made it out before throwing up right onto Forbin's boots.

"Damnation, Quane, do you know how much they charge us for a Laundry Spell on boots?"

Quane stood hunched over, hands on knees, trying to get his breathing under control. His lips were caked with puke, and his mouth tasted like something died in it. Pointedly, he ignored Forbin's question. Given what was on the ground in Cliff's End, his puke was the least of what was staining Forbin's boots on a given day.

Wiping his mouth with his glove, he stood upright, took a very deep breath, and walked back in.

Danthres was standing just on the other side of the door. "Lord and Lady, Quane, is this your first dead body?"

Swallowing down the leftover bile, Quane nodded.

"How did you— Oh, never mind, I don't even want to know." She pointed at a table. "Go sit down." She turned around and looked at the assembled multitudes before pointing at a human woman. "You, come over here."

The woman came over and sat down opposite Quane, Danthres taking a seat between them. "Tell me," she said, "what happened?"

She shrugged. "Dunno. Some dwarf and that man over yonder," she pointed at a red-haired man seated at the bar, "were tellin' war stories, and next thing I know, everyone's gone mad."

"Which dwarf?"

The woman looked about. "Dunno. Ain't here no more. Said his name was Zubering or summat."

"Did you see who killed the bartender?"

"Her name's Gava — she was a good woman."

Quane said, "I'm so sorry for your loss."

Danthres shot him a look.

The woman said, "It's everyone's loss. Other bartenders in this dump are shitbrains, but she knows how to pour. Anyhow, I didn't see who killed her. And if I did, I'd've cut him m'self."

Once they were done with her, Danthres called a human man over. He said more or less the same thing, though he had no idea what the dwarf's name was. Then a dwarf, who said that the dwarf who started the brawl was named Zorbanig. Then an older human man.

"I come in fairly regularly," the man said. "My name's Tam Kort, and I don't know who Zorbanig was — except that he was a dwarf who fought in the war — but I've never seen him before. Of course, I've never seen Mr. ban Wyvald over there before, either, but he didn't sneak out while the brawl was going on."

Danthres frowned. "You're sure he left then?"

Kort hesitated. "Not entirely, but I didn't see him at all after the fight ended. Stands to reason. Also, he and another person, a human, seemed to have some sort of prearranged movement where Zorbanig bumped him, and the man swung over his head and stumbled into a table with a bit of deliberate clumsiness."

"I can't help but notice that you're uninjured," Danthres said.

Quane shook his head. He hadn't even noticed that. Everyone else in the place had at least the beginnings of a bruise, if not a cut or two, except for this Kort gentleman.

Kort smiled sheepishly. "I'm afraid I'm of little use in a fight, and I'm a tremendous physical coward. I kept my head down and didn't engage."

Danthres then summoned the red-haired man over.

"Greetings, Lieutenants. My name is Torin ban Wyvald, and the person you wish to speak to is named Zorbanig. He's a dwarf, completely bald, with a mark on the left side of his head. His beard is brown with some gray, and very thick."

Danthres blinked. "That's—quite a bit of detail."

Ban Wyvald shrugged. "I was suspicious of him. He claimed to be from the Elmgren Regiment, which fought alongside my own 17th Company at Hobgoblin's Run. But his remembrances seemed vague at best, and when I mentioned Captain Birok's big charge, he nodded and said he remembered it well."

Danthres smirked. "I take it that Captain Birok did not charge during that battle?"

Smirking right back, ban Wyvald said, "That would be rather difficult, since he'd been dead for a month by the time Hobgoblin's Run occurred." The smirk fell. "After I finished the story, he picked a fight, despite all my attempts to defuse his anger. And then he and a compatriot appeared to deliberately provoke a table full of men."

"You seem to notice a great deal," Danthres said slowly.

"You seem suspicious of that, Lieutenant."

"Can you give me a good reason why I shouldn't be?"

Quane frowned. Danthres was talking like this man was a suspect, which was absurd, given how cooperative he was.

"I can, as it happens. I was raised in Myverin, and trained to be observant of my surroundings at all times."

"Myverin's real?" Quane blurted out. "I always thought it was a myth!"

"So did I," Danthres said. "Certainly, people who voluntarily leave Myverin are."

"An odd statement," ban Wyvald replied, "from someone who voluntarily left Sorlin."

Now Danthres smoldered. Quane found himself slowly nudging his chair away from her. Sorlin was one of those places in the south that Quane had heard stories about—something about elves experimenting on humans, maybe?—but he wasn't sure of the reality. He had no idea that Danthres was from there, or indeed if she really was. But ban Wyvald just mentioning the place obviously pissed her off.

Tightly, Danthres said, "We're not here to discuss me, Mr. ban Wyvald, but the bar brawl and the murder of a woman."

"I'm afraid two of the brawlers occupied my attention, to their detriment, so I did not witness the murder. However, you may be able to obtain assistance from the man you interviewed before me."

Quane blinked. "Mr. Kort already told us everything he knows."

"No, shitbrain, he didn't," Danthres said dismissively. "He merely answered what we asked him."

"Did he tell you that he's a wizard?" ban Wyvald asked.

Now Quane's jaw dropped. "He's not a wizard!"

"I'm afraid I must agree with my idiot partner," Danthres said. "Wizards generally announce themselves."

"I can't speak to why this Kort gentleman hid his true nature, but he spent the entire fight sitting on his stool at the bar, and was left completely untouched by it, even as all those around him were caught up in it whether they wished to or not. That could only have been accomplished by a spell he cast."

"That's amazing," Quane muttered.

Danthres gave her partner a withering look. "Hardly. He could have bought a Shield Spell."

But ban Wyvald just shook his head and pointed at the doorway to the Stone Kobold.

Turning around, Quane saw a sigil painted on the wall over the doorframe, though he had no idea what it meant.

"That symbol," ban Wyvald said, "can be found on most reputable taverns throughout—"

"Yes, yes, yes," Danthres said with a sigh.

Quane swallowed. "I've never seen it before."

"It's a ward, shitbrain." Danthres gave him another of her withering stares. Quane was already getting tired of them. "It prevents any store-bought magick from working where it's placed. But it won't stop natural magick, so wizards can still function where that ward appears."

At this point, Quane's head was swimming, as he hadn't known any of this. "All—all right then, if he *is* a wizard, how does that help us?"

"During the war, there was a court-martial of a soldier who claimed that a fellow soldier had been killed by an enemy scout, but nobody had seen this scout. There happened to be a wizard in camp, and he offered to cast a spell called Inanimate Residue. It can tell the wizard what has happened to certain inanimate objects, to peel back time on that object and reveal its past."

Frowning, Quane repeated himself. "How does that help us?"

Danthres was leaning forward. "This spell can be cast in a room?"

"He told me it could. It certainly can't hurt to ask this Kort person if he is capable of such."

"Assuming," Danthres added with a smile, "that he *is* a wizard."

Ban Wyvald smiled right back. "Assuming."

"You admit you might be wrong?" Danthres tilted her head quizzically.

"Of course," ban Wyvald replied matter-of-factly. "I'm only guessing—I might be mistaken, and Kort may simply be a *very* talented coward."

"That was, in fact, what he claimed," Danthres said. "We shall see. And I'm impressed. Most men would never admit to the possibility of being wrong."

"Then it would seem that I am not like most men."

Danthres snorted. "Doubtful. Is there anything else you wish to add?"

Shrugging, ban Wyvald said, "Only that the woman was obviously targeted, and Zorbanig's purpose was to provide a distraction that would allow him, or someone else, to kill her."

"Are you sure of that?" Quane asked.

Danthres looked to the ceiling in supplication, and Quane realized he'd screwed up yet again. "Lord and Lady, you stupid shitbrain, of *course* that's what happened! Gava was very carefully stabbed right in the chest where she'd be guaranteed to die almost instantly. That type of precision doesn't happen in a bar fight."

"I—" Quane started, but Danthres had already gotten up and walked over to Kort.

After following her progress across the tavern, ban Wyvald turned to Quane. "Is she always so—so direct?"

Quane snorted. "That's the polite way of putting it. I've only been partnered with her for a short while." And he wasn't sure he'd be partnered with her for much longer, though he didn't say that aloud. "Thank you for your cooperation," he added as he rose and went after her.

She was now standing in front of Kort. "Tell me, Mr. Kort—are you a wizard?"

Several of the other people in the tavern laughed at that. "He ain't no wizard!"

"Kort ain't no more a mage than I am!"

"Like a magick-slinger'd be caught dead in *this* place!"

Kort, however, just sighed. "How did you know?"

More expressions of shock and disbelief and outrage.

Quane was about to explain that ban Wyvald had figured it out, but Danthres talked over him. "That doesn't matter. What does matter is whether or not you are capable of casting an Inanimate Residue Spell."

Instead of answering directly, Kort just stared at Danthres. For her part, Danthres stared right back. Quane had to look away, but neither lieutenant nor wizard did.

Finally Kort sighed. "Now I'll have to find a new tavern—*again*."

"Is that a yes?"

"Yes, it's a yes. I'll need everyone to depart this tavern. The spell only will work if there is nothing alive in the space."

"But," Quane said, "aren't *you* alive?"

Danthres barked a laugh. "Congratulations, shitbrain, that's the first smart thing you've said in your entire life."

"The spellcaster, obviously, can be present," Kort said slowly. "If we're to do this, let's get it over with, so I can find a new tavern to patronize. I'll need half an hour to cast the spell."

Looking at Quane, Danthres said, "Let's clear the place out."

Stunned that she didn't call him "shitbrain" that time, Quane started to herd people out of the Stone Kobold. Within a few minutes, they'd cleared everyone onto Axe Lane. They were all muttering various importuning about how surprised they were that Kort was a mage.

With a sigh, Danthres looked at Forbin. "All right, I see no reason to stand around for half an hour, so you stay here, and when the wizard in there is finished, escort him to the castle."

"Uhm—" Forbin started.

"Is there a problem?" Danthres asked in a tone that made it abundantly clear that the answer to that question needed to be "no."

Forbin, however, did not catch the tone—or, more suicidally, didn't care. "Ma'am, I'm afraid I'm off-shift in a quarter-hour, and Sergeant Alvin made it abundantly clear that we cannot have overtime."

Danthres put her head in her hands. "Then send someone to Dragon and get a replacement!"

With that, Danthres stormed off. Quane gave Forbin a quick shrug, and then ran to catch up with her.

As soon as he did so, Danthres said, "You were utterly useless in there, shitbrain. Osric keeps insisting that I must have a partner, but a tree would've been more beneficial than you. At least it would provide shade."

Quane instinctively wanted to be outraged. That was the sixth time she'd called him a shitbrain today, and he was sick of it. But he couldn't muster up that outrage because in the back of his head he knew that she was absolutely right. For all that he'd been clever on the *Fool's Gold* case, he wasn't, it seemed, cut out to be a detective. That ban Wyvald fellow was of more use to the investigation than he.

TORIN

Torin ban Wyvald felt oddly nervous as he approached the castle that served as the seat of Lord Albin and Lady Meerka's demesne.

He had, over the past five years, left his childhood home—the only person to voluntarily leave Myverin in recent memory, or even not-so-recent—nearly died in the Forest of Orven during a particularly brutal winter, and fought in a war. He had done more than he ever could have imagined when he departed the safe haven of home for the greater world of Flingaria outside Myverin's cloistered walls.

So why was his stomach doing backflips at the notion of simply approaching a castle door?

Steeling himself, he entered through the portcullis, traversed the grand foyer—and then had no idea where to go next.

Conveniently, there was a man in armor standing near one of the doorways. The style of leather armor was the same as the other members of the Castle Guard he saw at the tavern. This one had a gryphon insignia on his chest, just like the two lieutenants, but no cloak, like the guard who'd been standing outside.

"Excuse me," Torin said to the guard, who had been staring straight ahead until Torin approached him.

"Yeah?" the guard asked.

"My apologies, but I'm here to see General Osric."

The guard squinted. "Ain't no General Osric here. 'Less Cap'n Osric's been promoted without tellin' nobody."

At that, Torin chuckled. "My apologies. Your captain and I served in the war together, and he was a general then."

"So I heard." He stepped away from the doorway and pointed down a corridor. "Head down 'at way, then hang yourself a left at the big dragon statue, then a right at the unicorn tapestry. Right through 'ere's th'squadroom."

Inclining his head, Torin said, "My thanks, kind sir," and then followed those directions.

Once he navigated past a hideous statue of a dragon and a pretty tapestry portraying a unicorn gamboling in the woods, he found himself in a large room filled with desks. A picture window filled the north wall, providing rather a nice view of the forest outside the city-state's outskirts. The east wall had a doorway, and three more doorways ran across the south wall.

He saw three people in leather armor that had the same gryphon insignia on the chest as Tresyllione and Quane from the Stone Kobold and the corridor guard, though he saw neither detective. None were wearing cloaks, but Torin noticed a pegboard on which hung five earth-colored cloaks. The three were each sitting at desks, writing on scrolls. One got up and went to the window, saying, "The Gerrin case."

The window then shimmered and twisted, the forest view being replaced with the bearded male face of an imp. Said imp spoke in a thin, reedy voice. "You don't need to say which case, you know. I'm perfectly capable of filing the scrolls in their proper place."

"Your optimism amuses me, Ep," the lieutenant said. "Just put these with the Gerrin case."

"Fine, fine," Ep said in what Torin imagined to be a long-suffering tone.

The lieutenant placed the scrolls in the imp's beard, and it disappeared shortly thereafter, allowing the view of the forest to return.

After that, the lieutenant turned to look at Torin. "You impressed with the view or the imp?"

"Oh, I've seen imps before," Torin said with a smile. "The boat I took to Cliff's End used one for announcements to the passengers, and I encountered more than one when I served in the army."

Returning the smile, the lieutenant said, "So it's the view, then?"

"It is a very pretty forest. It's called Nimvale, if I recall the area geography, yes?"

"Yes. Surprised you didn't learn that upon arrival—no, wait, you came by sea, you said."

Torin nodded. "I'm actually here to see Captain Osric. Is he available?"

"That depends on who needs him."

"I'm Torin ban Wyvald."

Offering his gloved hand, the detective said, "I'm Lieutenant Gef Linder."

Accepting the hand, Torin added, "I served under your captain when he was a general in King Marcus and Queen Marta's army."

Linder chuckled. "Ah, took on the Elf Queen with him, didja? Well, he'll be willing to make time for you, most likely." He leaned forward. "Tell me—did he really lose the eye fighting the Elf Queen's brother?"

Glancing sidelong at Linder, Torin asked, "Is that what he told you?"

"Oh, Wiate, no, he won't tell us a damn thing. No, it something that Sir Palrik told us once."

Torin blinked. "'Sir' Palrik?"

"You know him?" Linder shook his head. "Right, of course you do, you both served under the cap'n."

"I had no idea Palrik was of the nobility. He certainly never gave any indication of it during the war."

Linder snorted. "He hasn't given much indication of it here, neither. In fact—"

He was interrupted by the east-wall door flying open and three people walking out: Quane, looking relieved, Tresyllione, looking pissed, and Osric, looking—well, looking a great deal like Osric always did. Torin couldn't remember a time when his erstwhile commander didn't scowl.

A man wearing a green cloak came in from one of the other doorways. As he did, Osric said, "Sergeant Newcastle, take Lieutenant Quane to Sir Gevlin. He'll need to be processed out, as he's resigning his commission as a member of the Castle Guard."

Newcastle, the man in the green cloak, sighed. "C'mon with me, boy." The pair of them exited through the same west-wall door that Torin had come in through. Quane had been completely out of his depth in the Stone Kobold—the half-elf woman was doing all the work—but Torin had thought he was at least trying. Quitting seemed an extreme reaction.

One of the other detectives said, "Couldn't handle it, huh? Or couldn't handle her? Not that anyone can handle her. What's that, Danthres, ten partners?"

Osric and Tresyllione both gave that detective a nasty look. Then Osric did the scariest thing Torin had ever see him do.

He smiled.

"We'll have to see how good you are at handling her then, Iaian. As of now, you and Tresyllione are partners."

Iaian's face fell. The other two detectives chortled.

"Trust me," Tresyllione said in a low voice, "I'm as thrilled about it as you are."

"What did I do to deserve this?" Iaian asked.

"You're one of the more experienced detectives I have," Osric said, "and I want this murder solved. We have too damn many bar brawls as it is, now people are using them to shield a murder. I want it solved, and that means I need my best detective on it."

"Hey!" Linder said. "Since when is this shitbrain your best detective?"

"Thanks, partner," Iaian muttered.

Osric put his hands on his hips. "Since he closed the Gerrin case. And don't tell me you both closed it, I know for a fact that he was the one who found that gnome and interrogated him while you were taking a personal day."

Torin shook his head and chuckled. Osric hadn't changed a bit, it seemed.

At that point, Tresyllione was staring at Torin. "What are you doing here? Did you remember something else?"

Before Torin could reply, Osric also noticed him. "Lord and Lady, is that you, ban Wyvald?"

"Yes, sir. My apologies, Lieutenant Tresyllione, I'm afraid I'm not here about the incident at the Stone Kobold. Rather, I'd like to visit with my former commanding officer."

Osric looked at Tresyllione. "*He* was that witness you mentioned?"

"Yes," she said.

"Well, I'm afraid I'm going to have to disagree with your assessment of him as someone we shouldn't trust."

Torin shot Tresyllione a look. "Why not trust me?"

Iaian rolled his eyes. "Don't take it personal, mister. Danthres doesn't trust anyone."

"You needn't be concerned," Osric said. "There is no circumstance under which Torin ban Wyvald would be part of a conspiracy to commit murder. Take Iaian, go see if you can find the people the wizard found with that spell."

With a big sigh, Iaian got up from his chair and went to the pegboard. "What spell is that?"

"A damned impressive spell, actually," Tresyllione said as she headed toward the pegboard. "It peels back the events in a place and shows them to the wizard."

"Just the wizard?"

Tresyllione nodded. "It won't work if there are any other living beings around."

"So we have to take the wizard's word for it?"

"Yes, but—well, he's a wizard. They're completely trustworthy." Tresyllione spoke as if it were the most natural thing.

Iaian and Tresyllione moved toward the door as Iaian put his cloak on. "Yeah? What about Chalmraik the Foul?"

"Fine, members of the Brotherhood of Wizards are trustworthy. If they weren't, the Brotherhood wouldn't let them in, would they?"

"Hope so. Who're we looking for?"

The woman's answer was lost as they continued down the corridor and out of earshot.

"So, ban Wyvald," Osric said, "what brings you here?"

Suddenly conscious of the eyes of Linder and the other detective— not to mention the imp in the window—Torin said, "I'd be happy to answer that question—in private, if you don't mind."

Nodding, Osric said, "Of course not." He looked around the squadroom. "Linder, Karistan, I'm sure you have work you can be doing. And where the hell is Nael?"

Karistan said, "He's chatting with Jezz, that sailor friend of his, about the robberies on Sandy Brook Way."

"So why aren't you with him?"

"Jezz doesn't like me."

Osric shook his head. "All right. Don't you two need to talk to the magistrate first thing in the morning?"

"Yes, we're ready."

"You'd better be." Osric took a breath. "C'mon into my office, ban Wyvald."

Grinning, Torin followed Osric into the small office.

As the captain closed the door behind them, Torin said, "I see you still can't leave a room without shouting at each of your subordinates at least once."

"Can't let them think I'm not paying attention, now, can I?" Osric sat down behind the desk, and Torin took one of the facing guest chairs. "When did you get into Cliff's End?"

"Two days ago, on the Stars Rising. The boat's first mate was grumbling about how much harder it was to make an 'honest' living the last year, ever since old 'One-Eyed Osric' took over the Guard."

Osric snorted. "Good to know my reputation is preceding me."

"You definitely have been doing well for yourself. That first mate was not the only person who spoke highly of your Castle Guard." He grinned. "And you can afford a better eyepatch."

The captain's hand moved to the silk patch that covered his left eye, which was of much higher quality than the one he'd been using in the last days of the war. "Indeed. But I can't take complete credit. The Guard is entirely Lord Albin's work. I merely administrate it—though I will freely admit to doing a better job than my predecessor." He shook his head. "Then again, a dead goblin could do a better job than Brisban. I've been working to get rid of the detectives he thought were worth promoting and trying to promote up the ones who actually know their asses from their elbows."

"I suppose it's not going as well as you'd hoped, based on what just happened with young Lieutenant Quane."

Osric shrugged. "His sergeant back at Mermaid thought highly enough of him that I didn't want to just let him go." He chuckled. "So I paired him with Tresyllione, which I knew would have him quitting inside a week."

Slowly, Torin said, "She's—interesting."

"She's brilliant, is what she is, but she's also impossible. She's gone through half a dozen partners since I promoted her." He shook his head. "Brisban put her in Goblin as a rookie. Usually, we break people in by sending them to Unicorn, but—" He chuckled again. "Apologies, ban Wyvald, you don't know our system. Goblin Precinct is our poorest area, and Unicorn is where all the rich bastards live."

Torin nodded. "Of course."

"Brisban kept Tresyllione in Goblin, hoping she'd wash out. He felt she wasn't Guard material." He blew out a breath. "He may have been right, to a degree. She is constantly fighting with the nobility, and irritating witnesses, and just generally being difficult. But she also has the best instincts of anyone I've ever seen." A small smile pricked up the side of his mouth. "Enough about my travails, I doubt you wish to hear them. What have you been up to?"

Leaning back in the wooden chair, Torin said, "Less than I'd like to admit. Since my pension never materialized—"

That got a small growl from Osric. The army had a policy whereby, if someone died, the money set aside for their pension would be fed back into the army's coffers. What they neglected to mention was that they had done so for the living soldiers as well, so anyone lucky enough to live through the war did not receive their promised reward.

Torin went on. "—I've had to find work here and there. It hasn't been easy—there are far too many former soldiers and not nearly enough things for them to do."

"We've taken on several as guardsme—"

Osric was interrupted by a knock at the door. Then it opened to reveal the sergeant, Newcastle. "Sorry to interrupt, Captain, but I'm afraid Sir Gevlin needs to see you right away. Says it's urgent."

Standing up, Osric scowled deeply. "Very well. My apologies, ban Wyvald, but one of the first things I learned after I accepted this job from Lord Albin was that, when someone with the prefix 'Sir' has a request, it must be fulfilled immediately. Where are you staying?"

"The Flying Unicorn Inn—it's right next to the Stone Kobold. That was why I was drinking there, in fact."

"Why don't we meet for drinks at the Old Ball and Chain tomorrow night? We can catch up in a more civilized setting."

Torin grinned. "I would like that very much, Captain."

Osric tilted his head. "And shave, will you please? Your face looks like a ravaged forest."

As they exited Osric's office, Torin said, "I was thinking of growing a beard, actually."

"Well, make up your mind one way or the other, you look ridiculous."

"Says the man who always has stubble."

Rubbing his slightly hairy chin, Osric said, "Yes, but on me it works."

With that, Osric left through the west-wall door at top speed. Torin made his way toward that door more slowly, but Newcastle grabbed his shoulder.

"Yes?" Torin asked.

Newcastle removed the hand quickly from the shoulder. "You served with the captain?"

Torin nodded.

"Hmp. You should come by more often. He usually ain't that—that *human*."

IAIAN

Danthres was striding ahead of Iaian as they walked out of the Stone Kobold. One of the other bartenders recognized the description of the person whom Kort said killed Gava. It was a tall, skinny human with a large, hooked nose. They were now headed to where the bartender thought the man—whose name was Camrin—lived.

At Iaian's muttering, she stopped and turned around to face him. "What's ridiculous?"

"Besides your face?" He added a grin to make it look like he was kidding.

"Iaian, I'm perfectly happy to run you through and claim that some random person did it before I could stop them."

"Look, it's just not fair, okay? When I signed onto the guard thirteen years ago, it was simple. Sure, there was a shit-ton of crime, but it was all committed by morons. Now, though, the morons get caught, and most of 'em don't bother, 'cause the Castle Guard's all for maintaining law and order in the demesne." He said that last with as much sarcasm and bitterness as he could muster—a considerable amount, all things considered, as he was pretty well pissed off at the moment.

Danthres just stared at him with that really ugly face of hers. "And how is this a problem, exactly?"

"Because now the only people committing crimes are really smart people, and they're damn near impossible to catch. Take this murder— used to be, someone wanted to kill a bartender, they'd just kill her in front of everyone. Now, though, everyone's worried about getting caught by us, so they start a brawl to hide what they did and make it damn near impossible to find them. If there hadn't happened to be a wizard in the Kobold, we'd be shit outta luck. Wasn't so bad before, when Brisban was in charge, but now, with Osric? It's impossible to do police work."

"You mean impossible to take bribes."

"I don't know what you're talking about." He started walking again.

"You really think I don't know?" Danthres called after him.

"What I really think is that you're another one of Osric's holier-than-thou shitbrains who think that they're above it all. That's not how this city-state works, and it never has been."

With her ridiculously long legs, Danthres caught up to him quickly. "How city-states work is something that can change rather rapidly. Believe me, I know."

Iaian had no idea what that meant, and didn't care enough to ask. It had to do with whatever Danthres's past was, and Iaian found that that subject was very low on the list of things he cared about.

So he just kept walking.

They arrived at a boarding house where the bartender at the Stone Kobold was fairly certain Camrin lived. After knocking on the door, it opened to reveal a wizened old woman in a battered housecoat and wearing a kerchief over her hair. "Whaddaya want?"

"We're with the Cliff's End Castle Guard, ma'am," Iaian said.

"Yeah, I can *see* that, y'idjit. I ain't blind, y'know. Whaddya *want*?"

"Is there a man named Camrin living here?"

"S'what if there is?"

Iaian sighed. "*If* there is, we need to talk to him."

"An' if he ain't, you don't need t'talk t'him, that it?"

Whirling to give Danthres a "see?" expression, he then said, "Ma'am, if you could just tell us where Camrin is, so we can talk to him."

"That ain't whatcha said. Should say whatcha mean."

Danthres, Iaian noticed, was walking around to the other side of the boarding house. Iaian started trying to figure out how he was going to approach Osric about requesting to be put back with Linder—he'd been in the Guard as long as Iaian, and he knew how the job was done, dammit, including not abandoning your partner while he's questioning a crazy old woman—while he slowly said to the woman, "Look, ma'am, I'm trying to be patient, but if you don't just tell me if Camrin lives here or not, I'm gonna have to arrest you."

"I ain't done nothin'."

"No, you haven't—including answering my question. So tell me, right here right now —"

He was interrupted by a male voice screaming, "Oooof! Let go'a me you crazy bitch! Aaaaaaaaah!"

It was coming from around the corner, where Danthres had wandered to. Running in the direction of the shouting, Iaian turned to see his new partner kneeling on the back of a skinny human with a hook nose, having wrenched his arm behind his back.

Danthres looked up at him. "Want to help me arrest this shitbrain?"

Before Iaian could reply, Camrin cried out, "Whatcha arrestin' me for? I didn't do nothin'!"

"You killed Gava," Danthres said.

"I don't know nobody named Gava!"

She got to her feet, pulling Camrin up as well. "The bartender at the Stone Kobold."

"Ow! Is *that* what that bitch's name was? Huh. Bad enough she wouldn't sleep with me, but then she called me ugly."

Iaian rolled his eyes. "Hate to break this to you, chuckles, but you *are* ugly." Then he looked at Danthres. "How'd you know he'd be back here?"

"The woman had the same type of nose that Kort told us the killer did, so I thought she might be related to him—probably his mother. And she was obviously stalling so he could get away. So while you talked to her, I came around back, and sure enough, our murderer was climbing out a window."

The woman in the housecoat finally came around the corner and started screaming. "That's my boy! Y'can't take my boy away!"

"Shut up, lady," Iaian said, "or we'll keep you together by throwin' you *both* in the hole."

They led Camrin down the road toward Meerka Way. "You know, Iaian," Danthres said, "given that this imbecile just confessed to murder without a thought, and given that you fell for his mother's obvious delaying tactic, perhaps you should consider that the criminals aren't getting smarter, but that you're getting stupider."

Iaian just seethed, more determined than ever to ask for a new partner.

As they turned onto Meerka Way, Dru, a guard from Dragon approached them. "Lieutenants, I'm glad I found you!"

"What is it, Dru?"

"We got a message to find you two—there's been a murder down Alfar's Way. A wizard named Finnert got his throat cut right in front of his shop."

Iaian sighed. "We *got* a case."

Dru grinned. "Yeah, Sergeant Newcastle said you might say that, and he said to tell you that Cap'n Osric wanted you two on it. I can take your prisoner, put him in the hole till you're done."

Danthres practically threw Camrin at Dru. "Take him. C'mon, Iaian."

She strode up Meerka Way toward the intersection with Alfar's. Grumbling, Iaian followed her. "Who put the gargoyle up your ass?"

"It's a *wizard*. We need to solve this one quickly." Danthres sounded almost reverent.

"Have you ever even *met* a wizard?"

That earned Iaian one of Danthres's typical stares of annoyance, thrown over her shoulder as he struggled to catch up with her. "Just the one in the Stone Kobold yesterday. I've never really moved in the same circles," she added with a tone of bitterness.

"Trust me, they ain't exactly the paragons of virtue they pretend to be."

"As if *you'd* know," she said dismissively.

"Fine, ignore my years of experience."

"Gladly."

Iaian sighed again. Danthres had mastered the art of sarcasm, so he knew that she was not employing it just then.

They saw the crowd gathered in front of Finnert's Magick Shop more easily than they could see the shop itself. Iaian noted several guards from Dragon keeping people away from the area right in front of the store.

"What've we got?" Danthres asked.

The oldest of the guards, whom Iaian recognized as a lifer named Mannit, said, "Danthres? Mitre's left thumb, when'd *you* get promoted?"

Danthres then did something Iaian had never seen her do: smile. "Six months back. I see they finally put you on days."

"Yeah, thought I'd see the sun every once in a while. Not that you can see it with all the damn buildings. Anyhow, can you take a look at this stiff so we can get him off the street?"

Iaian had taken advantage of his partner's reminisce to look at the body. It was an older human, thick beard, silver-and-black hair, wearing the usual robes that wizards wore. His neck was sliced open, dried blood near the wound.

"You can get him off the street now," Iaian said. "This ain't the crime scene."

"What?" Danthres asked snappishly.

He pointed at the body. "His throat was cut. There should be blood everywhere, but there isn't. Someone dumped the body here."

Danthres turned to Mannit without even acknowledging that Iaian was right, which pissed him off more than it probably should have. "This is Finnert?"

Mannit nodded. "He owned the place, and his clerk found him just lyin' there on the street when he came out to close up."

"All right. Can you talk to these people, see if any of them saw anything, and get a detail to take the body to the shop? And keep that clerk around."

"Right." Mannit moved off to give instructions to the other guards to take care of that. Iaian didn't envy whoever had to carry Finnert's body to the cave outside the Cliff's End city limits — that was where bodies were kept and generally incinerated, unless someone had specific instructions on how to dispose of their remains otherwise. Visiting there was Iaian's least favorite duty.

Looking over at Danthres, he amended that to second least favorite.

"Let's go inside," she said.

"Why didn't I think of that?"

"Are you always this disagreeable, or only when you have women partners?" Danthres asked.

"You're one to talk."

They went inside the small shop. It was a fairly standard setup: shelves lined with potions and scrolls and such on the walls of either side, a few stands with other items dotting the floor, and a desk in the back behind which the clerk stood. Behind that desk was an entryway to a rear room that probably included offices and storage.

"Surprised the killer left the robes on," Iaian muttered.

"What do you mean?"

"Well, wizards are always wearing those stupid robes."

"They're not stupid," Danthres said defensively. "They wear those robes for the same reason that we wear armor."

Iaian snorted. "We wear armor to protect ourselves from the crazies."

Danthres snarled. "Why we wear *decorated* armor, then. Plain armor would protect us, but our cloaks indicate our rank and the shields on our chests and cloaks signify our assignment. The robes let everyone know that they're wizards."

"Yeah, like going around shooting fireballs and turning people into newts doesn't do the trick." He stared at his partner. "I'm not seeing any sign of a struggle or any blood."

Nodding, Danthres said, "We should check the back."

"No!"

Whirling around at that voice behind them, Iaian saw another older human in blue robes, though he had no beard and darker skin.

"Who the hell are you, and what're you doin' in our crime scene?"

Danthres shot Iaian a look. "Please excuse my partner, sir—he takes himself a little too seriously. I assume you're here as a representative of the Brotherhood of Wizards?"

"Yes. I am Myk Dourti, and you may not enter the rear room of this shop. There are things back there that you are not fit to see."

"One'a yours was killed," Iaian said, "and we gotta find out what happened."

"Actually, you do not. This is now Brotherhood business. You will leave this shop at once, and inform your thugs not to touch Finnert's body."

Danthres moved forward. "I'm sorry, Mr. Dourti, but I'm afraid that, for once, my partner is right. When a body falls in Cliff's End, the Castle Guard's mandate is to investigate."

Dourti folded his arms over his robed chest. "Not when the body belongs to the Brotherhood. You will remove yourself from this site or I will remove you."

"Look," Iaian started—

—and the next thing he knew, there was a bright light, and when it dimmed, he was in the squadroom blinking spots out of his eyes.

Danthres was standing next to him, while Nael and Karistan both dropped the scrolls that they were carrying over to Ep in shock.

Suddenly, Danthres turned a bit green, then doubled over and threw up on the floor.

Osric came in from the kitchen, a pastry in his hand, Newcastle right behind him. "What the hell just happened? I thought you two were on the wizard murder."

"We were," Iaian said, watching with amusement as Danthres wretched. "The Brotherhood took us off it."

"What does that mean, exactly?" Osric asked in a low, dangerous tone.

Iaian just threw his hands up. "Take it up with Myk Dourti. He's the Stupidhood of Wizards rep that teleported us here."

Shaking his head, Osric yelled, "Dammit!"

"Cap'n, can I talk to you for a sec?"

Osric nodded, then turned to Newcastle. "Make Tresyllione some tea, would you, please? Teleport Spells tend to be hard on the stomach. And get someone to clean that up."

"Good thing I've drunk my belly into submission," Iaian said with a grin.

Iaian then followed Osric into his office and closed the door. "What do you want, Iaian?"

"A new partner. Or better yet, my old partner."

"Tresyllione needs someone to work with. Everyone else has quit, or refused to be paired up with her. You're my last resort."

"Fine, then I quit."

Osric regarded Iaian quizzically. "Really? You can barely do *this* job, Iaian, what makes you think you'll be able to do another one at your age?"

"I ain't *that* old." Iaian shook his head. "You're right, I don't want to quit, but I can't take workin' with that bitch. Look, I'll help finish off the Gava murder, but that's it. I'm done with her. I don't know why the hell you promoted her."

"Because if she can get her attitude in check, she'll be the best detective in that squadroom."

"Yeah, well, you must see a lot more with one eye than I can with two, 'cause all I'm seein' is the attitude."

Osric shook his head. "Fine, finish Gava, and then you're back with Linder. With Quane quitting, I need to bring in someone new in any case."

"You partner the new guy with her, they won't stick around much longer'n Quane did, you ask me."

His scowl deepening, Osric said, "I don't recall asking you, Iaian. In fact, what I asked you was to partner with Tresyllione, which you couldn't manage for more than a day."

"Cap'n—"

"Get out of my office." Osric pulled out his dagger and started sharpening it.

Knowing better than to even try talking to the captain when he was in a sharpen-his-dagger mood, Iaian got up and left.

He wondered if he'd be able to stand another twelve years of this shit.

NEWCASTLE

BEL NEWCASTLE RUBBED HIS JAW, TRYING TO IGNORE THE ACHE THAT CUT through his mouth. He knew he should have gone to a healer, but it wasn't *that* bad at first, and he figured it would get better in time. Instead, it got worse, and now his wife Rhi was bugging him to see a healer already, but he didn't really have time, and besides, the place would fall apart without him.

At least, that was what he kept telling himself. It wasn't really so much the case anymore. When Brisban was the captain, the office was a disorderly mess, but Osric had brought his military efficiency to the running of the Castle Guard. Newcastle appreciated it, he really did, especially since it made his life easier. He didn't move as fast as he used to since he started having problems with his knees, after all.

Today he'd been busy, processing the paperwork on poor Quane's departure. Newcastle hadn't really expected the boy to be able to handle being a detective, and it was his considered opinion that it had just been dumb luck that enabled Quane to figure out who hijacked that boat.

But nobody ever listened to Newcastle's opinions. They just had him handle the paperwork and keep track of assignments and fetch tea for the detectives when wizards hit them with Teleport Spells that made them throw up. He was okay with that.

Besides, two more years, and he could retire with a full pension. Then maybe he could take Rhi on that cruise.

Danthres and Iaian came into the squadroom from one of the interview rooms just as he filed the last of Quane's paperwork with Ep. The poor kid hadn't even been in the Guard long enough to earn any kind of pension, so he was going out into Cliff's End with nothing but whatever he'd saved. He made a mental note to check up on the boy, which he always did when someone left the Guard. Some day, he'd *actually* check up on someone . . .

"Camrin gave up his accomplices," Danthres said. "He hired a dwarf and a human to start the fight so he could kill Gava." She shook her head. "He wasn't even sorry that he killed her."

"Yeah, well, whaddaya expect? We were at war with the Elf Queen for so long, nobody thinks life means nothin'."

"What a ridiculous statement."

"Kiss my ass."

Newcastle shook his head. "Do you two do nothing but argue?"

Iaian grinned. "Not anymore. As of this confession, I'm done with you, Danthres."

"Except for the paperwork," Newcastle said quickly.

"Yeah, yeah."

Sighing, Newcastle went over to the kitchen to see if there were any pastries left. Rhi was more likely to convince him to go to the healer than Iaian was to get his paperwork done in a timely manner.

Osric then stuck his head out of his office and bellowed, "Newcastle! My office!"

Again, Newcastle sighed. It was never good when the captain bellowed your name followed by "My office!" It usually meant an unpleasant conversation. Of course, at least Osric was good enough to give you fair warning that it was going to be unpleasant. Brisban never gave any indication that he was going to tear you a new one until after you were already in the room.

To Newcastle's relief, Osric didn't close the door, so it wasn't going to be *that* kind of talk. Once he sat down in his chair, and Newcastle parked himself in the guest chair, the captain said, "We need to bring in a new detective."

Newcastle nodded, not sure where Osric was going with this.

"The problem," the captain continued as he took out his dagger, "is that nobody's ready yet. There are some promising guards, but nobody who's as ready as Sergeant Lorenz thought Quane was, and he couldn't handle it, either."

Speaking very tentatively, Newcastle asked, "Can I make a suggestion?"

"That's why I brought you in here, Newcastle." Osric started sharpening his dagger, which did nothing to alter Newcastle's tentativeness.

"I think we should just let Danthres work on her own. She—"

"No."

Newcastle frowned. "Sir, she —"

"No. You can't solve crimes by yourself. You let yourself get caught up in a pet theory and pursue it to the detriment of other possibilities. That's too easy to do if you're working alone. Plus, the interviewing of witnesses and suspects takes twice the time with one detective." He shook his head. "Besides, if Danthres has to deal with people by herself, either she or the people she deals with or both will be dead before too long. Someone needs to be a calming influence on her."

"I'm not sure that's entirely possible, sir."

"Yes, but we have to at least —"

Whatever it was they had to do, Newcastle would never know, as they were interrupted by a bright light that heralded the sudden appearance of an older human in their midst, wearing blue robes, and carrying a stern expression. Newcastle had to blink spots away from his eyes after the light burst.

"Captain Osric, the Brotherhood of Wizards requires your assistance."

Osric rose to his feet, pointing his dagger at the wizard. "The Brotherhood of Wizards should keep out of my damned office when I'm having a meeting."

"Your meeting can wait," the wizard said. "I am Myk Dourti, the representative for the Brotherhood for this region."

"I'm glad you're here," Osric said with what Newcastle could tell was utterly false sincerity. "Lord Albin wishes to speak to you about the manner in which you summarily dismissed the officers in his Castle Guard."

"There is no time for such trivialities."

"I doubt, sir," and now Osric was waving the dagger about, "that Lord Albin considers it trivial. I doubt King Marcus and Queen Marta would, either."

"It is trivial by comparison to this: another wizard has been killed. And — against, I might add, my own recommendation — the Brotherhood has requested that your Castle Guard investigate this murder, as it appears to have been committed by the same perpetrator as Finnert. This second wizard also owned a shop, his throat was also cut, and his body was also left in front of it."

"Does that mean you'll permit us to *properly* investigate Finnert's murder as well?"

Dourti let out a very long sigh. "Yes, we will permit your detectives to examine Finnert's shop—however it must be supervised by the new manager, who has purchased the location from the Brotherhood following Finnert's death."

"That's fine. I'll have Lieutenant Tresyllione—"

"No."

Osric scowled. "Excuse me?"

"Neither Lieutenant Tresyllione nor Lieutenant Iaian may be the lead investigator in the case. We have examined their records, and the former is too inexperienced, the latter with a troubling record. We are not enthralled with Lieutenants Karistan or Nael, either, and Lieutenant Linder's casework also leaves quite a bit to be desired."

Newcastle winced. He had just listed all the detectives.

"As it happens, we have a new hire in the squad, who is starting tomorrow," Osric said.

Somehow, Newcastle managed to restrain himself from gaping at his captain. Bluffing a wizard could not possibly have been a good idea.

"We will need to examine this man's record."

"He doesn't have one—"

Dourti frowned, and started to speak, but Osric kept going.

"—in Cliff's End. He served with me in the army when we fought the Elf Queen, and he helped me develop the strategy that won the day at the Nemerian Wastes."

At that, Dourti blinked. "He was your aide?"

"Absolutely. The finest soldier who served under me, with one of the keenest minds I've ever encountered. He will handle the investigation."

"What is this guard's name?"

"Lieutenant Torin ban Wyvald."

"From Myverin?"

"Yes."

Dourti nodded approvingly. "Very well. If he's from Myverin, he must be a very thoughtful individual. We have preserved the body and the shop with a Stasis Spell, which will only last a day. It's Kort's Spell Emporium on Boulder Pass."

Newcastle blinked. "The wizard who died is Tam Kort?"

Dourti stared at Newcastle as if only noticing he was even in the room for the first time. "Yes. Why?"

"He was a witness in a recent case we had," Newcastle said quietly. "The murder of a woman named Gava in the Stone Kobold."

A look of distaste came over Dourti at that. "Yes, Kort was fond of — of such establishments. I always thought he'd be killed in one of them. I never imagined he would instead be killed in his own shop." He turned to Osric. "Your Lieutenant ban Wyvald will report to the shop first thing in the morning?"

Osric nodded. "Absolutely."

"Good." With that, Dourti gestured and disappeared in a flash of light.

Before Osric could say anything, Newcastle said, "I'll send someone to fetch Mr. ban Wyvald right away."

"He's staying at the Flying Unicorn."

Newcastle nodded, and got to his feet even as Osric sat down and went back to sharpening his dagger. He hesitated before moving to the door. "Captain — what if ban Wyvald doesn't take the job?"

"He'll take it." Osric spoke with confidence.

"What if he *does* take it?"

Now Osric frowned. "I beg your pardon?"

"Every detective in here came up through the ranks. They may resent someone being given a lieutenant's cloak without earning it."

Osric stood back up, pointing at Newcastle with his dagger. "Torin ban Wyvald was one of the only reasons why we even survived the Nemerian Wastes. I exaggerated to Dourti about his helping with strategy there, because I needed to convince him. But ban Wyvald's quick thinking and observational abilities were a big part of why the 17th lived through that winter. Trust me, he's done his time in the trenches — just not the trenches *here*."

"I understand, Captain, but — "

After Newcastle's hesitation went on for a second, Osric prompted him: "But what?"

"I'm not the one you have to convince, sir."

Instead of responding, Osric just sat back down and picked up the sharpening stone.

Which, Newcastle figured, was answer enough.

Rubbing his jaw, he went out into the squadroom on aching knees to find someone to fetch their new detective.

DANTHRES

THE LAST THING DANTHRES EXPECTED TO SEE WHEN SHE WALKED INTO THE squadroom to start her shift was the primary witness in the Gava murder.

She especially didn't expect to see him wearing Guard armor with a gryphon crest and wearing a brown cloak. He was seated at Quane's old desk. Nobody else was in the squadroom, which wasn't much of a surprise. The shift was just starting, and the only detective other than Danthres who had ever come in on time in the past six months was Quane.

Staring at Torin ban Wyvald, she said without preamble, "You do know that impersonating a guard is a crime in this city-state, yes?"

Rising from the chair, ban Wyvald smiled. "A pleasure to see you again as well, Lieutenant Tresyllione."

Osric and Newcastle came in from the former's office. "Ah, good, Tresyllione, you're here. I believe you've already met your new partner."

Danthres's gray eyes widened. She didn't even understand what ban Wyvald was doing in Guard armor, and now she was supposed to be partnered with him?

Speaking slowly, she said, "I've met Mr. ban Wyvald, yes, as a witness in a case that hasn't even gone before the magistrate."

"And he still will be." Osric walked toward the two of them. "Only he'll be testifying as a lieutenant in the Castle Guard, which should make him a much more impressive witness."

While Danthres had to concede that the magistrate tended to put more stock in statements made by the Castle Guard and the nobility than he did ordinary citizens of the demesne, it didn't explain what this idiot was doing as a lieutenant. "Is this some kind of joke?"

Osric glared at her with his one good eye. "Have you ever known me to joke, Tresyllione?"

"No, sir," Danthres said. "Your humorlessness is legendary."

That prompted a snort from ban Wyvald.

The captain turned his glare to Torin, and then said, "You two are to report to Kort's Spell Emporium on Boulder Pass."

Ban Wyvald stood, and immediately winced.

With a grin, Danthres asked, "The boots, right?"

"Yes." He sounded surprised.

"It usually takes at least a month to break the damn things in. Not that I expect you to last that long."

"Your confidence is touching."

"The shop," Osric said, "and Kort's body are being preserved with a Stasis Spell by the Brotherhood until you two arrive."

Both Danthres and her new partner's jaws dropped at that. The latter said, "Kort is dead?"

Nodding, Osric said, "His throat was cut, same as Finnert. This time the Brotherhood has specifically asked for our help."

Danthres couldn't believe it. One wizard being killed by so mundane a manner as having his throat cut was difficult to credit—two was almost impossible.

Then Osric said, "Also, ban Wyvald is to be the lead investigator on this—at least whenever you're in the presence of any mages."

"What!?" Now Danthres was convinced that this *had* to be a joke.

Holding up a hand, Osric sounded aggravated when he explained. "It was the only way to get the Brotherhood to agree to an investigation at all. They were not happy with your behavior at Finnert's murder scene, nor with how much experience—"

"What's wrong with my experience?" Danthres blurted out. She wasn't surprised that a wizard would think poorly of her behavior at the scene, though the Brotherhood should have had more of an issue with Iaian. Then again, at least she was on the case, which Iaian wasn't, so she supposed that counted for something.

"The issue with your experience is that there's not enough of it."

She pointed at ban Wyvald. "It's a year-and-a-half more than he's had."

"She has a point, sir," ban Wyvald said. "I think it would make more sense—"

Osric's scowl was almost glowing. "I can assure both of you that right now I have a very minimal interest in what either of you think. Now get to Boulder Pass."

Danthres was unhappy, but based on Osric's attitude, this was as much politics as anything. However, she did have one last question. "Will we also be able to look at Finnert's shop?"

Nodding, Osric said, "The shop is remaining closed and two guards from Dragon are keeping an eye on it until you get there. But go to Kort's first. Any questions? No? Good." With that, Osric turned to go back into his office.

With a sigh, Danthres turned to leave, not bothering to see if ban Wyvald came with her.

As it happened, he did, though he walked gingerly thanks to his new boots. "I see Osric is still pretending to ask if anyone has any questions without actually allowing time to ask them. He used to do that in the army as well."

Not looking at her partner, she said, "Don't even try to make small talk with me. I don't care to get to know you, and I'm still not sure I entirely trust you."

"Whyever not?" He sounded surprised at that.

Now she did look at him. "You need to ask that? You were my prime suspect in Gava's murder until Camrin confessed, and I'm still not entirely convinced that you didn't have something to do with it."

"Why is that?" he asked defensively.

Smiling wryly as they exited through the portcullis, Danthres said, "Because in the year and a half I've been with the Guard, I have never had a single witness provide as much detail about a crime as you did who wasn't intimately involved with the crime."

Shrugging, ban Wyvald said, "I was trained to be observant."

"In Myverin?"

"Yes."

"I always believed that place to be a myth."

At that, ban Wyvald grinned. "That puts you in company with the vast majority of the people I've met outside Myverin."

Staring at his smile, Danthres shook her head. "On the other hand, it probably is everything people say it is, if you came from there with such perfect teeth."

Laughing, ban Wyvald said, "Indeed. Listen, Lieutenant, I understand that you do not wish me to be here. I must confess to being rather stunned that Osric offered me the job. But I was hardly in a position to decline the opportunity."

"Oh, I don't blame you for taking the job. Worry not, though, I'm sure I'll find plenty to blame you for as we proceed. Which won't be for long."

"That's the second time you've said that. What make you think I won't last?"

"Six months of experience. I'm hoping that, once you—Osric's pet soldier—run screaming from the castle, the captain will finally see the wisdom of allowing me to work alone."

They were proceeding down Meerka Way, moving past the mansions of Unicorn Precinct. "I'm hardly Osric's pet anything," ban Wyvald said. "And you might be underestimating me."

Danthres would have expected him to be more exasperated or annoyed or angry—but no, he was speaking in the same pleasant tone he'd been using every time she talked to him. It was starting to seriously piss her off.

She whirled on him. "You're not a detective. You're not even a member of the Guard. You're a friend of the captain who got lucky, and it is my considered opinion that you'll wash out of here faster than Quane did—and Quane was the biggest idiot I've ever been partnered with. This job is *important*, ban Wyvald—we speak for people who can't speak for themselves."

And then she turned and continued to stride down Meerka Way.

"Interesting," ban Wyvald said. He was able to keep up with her stride, which she found annoying. "I hadn't really thought about the job in that way. But then, I've had very little time to think of it at all, as Osric came to me last night and had me come to the castle and be fitted for this ill-fitting armor."

Danthres couldn't help but smile at that. It had taken Lady Meerka's armorers seven tries to get hers to fit properly.

Ban Wyvald continued: "I came to Cliff's End because I had nowhere else to go. I went to Osric simply because he was someone I knew. I never imagined he'd offer me a job."

For a moment, Danthres was bitterly amused that ban Wyvald came to Cliff's End for the same reason she did. But the moment passed, as most people came here for that reason. They were neither of them unique in that.

They passed Oak Way, and ban Wyvald then asked, "We're now in Dragon Precinct, yes?"

"Yes," Danthres said simply. The conversation was only irritating her more, and she was at the point where she wanted to keep it brief.

They turned onto Boulder Pass. A crowd was gathered near the magick shop, but it was a smaller one than what she saw around Finnert's place. Since Kort's was surrounded by a glowing blue sphere, Danthres couldn't bring herself to be overly shocked that people were gaping.

As soon as they approached, the same wizard who'd kicked them out of Finnert's appeared suddenly in a flash of light. "About time you arrived," he said without preamble. "The spell was only going to last another hour." With a gesture, the blue sphere dissipated, prompting a gasp from the onlookers.

One of them stepped forward, moving close to Dourti. The wizard said, "Ah, good, you're here. This is Yan, he's the manager of the shop. He will handle whatever you need—I have other, more important, business to attend to." With that, he gestured and disappeared in a flash of light.

Danthres had been hoping the wizard would stick around. Disappointed, she turned to Yan, a dwarf wearing a bright yellow tunic that almost blinded Danthres. "Where's the body?"

"It was discovered on the street," the dwarf said, "though we removed it in short order."

She sighed. "You *really* shouldn't have done that. It will be a great deal more difficult to ascertain who killed Kort if his body's been moved."

However, ban Wyvald was peering at the dirt road—while the main thoroughfares of Cliff's End were cobblestone, side streets like this were still glorified pathways—and said, "It doesn't matter. This *isn't* where Kort was killed."

Danthres couldn't believe this. "Excuse me?"

Ignoring her, ban Wyvald looked at Yan, pointing at a spot in the dirt. "This is where you found the body, yes?"

Sounding impressed, Yan said, "Yes, Lieutenant, that is precisely where his body was. How are you aware of that?"

"There's a body-shaped impression in the dirt. The impression is exactly the same size as a person's body, without any variance—which means he didn't fall, as that usually leaves an impression that does not perfectly conform to a person's shape. When people fall, they twitch or thrash about or try to stop their fall, or do something else to pervert the shape of the impression."

After blinking, Danthres stared down at where ban Wyvald was pointing. It just looked like dirt to her.

"Also," he added, "there's only one set of footprints between the door and here, heading to and from, and there's also only a little bit of blood on the ground. The body was placed here after Kort was killed. If, as you say, his throat was cut, had he been murdered on this pass, there would be far more blood."

Now Danthres rolled her eyes. She was almost starting to respect ban Wyvald's observations, but now he was just parroting Iaian. "You don't know that."

"I do, actually. Believe me, I've seen more than my share of cut throats in my time — the blood tends to spray." He turned to Yan. "May we see the inside of the shop, please?"

Yan nodded and walked toward the shop's entrance. "Please come with me." He glanced up at Danthres. "You must feel very fortunate to have so knowledgeable a partner."

Danthres didn't even dignify that with a response. When she caught ban Wyvald smiling, she glowered at him.

However, the inside of the shop told them nothing more than Finnert's did. It had a similar arrangement to the other one, except the desk was along the side wall, running the length of the shop, with a doorway covered in beads leading to the rear storage.

This time, Danthres went into the rear while ban Wyvald continued to look fruitlessly at the main floor.

The back was filled with floor-to-ceiling shelves filled to bursting with boxes, scrolls, jars, and more. She glanced at something in one of the jars that looked really disgusting, and decided not to peer at it too closely.

Besides, the door that went to the area behind the shop caught her eye: it was covered in blood.

Leaning back, she cried out, "Ban Wyvald!"

He came in a moment later. "What is it?"

She pointed at the door.

"Ah. Yes. As I said, cut throats tend to spray blood."

"But everything's in place, neatly on the shelves." Danthres shook her head.

"There's no indication that there was any kind of struggle. I can't imagine that a wizard would just *let* someone cut his throat."

"Indeed." Then ban Wyvald chuckled. "A pity, really."

"What is?" Danthres was confused, as she found nothing humorous about anything that had happened since she walked into the squadroom this morning.

"Under other circumstances, we could ask Kort to cast the Inanimate Residue Spell that would peel back the scene. If Dourti ever deigns to speak to us again, perhaps we can ask him."

"Perhaps." Danthres shuddered at the notion. She'd already dealt with wizards more in the last week than she ever expected to in her entire life. Mages did not consort with the likes of her, after all. But then, wizards didn't usually get killed, either. "I believe we shall speak to him again, but until then, we've learned all we can from this scene."

"Have we? I don't see that we've learned much of anything beyond the fact that Kort was killed here and taken outside."

Now Danthres grinned, looking forward to showing this neophyte how detective work was done. "We know that he was killed by someone he knew and trusted. It's not possible for a wizard to be caught unawares by a stranger, so he must have allowed his killer to get very close to him. The killer then wanted everyone to know that he'd killed a wizard, so he left the body outside in front of the wizard's shop where it was guaranteed to be seen in very short order. Our killer is someone who is bold, a friend to both victims, and who has something to gain by their very public deaths."

Nodding, ban Wyvald said, "Yes, I can see that. Thank you."

To Danthres's annoyance, he sounded completely sincere.

Grumbling, she turned on Yan. "We need to investigate the other store, but we may need to come back here, so do not open up just yet." Glancing at ban Wyvald, she said, "We'll need to contact the manager of Finnert's store."

"Oh, that's easy enough," Yan said. "I'm the manager of both stores."

Danthres whirled on him. "Really? When did that happen?"

"Just last week, actually. Why?"

YAN

Yan had been sitting in the interview room for what seemed like hours. He couldn't hear the timechimes in here, and there were no windows, so he had no idea how long it had really been.

All he'd said was that he was the manager of both stores. Then they took him to Finnert's store, and then they had the guards who were watching Finnert's take him back to the castle under arrest!

That wouldn't have been so bad, but then they put him in this damn room. The only illumination came from a lantern providing insufficient light, a table, three stools, and a door, which remained opened just a crack. Yan could hear voices and footfalls, though none of the former were distinct enough to make out actual words.

He dabbed the sweat that was beading off his high forehead. When those two lieutenants came in here, he was going to give them a piece of his mind, you could bet the house on that! He had been rehearsing the harangue he would give those two in his head for the last however-bloody-long he'd been in here, and once they showed up . . .

And then, finally, the pair of them came in, their cloaks swirling imperiously behind them as they walked through the door.

Opening his mouth and holding up a finger, Yan promptly forgot what he was going to say to the two of them.

"Our apologies," said the male detective while Yan sat there stupidly with his mouth open, "but we needed to check on some things before we could speak to you."

"Check on what things?" Yan's voice came out as a croak. He'd been hoping to come across as aggrieved, and instead he sounded like he'd just woken up.

The ugly female detective said, "We needed to confirm a few things with the records office in the castle's other wing and speak to some people."

"What people?" Yan really hoped they didn't talk to his wife.

Unfortunately, the woman didn't answer the question. "Imagine our surprise to learn that you were the one who inherited ownership of *both* shops."

Yan swallowed. "Yeah, I know that. You coulda just asked me."

"Really?" The woman sounded amazed. "You would have volunteered information that gives you an excellent reason to have killed Kort and Finnert?"

"Are you nuts? Why would I want to kill those two?"

The man smiled, showing teeth so nice, Yan thought *he* might be a wizard. "I believe Lieutenant Tresyllione just explained that."

"You see," the woman—Tresyllione—said, "you've gone from being the manager of one shop to the manager of two shops to the owner of two shops. In my experience, the owner makes more money than the manager."

Yan shook his head. "Yeah, well, there's some shit that money can't buy. I'm already lookin' to sell."

Tresyllione blinked. "What?"

"Which shop are you selling?" the red-haired man asked.

"Both." Yan shuddered. "I only been at this a day and I already can't take the nonsense from the damn Brotherhood. They got rules, they got regulations, and for Xinf's sake, have they got paperwork. I can barely *write* in Common, and they're asking me to fill out all these scrolls with requests and permissions and work orders, and I just can't *take* it! Worst thing that ever happened to me was those mages getting killed."

The man shook his head. "It seems I was wrong about him."

After staring daggers at her partner for reasons Yan wasn't too clear on, Tresyllione turned to Yan. "Who are you selling to?"

"I ain't sold it yet," he said with a sigh. "If you know anybody who wants to buy a shop or two, send 'em my way, willya? There's only three stores sellin' those new Bags of Holding, and I own two of 'em."

"You know, it's easy for you to *say* that you wish to sell the stores," Tresyllione said, "but it's been my experience that murderers lie. Besides, we also spoke to your wife."

Yan winced.

Tresyllione continued: "She told us that you weren't home when the murders took place. And—"

The other detective interrupted. "The murders were also committed—" Then he realized what he'd done. "My apologies, Lieutenant, please, go ahead."

"As Lieutenant ban Wyvald began to say," Tresyllione said, sounding a bit exasperated, "the murderers were committed in the shops when they were closed, by someone whom the victims knew and trusted."

"That perfectly describes you, doesn't it?" the man—ban Wyvald—said.

After giving another look to her partner, Tresyllione said, "I'm afraid we'll need to know where you were when the two wizards were killed."

Yan started fidgeting on the table. He really was hoping to avoid this.

But he couldn't get arrested for murder. That would get him hanged.

"Talk to Suzett," he said with a heavy sigh. "She runs a place on Sandy Brook Way. I been there pretty much every night the last month." He leaned back in his chair. "Myna's gonna kill me."

Ban Wyvald said, "Myna would be your wife?"

"Yeah." Yan frowned. "Hey, wait, you said you talked to her!"

Tresyllione grabbed ban Wyvald by the arm and led him out of the room, muttering, "Next time, keep your damned mouth shut."

Putting his head in his hands, Yan muttered to himself. Myna was *definitely* going to kill him. Still, better that than a death sentence.

Though not by much . . .

BONEEN

Boneen stared at the body of his old friend Javy Marta.

In his life, Boneen had only seen two dead wizards before today, and both of them died in their beds. Seeing Javy lying in front of his magick shop on Maple Path was the most repugnant sight he'd ever seen. His throat cut open, dried blood caked on the wound, and his body just—just *lying* there.

He looked up at the guard from Unicorn Precinct who'd responded initially to the call for help. "Have you ever noticed, young man, the major difference between a dead body and a living one?"

"Erm." The guard frowned, clearly confused. "One's dead and one's alive?"

Boneen sighed. "Dead bodies don't move at all. Living bodies move in so many subtle ways. The ironic part is that Javy here is the one who showed me that. His father died a while back. His father wasn't a wizard like we were, so he only lived a normal lifespan." He shook his head. "The funny thing is, I was the only other wizard there. None of the others could be bothered, not even the wizard Javy was apprenticed to. Never understood that. In fact—"

He cut himself off when he heard voices coming down Maple Path.

"You shouldn't have interrupted me."

"My apologies, but I had no idea you were going to continue speaking."

"And that idiotic 'and that's your wife?' question. I told you when we went in that we were going to lie about the wife."

"Actually, you said no such thing."

"I didn't?"

"No. I thought you *had* spoken to the wife while I was looking up the records."

"I don't believe—"

"Ah, hello," said the man, who had red hair. He and his companion, a hideous woman who was obviously half elf and half human, both wore guard armor with brown cloaks. Boneen had no idea what the cloak symbolized.

"I'm Lieutenant Danthres Tresyllione," the woman said. "We're with the Cliff's End Castle Guard, and we're here to investigate the murder."

After a sidelong glance at Tresyllione, the man said, "I'm Lieutenant Torin ban Wyvald. You found the body?"

"Yes. My name is Boneen. That's Javy Marta, and he and I were friends. We were meeting for lunch."

"You're also a wizard?" ban Wyvald asked.

Boneen nodded. "I didn't realize the Castle Guard had investigators—or that the Brotherhood would permit you to be involved."

"This is the third murder of a wizard in the last few days," ban Wyvald said.

"Hadn't you heard?" Tresyllione asked, sounding suspicious.

Shaking his head, Boneen said, "I've been vacationing in—well, it's hard to explain, exactly, but suffice it to say, I have not been anywhere nearby for the past month. I only came back to Barlin this morning, and used a Teleport Spell to meet up with Javy here in Cliff's End." He snorted. "He mentioned that he had some gossip about two other wizards who also apprenticed with the same . . ." He trailed off, as something horrible occurred to him. "Tell me, were the other two deaths Finnert and Tam Kort?"

Tresyllione frowned. "You know them?"

"Only by name. Javy, Finnert, and Kort all apprenticed with Myk Dourti about fifty years ago."

That got the two cloaked guards to exchange surprised glances. Tresyllione then looked at Boneen. "You're saying that all three of the victims apprenticed with the local representative of the Brotherhood?"

Boneen made a face. "When did they appoint that idiot to be the local representative?" He shook his head again. "Never mind, nothing those imbeciles do surprises me anymore. In any case, Lieutenants, I wish I could be of more service, but I attempted to cast a spell known as Inanimate Residue on the vicinity."

Nodding, ban Wyvald said, "We're familiar with the spell, yes. In fact, Kort cast one for us on an earlier case."

Tresyllione glared at ban Wyvald. "It wasn't for 'us,' you weren't—Oh, never mind."

"In any event," Boneen said quickly, not knowing nor caring what burr got in this pair's armor, "the spell was inconclusive, which means that some form of magick was involved."

Tresyllione stared at Boneen. "So does that mean a wizard killed him? That's insane!"

"It's *not* insane," Boneen said sadly, "though it's rare, especially these days. But no, that's not necessarily what happened. There are several types of magickal creatures that can affect the spell adversely, as can a store-bought spell."

"All right," Tresyllione said, "we need to look inside. Can you remain here, in case we have more questions?"

"Absolutely. I want to know who killed him." Boneen stomped toward the door, wanting to be there when the lieutenants looked around.

Inside, the shop looked pretty much the same as it did when Boneen had last been here—which was when Javy opened it. He'd rearranged things a bit, giving the potions more prominent shelf space near the desk, and having a door to the rear where there used to be beads.

The two detectives went into the back room while Boneen studied the inventory. All the usual items, including those ridiculous love potions that people kept buying even though they never worked the way the people buying them hoped they would.

He heard the two lieutenants muttering about blood through the door. Ignoring them, he looked around for the display for the Bags of Holding.

Frowning, he didn't see them.

Muttering a quick incantation, he cast a Search Spell to find the bags.

The spell revealed no such item anywhere inside the store—not even in the storage area.

"Lieutenants!" he cried out.

The two detectives poked their heads out from the back room. "What is it?" Tresyllione asked.

"The Bags of Holding aren't here."

They exchanged a look and then walked in. "Bags of Holding?" ban Wyvald asked.

"They're bags that are a portal to another dimension—they enable one to store considerably more than the bag's external capacity. It's only limited by what will fit through the mouth of the bag."

Tresyllione asked, "And Javy sold these?"

"The entire reason he and I were having lunch today was so he could show off the Bags of Holding. The magick required to make them work is incredibly difficult. Javy was very proud that they'd finally found a way to make it work."

"Who's 'they' in this context?" ban Wyvald asked.

"No idea." Boneen shrugged. "Javy just said he was working with other wizards on it. I didn't really care all that much, so I didn't ask. But he said they went on display last week." He opened his arms wide, as if to take in the entire shop. "So where are they?"

DANTHRES

Danthres stared at Torin ban Wyvald, and tried to come up with a way to get him to not join her in the interview room.

After the disaster with the dwarf, she wanted to just go it alone. While she'd only been a detective for half a year, she had developed a methodology, and ban Wyvald was completely spoiling it with his amateur idiocy.

Newcastle had given Quane's old desk, which was behind Danthres's, to ban Wyvald. He was looking over a scroll, and then turned around.

"Lieutenant Tresyllione, may I make a request?"

She blinked. "I suppose."

"I was wondering if I might interview Mr. Dourti alone."

Unable to help herself, Danthres burst out laughing. "Excuse me?"

"When I was in the army, I was one of the people in charge of interrogating prisoners. Over the years, I developed a methodology, and I'm afraid that your own interrogation methods are spoiling my own. And this amuses you?"

"You really think interrogating suspects is the same as interrogating prisoners of war?"

"Yes, actually. Both are inherently hostile, both are utterly uninterested in telling you anything, and both need to be tricked into revealing things they absolutely do not wish to reveal to someone who has the power of life and death over them."

That brought Danthres up short, as she had no clever retort for it.

From Osric's office came the captain's voice. "You'll both be interrogating Dourti."

With a sidelong glance at her partner, Danthres said to Osric, "That's a mistake, Captain. I hate to admit it, but ban Wyvald's right—except it should be me in there."

"It will be both of you, and that is final." Osric took a breath and walked over to the two of them. "I don't think you two understand the importance of your newfound partnership, so I'll explain it to you. You see, Lord Albin believes very strongly in the Guard, and he took a big risk hiring an outsider like me to run it. As a result, for the past ten months, he has meticulously read every single scroll that has gone through this squadroom to make sure I'm doing as good a job as he had hoped I would do when he hired me to replace Brisban."

Danthres had to resist the urge to spit. There were a lot of people in this world whom Danthres hated with every fibre of her being, but Brisban had always been second from the top of that list, surpassed only by her cousin Sicund. The happiest day of her life since arriving in Cliff's End was the day Brisban died.

Osric continued: "One of the things Lord Albin has noticed is the heavy turnover rate of people whose job description includes being your partner, Tresyllione. So ban Wyvald is your last chance. If you can't make it work with him, you're finished in the Guard."

Swallowing, Danthres said, "Captain, I—"

But Osric wasn't done. He turned his one-eyed gaze upon ban Wyvald. "As for you, you've been granted a very special privilege, bypassing the usual promotion structure because I firmly believe that you're the only person in all of Flingaria who can save this woman's job. And if you can't, you'll be back on the streets with her looking for work."

Nodding, ban Wyvald said, "I understand."

"I don't!" Danthres stood up. "I've done a damn good job of—"

"You've done a decent job, Tresyllione, yes. But if you close this case? You'll be wearing magick armor. Prior to Finnert's murder, there had been no reported unnatural deaths of a wizard that weren't during a time of war. The people who solve this will be well set, believe me."

Before Danthres could reply to that, a familiar voice sounded from the west-wall doorway. "Excuse me."

Whirling around, Danthres saw Myk Dourti.

"Welcome back, Mr. Dourti," Osric said in what Danthres recognized as his most insincere polite tone.

"I do not feel especially welcome. Why has this castle been warded against Teleport Spells?"

"My apologies," Osric said unapologetically, "but Lord Albin purchased the wards after a wizard presumptuously teleported into his castle unannounced."

Dourti scowled. "I was told you wished to speak to me about the murders. I have better things to do than waste time with the likes of you."

Danthres bridled, while ban Wyvald said, "We understand, sir, truly, but there are questions that we must pose if we are to learn who killed Kort, Javy, and Finnert."

"You yourself told Captain Osric," Danthres added, "that the Brotherhood wanted us to solve these murders."

With a sigh, Dourti said, "Very well. Pose your questions."

Indicating one of the interview rooms with a hand, ban Wyvald said, "If you'll come this way, sir. I believe it would be best if this conversation took place in private."

"That, Lieutenant, is the first thing you've said with which I've completely agreed." The wizard stormed past both detectives and went into the interview room.

Danthres exchanged a look with ban Wyvald, then looked at Osric.

The captain merely said, "Get it done, you two."

After Danthres walked in, ban Wyvald right behind her, she saw Dourti standing at the table. "Where, exactly, am I to sit in this dreadful room?"

Pointing to the stool behind the table, Danthres said, "Right there, Mr. Dourti. We just have a few questions, and I'm sure this will all be resolved very quickly."

"I hope so." Dourti sat on the indicated stool. "I have a great deal of *important* work to be doing."

"Fascinating," ban Wyvald said.

"Excuse me?" Dourti asked archly.

Shaking his head, ban Wyvald replied, "My apologies, but that's far from the first time you've indicated that there's work more important than this. And yet, we've spoken with several other wizards—"

Dourti stood up. "You did *what*?"

"Is there a problem?" Danthres was now leaning against the wall, and at the mage's outburst, she raised an eyebrow. "It is standard procedure for detectives to question people who knew the victim of a homicide."

"You should not have questioned members of the Brotherhood without checking with me first."

"Why?" ban Wyvald asked. "They are all private citizens who are free to speak to whomever they wish. None of them seemed to have an issue with discussing what they knew of Finnert, Kort, and Javy. Indeed, by talking to them, we were able to determine what the three of them have—or, rather, *had* in common."

In fact, aside from Boneen, they all had great reluctance to discuss anything with the two of them. Danthres hadn't realized how incredibly snotty wizards could be. She was glad that ban Wyvald had the good sense to lie to Dourti about that.

"You already know what they have in common," Dourti said dismissively as he sat back down, folding his arms over his robed chest. "They all owned shops."

"Yes," ban Wyvald said, "and they were also killed by someone who knew them all well and had access to the back rooms of their shops."

Dourti cocked his head to the side. "Interesting. You suspect Yan, don't you?"

A bit mockingly, Danthres matched his head gesture. "Why do you say that?"

"Do not attempt your tiresome rhetorical trickery on me, Lieutenant. Yan is an obvious candidate for committing these murders, as he fits the criteria you just listed."

"Yes, he does." Danthres came away from the wall. "And indeed, we did interview Yan, only to discover that he can account for his whereabouts during the times that the murders took place."

Rolling his eyes, Dourti said, "I'm not surprised that you just *believed* him."

"Oh, we didn't. But we checked, and there are about half a dozen witnesses at Suzett's on Sandy Brook Way."

Smiling, ban Wyvald added, "Quite helpful, was Suzett."

"He could have paid those concubines off," Dourti said, pointing a finger at Danthres. "He owns the shops now, so he'd be motivated to spend the money."

"Unfortunately, that doesn't *quite* work," Danthres said, "because Yan had no such motivation to commit Javy's murder—and he has an even better alibi for that one, as he was in our holding cell when it happened."

Taking a seat in one of the stools opposite Dourti, ban Wyvald leaned on the table with both elbows. "Besides, we actually were not done enumerating the commonalities among the victims. For example, they were the only three shops in all of Cliff's End that sold Bags of Holding."

"A very popular item," Danthres put in, "especially for people who shop down Jorbin's Way. Much easier to carry multiple items from many stands home if you can put it all in a single container."

"I'm sure they also all sold the same type of love potion." Dourti stood up. "Lieutenants, you are wasting my time, which is far too precious to be wasted on the likes of you. If there's nothing else."

Standing up to face him, ban Wyvald said, "There's just a few more items, sir, please, if you'd sit down."

Declining the invitation to sit, Dourti instead started to pace. "You said you had questions to ask me. Thus far, your only questions have directly related to things I've said rather than the solving of these murders."

"Fine," Danthres said, "here's one. Why didn't you tell us about the most important commonality the three victims had?"

Derisively, Dourti said, "You already knew they all owned shops."

"I meant that they *all* apprenticed under you."

Stopping in mid-pace, Dourti whirled upon Danthres with outrage. "How did you know that? The bond between apprentice and teacher is sacred! Such as you should never be privy to such private information!"

"You may wish to speak to your fellow wizards about that," ban Wyvald said. "The information was provided to us without hesitation."

"By whom?"

Before ban Wyvald could respond, Danthres quickly said, "We ask the questions in this room, Mr. Dourti, and right now I would ask you to sit down."

Dourti put his hands on his hips. "I demand to know who provided this intelligence to you! It is a dire breach of protocol!"

Stepping between Dourti and Danthres, ban Wyvald said, "Policing the Brotherhood of Wizards is outside our purview. Our goal is to discover who killed three of your fellows."

"You don't understand—"

Talking over ban Wyvald's shoulder, Danthres said, "No, *you* don't understand. Put your house in order on your own time. You're on ours right now, and we're not done talking to you."

"Please sit down, Mr. Dourti," ban Wyvald said quietly but firmly.

With a snarl, Dourti sat down. "This is ludicrous."

Danthres and ban Wyvald both sat down opposite Dourti. The latter said, "You do not deny that all three victims were your apprentices? Bear in mind that lying to us is an offense within this city-state."

Somehow, Danthres managed not to snort. Nobody who sat on that stool ever worried about that — but then, that was usually because they were arrogant enough to think they wouldn't get caught. In six months, Danthres hadn't seen anyone sit on that stool who was anywhere near as arrogant as this mage.

"Yes, I trained all of them. What of it? I've lived for two centuries, Lieutenants, and I've trained many wizards."

"And you worked with all three of them on creating a Bag of Holding," Danthres said.

"Quite a difficult endeavor, we've been told," ban Wyvald added.

"You never managed it, with any of them."

"Not for lack of trying, certainly."

"No, and yet they managed it without you."

Dourti cried, "They did no such thing! It was my research that led to the creation of the bags! Mine! They had no right to cut me out of the profits! You think any of those three idiots would have even come close to the right spell without my guidance? And were they grateful?"

"So that's why you killed them?" ban Wyvald asked.

Danthres winced, as asking the direct question always made people stop talking.

But Dourti, still screaming, replied. "Yes! They deserved to die for betraying me like that! I showed them love and affection far more than any other wizard would have! And this is how they thank me?"

Quickly, Danthres stood up. She said formally, "In the name of Lord Albin and Lady Meerka, I hereby place you, Myk Dourti, under arrest for the murders of Finnert, Tam Kort, and Javy Marta. Other charges to be added as necessary."

Dourti scoffed. "I do not recognize your authority to arrest me, mortals." With that, he gestured.

A moment later, tendrils of energy surrounded all four of his limbs, pulling him outward and upward so that he floated several handslengths over the floor, his arms and legs splayed.

His eyes blazing, spit flying from his mouth, Dourti cried out, "What is the meaning of this? I will *not* be restrained in this manner!"

Smiling, ban Wyvald said, "We did warn you that the castle was warded, did we not?"

The door to the interview room opened, and Osric stepped inside, along with Sir Gevlin, Boneen, and another one of the wizards they'd spoken to, Lord Ythran.

Dourti stared right at Boneen. "I should've known. You've never understood the bond between apprentice and teacher, Boneen. As soon as these two mortal imbeciles told me that I was betrayed—"

Boneen sneered. "Everyone knows who you took on as apprentices, Myk, stop being such a fool."

Ythran stared daggers at Boneen. "You revealed his apprentices?"

"Of course I did," Boneen said, sounding confused as to why it was an issue—a confusion Danthres shared.

"We will discuss that later." Ythran regarded Danthres and her partner. "The Brotherhood of Wizards thanks you for your hard work, Lieutenants. We shall deal with this murderer ourselves."

Sir Gevlin stepped forward, holding up a rune. "I'm afraid not. Mr. Dourti is in our custody now."

He touched the rune while he muttered something, and Danthres quickly covered her sensitive eyes. Through her eyelids she could tell that there was a flash of light. When she opened them, Dourti was gone.

Angrily, Ythran asked Gevlin, "Where is he?"

"He is now in our holding facility beneath the castle."

"That was *not* our arrangement." Ythran's dagger-stare was now fixed on Gevlin.

The noble was taken aback. "Er, I'm sorry, my lord, but I am performing my duties as instructed by Lord Albin and Lady Meerka. I'm afraid that you must register any objection with them."

"Oh, I shall, rest assured." With that, he stormed out.

Biting his lower lip, Gevlin muttered, "I'd best go with him," and ran after the mage.

Danthres noticed that ban Wyvald was shaking his head. "What is it?" she asked.

"It's just sad, is all. You could tell he really cared about those three. He said he gave them love and affection—and they went and created their lucrative product without him."

"Love and affection?" Boneen asked. "He said that about his apprentices?"

"Yes, he did," ban Wyvald said. "Why?"

"The very last things a wizard should show an apprentice are love and affection." He shuddered. "It seems the rumors were true about him."

"What rumors?" Danthres asked.

"Never mind. I'd best follow Sir Gevlin and Lord Ythran. Well done, Lieutenants."

The diminutive wizard waddled out of the interview room, leaving Danthres with her new partner and her captain.

She smiled at Osric. "Magick armor?"

Osric snorted. "If you're lucky. Good work, you two."

As the three of them went out into the squadroom, ban Wyvald said, "I owe you an apology, Lieutenant."

Danthres whirled on him. "Oh, you do, do you?"

He grinned. "Indeed, I do. You're an excellent interrogator. It was a pleasure to partner with you on it."

She sighed. "Much as it pains me to admit it—I feel the same way. Perhaps you'll last a *bit* longer than Quane did."

Speaking over his shoulder as he headed to his office, Osric said, "You'd better hope it's a lot longer!"

Carefully waiting until the captain was out of earshot, Danthres said, "What I hope is that I can work alone. Since that seems to be rather a forlorn hope indeed, I suppose I could do worse than partnering with you, ban Wyvald." She chuckled, looking over at Iaian's desk, currently empty. He and Linder had taken a call earlier. "In fact, I have done worse, quite recently."

"Well, thank you for that, Lieutenant Tresyllione. And please, call me Torin. Being called 'ban Wyvald' reminds me of—of something I'd prefer not to be reminded of."

Frowning, Danthres said, "But that's how Osric refers to you."

Ban Wyvald—or, rather, Torin—smiled ruefully. "Yes, he does. I gave up asking him to call me by my given name after a month."

Danthres chuckled. "Very well—Torin. And you may call me Lieutenant Tresyllione."

Torin's face fell, and Danthres found she couldn't hold in her laughter. She added quickly, "Or Danthres is fine, as well."

They sat down at their respective desks to start filling out the paperwork that would be needed so Dourti could be properly prosecuted. Rather, Danthres filled it out while Torin, who as yet had had no instruction in same, watched and learned how to do it.

By the time Danthres was done, and had finished answering Torin's many — and, she had to admit, intelligent — questions about the procedure, a pageboy entered the squadroom. "L'tenants Tresyllione and Binwid?"

Torin gently corrected him. "That's 'ban Wyvald.' What may we do for you?"

"You two an' Cap'n Osric need t'be comin' wif me. Lord Albin needs t'see you."

TORIN

Torin found himself to be very impressed with the statuary that lined the corridors of the central area of the castle. The eastern wing where the Castle Guard's squadroom was kept was functional and utilitarian, with only a few bits of decoration—the ugly dragon statue, the pretty unicorn tapestry.

The quality of the sculpture, however, improved tremendously in this section. The pieces displayed on marble stands here were more elegant than anything Torin had seen since leaving Myverin, where he'd been training to replace his father as Chief Artisan. That training was ended abruptly by Torin running away from Myverin as fast as he could go.

He made a mental note to ask someone in the court who the sculptor was, when the opportunity presented itself.

For now, the pageboy led him, Danthres, and Osric toward a set of large wooden double doors.

Leaning over to Danthres, he whispered, "So I'll get to meet the lord and lady?"

"We both will," Danthres whispered back, "and just the lord. Lady Meerka would only be in the meeting if it involves the treasury, from what I've been led to understand."

Torin raised an eyebrow. "You haven't met them yet, either?"

"I'd been hoping to continue to not have done so. The captain's always in a foul mood after he talks with Lord Albin."

Further conversation was ended by the pageboy opening the double doors to reveal an opulent room filled with comfortable furniture— including a large chair and a sofa—more statuary as well as a lovely tapestry on one wall, and a fireplace, currently inactive.

Seated on the sofa were the two wizards, Boneen and Lord Ythran, the former's legs dangling above the floor. A bald man with a thick mustache and a hawk nose that rivaled Torin's own aquiline proboscis for size sat in the large chair. Since the meeting was with Lord Albin, and since the bald man was the only one in the room Torin didn't recognize, he had to be the most powerful man in the demesne. Next to his chair was a small sideboard on which sat a crystal goblet about a third filled with an amber liquid.

"Ah, Captain Osric, thank you for joining us."

Osric inclined his head. "Of course, my lord."

The captain's words confirmed it, and the lack of a woman in the room besides Danthres confirmed his partner's opinion that Lady Meerka was not present.

"This," Osric continued, indicating the two lieutenants with a gesture, "is Lieutenant ban Wyvald and his partner, Lieutenant Tresyllione. They were the ones who closed the case."

"Welcome to the Castle Guard, Lieutenant ban Wyvald," Lord Albin said jovially. "It seems you had quite the first case."

Testily, Lord Ythran said, "If we may dispense with the tiresome formalities, we need to resolve this immediately."

"I don't see that there's anything to resolve," Albin said equally testily. "You asked us to find the person who killed three wizards. Lieutenants ban Wyvald and Tresyllione did so."

"Yes, and Dourti's apparent guilt—"

"Apparent?" Danthres's parroting of Ythran echoed off the stone walls of the room.

"Yes, 'apparent,' and if the mortal would please be silent," Ythran said with a sneer, "we may continue. Dourti's apparent guilt would explain why he was reluctant to involve the Castle Guard in this case. I will admit that it would not have occurred to us to suspect one of our own."

Boneen muttered, "Wouldn't have occurred to *you*, perhaps."

Torin tried not to snort at that. He was mostly successful.

"But Dourti *is* one of ours," Ythran said, "and we must be the ones to dispense justice."

Albin shifted in his chair. "Hardly your place after asking us to step in. The law is crystal clear on this matter. If the case involves magick, it falls within the Brotherhood's jurisdiction, but if you refuse to accept that jurisdiction, it becomes the purview of the Castle Guard. When you requested that my detectives investigate—"

"Yes, I understand that." Ythran waved his arms back and forth dismissively. "But that was before we discovered that the perpetrator—"

"We're going around in circles," Albin said, interrupting the wizard right back. "Lieutenant ban Wyvald, can you confirm that Myk Dourti is the perpetrator of those crimes?"

Torin nodded. "Yes, my lord. He, in fact, admitted it to Lieutenant Tresyllione and myself, and then attempted to escape arrest."

"And you will both testify to that before the magistrate," Albin asked, "making his guilt a matter of public record?"

Danthres said, "Absolutely, my lord," while Torin simply nodded.

Now Ythran was squirming, and Torin started to see what the lord of the demesne was getting at.

"We do not wish—" Ythran started, then hesitated.

Boneen rolled his eyes. "Dammit, Ythran, the man killed his apprentices! Over commerce!"

Ythran snapped, "And that is not a fact that it would be well for the general public to be aware of."

"Yes, it would be just *terrible* if they knew that we were fallible."

"It would, in fact." Ythran was gesturing like mad as he ranted. "The Brotherhood was formed in part to reassure the people that wizards are very much infallible, that the days of megalomaniacal wizards like Chalmraik the Foul and Mitos are a thing of the past!"

Torin shuddered. He'd never encountered any of the crazed wizards that had tried to take over Flingaria over the decades, though he'd heard quite a bit about them growing up in Myverin. Indeed, one of his father's (many) arguments for why he shouldn't leave the safety of Myverin was that he was far less likely to be enslaved by a mad mage if he stayed home.

Albin leaned forward. "Understand something, Lord Ythran. If you do not allow us to bring Dourti to justice, if you do not allow our magistrate to pass judgment upon someone who killed three of Cliff's End's merchants, then we will let it be known far and wide that the Brotherhood of Wizards is a sham that hides its mendacity behind arrogance and falsehood."

Torin wasn't sure that entirely made sense, but he wasn't about to correct the lord's syntax in this setting. Or ever, truly.

Besides, his words seemed to have an effect on Ythran, who looked as if he'd been asked to swallow a live snake.

Danthres, for her part, looked satisfied. Torin was impressed with her zeal for justice, and he wondered where that came from, exactly. Half elves who lived past the age of three days were almost always from Sorlin, a little colony to the south that was generally considered to be peaceful and orderly. Of course, that very peace and order may have led to her striving for it outside Sorlin's borders. He made a mental note to ask her about it.

"What is it you want then, Lord Albin?" Every word was practically spit by the wizard.

Albin leaned back in his chair and grabbed the drink off the sideboard. "If you wish to take Dourti into your custody and if you wish the truth of his crime to be kept from the people in order to keep your precious reputation intact, we will require the cooperation of the Brotherhood." He turned to Danthres. "Lieutenant Tresyllione, your report on the murder of that poor young woman who tended bar at the Stone Kobold indicated that a mage was able to cast a spell that revealed the events of the recent past?"

"Uhm—" Danthres swallowed, looking less pleased. "Yes, my lord. It was a wizard named Kort—he was a witness to Gava's murder before he was killed by Dourti. For that matter, Boneen here cast the same spell at one of the wizard murders, but it was inconclusive due to a mage being the murderer. Magick can apparently interfere with the spell, and that was one of the things that led us to Dourti as a suspect."

"Interesting. Thank you, Lieutenant." Lord Albin turned back to Ythran. "We will keep the Brotherhood's secrets, but only if you provide the Castle Guard with a wizard who can serve as a sort of examiner, who will cast this peel-back spell that Lieutenant Tresyllione described."

Ythran folded his arms. "So it's to be extortion, is it?"

"Simply an acknowledgment that actions have consequences, my lord."

Torin noted that Lord Albin didn't start referring to Ythran as "my lord" until he made his request.

For several seconds, Ythran simply sat with his arms folded, before speaking again. "And if I tell you that the Brotherhood does not respond well to extortion, and that your attempt to bargain with us will result in your demesne being sanctioned by the Brotherhood?"

Albin took a sip of his drink before replying. "That would be your prerogative. But considering how much unlicensed magick there is in this city-state, I would think you'd jump at the opportunity for one of your own to be part of the process by which it's pursued and stopped. However, if you wish to sanction us, then by all means, do so. We'll put Dourti on trial and reveal his crimes for all to see. And I'm sure there are plenty of merchants who will eagerly jump at the real estate opportunities provided by eighty-three magick shops that will have to close once you sanction Cliff's End. I'm also sure that you will be hard-pressed to replace the lost revenue from the sudden shuttering of those shops, not to mention all the mages who hire themselves out privately." Albin smiled. "It's entirely up to you. And keep in mind that sanctioning Cliff's End for the devastating crime of following the law will not be looked upon favorably by the king and queen, either."

Putting his head in his hands, Boneen said, "Oh for pity's sake, Ythran, just accept the offer. It's not as if you have a choice."

Witheringly, Ythran said, "There is always a choice, Boneen. If you had simply kept your mouth shut—" He shook his head. "Fine. You believe we have no choice, then you may serve as this—this magickal examiner that Lord Albin suggests."

"What?" Boneen rose to his feet, but his diminutive height made him no taller while standing than he was sitting on the couch. "Why am I to perform this ridiculous task?"

Ythran shrugged. "You know Inanimate Residue. You've already proven you can work with the Castle Guard, since you were so incredibly cooperative with them."

"But—"

Gesturing, Ythran stood up. "It is done. Boneen shall be your new magickal examiner. I assume you will find accommodations for him here in the castle. In exchange, I expect the wards to release Dourti into my custody."

Sir Gevlin stepped forward. "With my lord's permission, I will take care of that."

Albin nodded, and Gevlin indicated the door. "Come this way, please, Lord Ythran?"

Torin smirked. Gevlin, it seemed, did not consider Ythran to be "his" lord.

As soon as Ythran and Gevlin departed, Danthres exploded. "That's *it?*"

"Is there a problem, Lieutenant?" Albin's tone lowered the temperature in the room.

"We can't just let Dourti *go!*"

"On the contrary, Lieutenant, we had little choice in the matter. Wizards are stubborn creatures, and if we attempted to hold Dourti and subject him to our laws, the backlash would have been vicious."

"But what about justice for his victims?"

"They were also wizards." Albin shrugged. "I appreciate your zeal, Lieutenant, but this was the best possible outcome. Trying to keep Dourti here would have started a war between the Brotherhood and King Marcus and Queen Marta. We only just finished fighting the Elf Queen, I doubt that a new conflict would benefit anyone. This way we were able to get a killer out of our city-state, and gain ourselves a valuable asset."

That got a sneer out of Boneen. "How nice to see that, at my age, I'm reduced to being an asset."

"Oh you will be quite the asset, Boneen, believe me. When Sir Gevlin returns, speak to him about what arrangements you require here at the castle." He looked at Torin, Danthres, and Osric. "Thank you, Captain, Lieutenants. You've done *very* well today. That will be all."

Danthres just stood there while Osric and Torin headed out. Gently, Torin touched her shoulder, at which point she shook her head and followed them out.

"I don't know what disgusts me more," she said, not bothering to wait until they were out of earshot of Albin's sitting room, "that the Brotherhood are so much more interested in preserving their image that they'd barter with justice like that, or that Lord Albin would go along with it for his own benefit."

"Our job is to keep the people of Cliff's End safe, Tresyllione," Osric said. "Justice is simply a fortuitous side benefit—and one we didn't get this time. But you caught Dourti and he *will* be punished. I doubt we did him any favors by turning him over to the Brotherhood."

He stopped, turned, and smiled at them. Osric didn't smile very often, and Torin could tell that he wasn't any better at it now than he had been on the front lines.

"I knew I was right to put you two together. You did excellent work. Now go home and take the rest of the day off. First case tomorrow's yours, and I expect you both to close it."

With that, he turned and walked down the corridor.

Danthres still looked aggravated — though, Torin supposed, that was her normal look. "Are you all right, Danthres?"

She let out a very long breath. "I will be. I suppose. But I'm really starting to learn to hate magick."

THE DRAGON PRECINCT CHRONOLOGY

FOR THEM THAT CARE ABOUT SUCH THINGS (YOU KNOW WHO YOU ARE), HERE'S a list of all the Cliff's End Castle Guard stories in chronological order.

"Heroes Welcome" (flashbacks). Gan Brightblade and his friends follow a lead to Mitos the Mage in an abandoned castle outside Treemark.

"Gan Brightblade vs. Mitos the Mighty" (flashbacks). Gan Brightblade and his friends have their final confrontation with Mitos in his mountain redoubt near Shael's Haven.

"When the Magick Goes Away." Torin and Danthres's first case together, solving the murder of three wizards.

"Baker's Dozen." Danthres and Torin's second case together, as several bakeries are vandalized.

"Blood in the Water" (flashback). Hawk works with the vampire hunter Corvin to bring down a couple of vampires who have committed multiple murders.

"Crime of Passion." Torin and Danthres can't find the hrancit demon that killed a woman and her children.

"A Clean Getaway." A closet in the Jaros house explodes with muck — a closet that wasn't there previously — and Danthres and Torin must find out who put it there.

"Catch and Release." One of Iaian's old cases comes back to haunt him.

"Getting the Chair." A wizard who animates furniture is murdered, and his sofa, chair, and lantern are the only witnesses—Torin and Danthres must figure out which one is lying.

Dragon Precinct. Danthres and Torin investigate the murders of one Flingaria's greatest heroes, Gan Brightblade, and three of his comrades.

"Fire in the Hole." The dragon who appears every midsummer breaks the routine and incinerates a house and several people, and Torin and Danthres must find out why.

"Heroes Welcome" (present-day portions). The survivors of Gan Brightblade's gang of heroes, Genero, Bogg, and Ubàrlig, must figure out what to do in the wake of the murders of their friends.

"House Arrest." Torin interrogates a house faerie about the death of one of the residents.

Unicorn Precinct. Arra Cynnis is killed on the eve of her wedding by an illicit lover who can't be identified via peel-back, and Danthres and Torin must find the killer while navigating the upper-class minefield.

"Blood in the Water" (present-day portions). There's a vampire in Cliff's End, and Dru and Hawk must find Corvin the vampire hunter to help stop it.

"Brotherly Love." Danthres interviews a man about the murder of his sister.

Goblin Precinct. A designer drug is sweeping through Cliff's End, and Torin and Danthres must find out who designed it.

Gryphon Precinct. The death of Lord Albin means sweeping changes for the Cliff's End Castle Guard.

Mermaid Precinct. The infamous Pirate Queen is found murdered.

Phoenix Precinct. A crime wave strikes the newest precinct in the city-state.

Manticore Precinct. A breakout occurs on the prison barge, and the detectives must find out who orchestrated the prison break as well as track down the fugitives.

ABOUT THE AUTHOR

KEITH R.A. DECANDIDO IS A WHITE MALE IN HIS EARLY FORTIES, APPROXImately 200 pounds. He was last seen in the wilds of the Bronx, New York, though he is often sighted in other locales. Usually he is armed with a laptop computer, which some have classified as a deadly weapon. Through use of this laptop, he has inflicted more than fifty novels, as well as an indeterminate number of short stories, comic books, nonfiction, novellas, and anthologies on an unsuspecting reading public. Many of these are set in the milieus of television shows, movies, games, and comic books, among them Star Trek, Cars, Doctor Who, Supernatural, World of Warcraft, Orphan Black, Alien, Marvel Comics, and many more. We have received information confirming that more stories involving Torin, Danthres, and the city-state of Cliff's End can be found in the novels *Unicorn Precinct*, *Goblin Precinct*, *Gryphon Precinct*, and the forthcoming *Mermaid Precinct*, *Phoenix Precinct*, and *Manticore Precinct*, as well as the short-story collection *Tales from Dragon Precinct*. His other recent crimes against humanity include the urban fantasy novel *A Furnace Sealed*; the Orphan Black coffee-table book *Classified Clone Report*; the Alien novel *Isolation*; the *Tales of Asgard* trilogy of prose novels featuring Marvel's Thor, Sif, and the Warriors Three; short stories in the anthologies *Aliens: Bug Hunt*, the two *Baker Street Irregulars* volumes, *The Best of Bad-Ass Faeries*, *The Best of Defending the Future*, *Joe Ledger: Unstoppable*, *Nights of the Living Dead*, *The X-Files: Trust No One*, among others; and writing about pop culture for Tor.com and Patreon. If you see DeCandido, do not approach him, but call for back-up immediately. He is often seen in the company of a suspicious-looking woman who goes by the street name of "Wrenn," as well as several as-yet-unidentified cats. A full dossier can be found at DeCandido.net.